M000083104

Let the Ghosts Speak

Let the Ghosts Speak

By
Bryan Davis

To Amy,

Bryan Davis

MOUNTAIN**BROOK**FIRE

Let the Ghosts Speak
Published by Mountain Brook Ink under the Mountain Brook
Fire line
White Salmon, WA U.S.A.

All rights reserved. Except for brief excerpts for review purposes, no part of this book may be reproduced or used in any form without written permission from the publisher.

The website addresses shown in this book are not intended in any way to be or imply an endorsement on the part of Mountain Brook Ink, nor do we vouch for their content.

This story is a work of fiction. All characters and events are the product of the author's imagination. Any resemblance to any person, living or dead, is coincidental, other than people mentioned in the Author Note.

Any scripture quotations are taken from the King James Version of the Bible. Public domain.

ISBN 978-1-943959-61-7
Published in association with Cyle Young of the Hartline
Literary Agency, LLC.
© 2020 Bryan Davis

The Team: Miralee Ferrell, Alyssa Roat, Nikki Wright, Cindy Jackson
Cover Design: Indie Cover Design, Lynnette Bonner Designer

Mountain Brook Fire is an inspirational publisher offering worlds you can believe in.

Printed in the United States of America

Discovered in a time capsule unearthed in Paris in 1962, this manuscript was part of a police-case dossier, filed and forgotten until a friend learned of my interest in nineteenth-century jurisprudence and passed it along to me.

The first portion, which is the lion's share of the manuscript, was written by a hasty hand in English with an occasional French word or phrase. Because of its progressively illegible script, I did more than simply copy it into a decipherable form. I translated it into something modern readers of English could understand while keeping the more easily recognizable French words the author chose to employ.

I did not, however, alter the author's measurement conventions. Although he lived in France, which used the metric system at the time, he provided distances in Imperial units, most likely for the sake of his mother, an Englishwoman. In contrast, I opted for American spellings of words, since I am providing this translation for a largely American readership.

In addition, at all times, I was careful to be true to the author's style, his mindset, and his apparent madness.

The second portion, a police officer's addendum, was written entirely in French, and I employed the same method in translating that author's words.

Although I find the story contained herein to be doubtful at best, I respectfully submit it for public review, faithfully preserved with appropriate chapter divisions.

Henri M. Bellamont, translator

Chapter One

I have forgotten love. My chains have driven it from me. Loneliness has leached it from my bones and left behind only regret.

It is daylight once again, and I am sane today. This time I am certain of it, though the hauntings of the night continue to test my confidence. Therefore, while my mind is clear, I must take pen and ink, so kindly provided by my only friendly visitors, and begin my story. I cannot say how long this season of sanity will remain with me, so I will write quickly and continue during every day of clarity until I finish this account for the court.

Although you might be dead by now, dear Mother, I am including occasional personal side notes to you, and I dedicate these recollections to your memory, for your lullabies echo from these bare walls. Perhaps you alone knew what love really is. The ghosts tell me that few remember.

I see a world of children who walk in darkness, their bony hands stained with blood not their own, the blood of the innocent. I have been led by such hands, the frail hands of schoolboys in this realm of shadows. Will the rest of the world learn from their schoolmasters?

Alas. Forgive me. I am getting far ahead of myself. A sane man begins his tale at the beginning, so I shall relate where this story of heartbreak has its origins, in Paris where I, Justin Trotter, shared a one-room flat with Marc Noël.

You would have approved, Mother. The room was austere and clean, only a bed and a desk for each of us, situated above a police commissary and within walking distance of the theater and our university. Although Marc's family could have afforded more opulent lodging, he chose a simple life, often to his mother's vexation.

As part-time students with thespian hearts, we spent our waking hours working for our employers, attending a class or two, studying for exams, and rehearsing our respective roles in whichever play the community theater offered. Regarding employment, Marc conducted research for a law firm, while I translated manuscripts from English or Gaelic to French for a publisher in Paris.

Our jobs were tedious, often mind-numbing, but they provided income that I sorely needed, especially because of my dear sister, Justice.

On a fateful day in early November of 1860, Justice visited my flat, hoping to escape her dismal fortunes, at least for a few hours. As always, we laughed together and wept together. The respite provided solace and hope for her and joy for me. Her smile brightened any room, and her eyes danced with delight, in spite of their blindness.

Mother, I realize this is shocking news, but Justice went blind at the age of ten after a bout of smallpox, which almost took her life. If she had died, I would have been lost, alone. She always remained my best friend, my closest ally during our trials when we had to leave England. Even blind, she was the steady guide who kept me on the pathway of sanity. And I adored her.

Late afternoon rain threatened as I helped Justice walk toward the carriage that would transport her to Montreuil. Fortunately, it was covered, so she would stay dry during the journey. Earlier storms had left deep puddles scattered here and about, forcing us to step over or around them in a meandering path.

When I boosted her into the carriage, I tucked the skirt of her dress inside to keep it from getting caught in the door. Loose threads dangled at the hem, and a gaping hole in her knitted shawl revealed a sleeve that had been mended with darker thread, obvious to anyone but a blind seamstress, though Madame Dupont probably noticed and never said anything. The shrewish woman couldn't be bothered with even the smallest act of kindness.

How could I once again send Justice to such a heartless caretaker? She demanded complete obedience to her insufferable and constantly changing rules while steadily increasing the charge for Justice's care. Still, I sent the money each month without fail, though it left me with barely enough to survive.

When I leaned in and kissed Justice's pale cheek, she broke into sobs that shook her thin frame. "Justin, I don't think I can stand another moment in that horrid woman's house. When will we be able to have a place to ourselves?"

I stroked her long, dark curls. "I don't know. Without Marc's help, I couldn't afford anything outside the beggars' slums, and I would never take you there."

"Or the institution."

"No. The rumors I hear are ... well ... rife with nightmares. You need not worry about going there."

She gestured with her hands as if making something. "My basket weaving is much improved, and I am learning how to cane chairs. I also learned how to sew well enough to repair clothing. I can earn money now."

Her determined brown eyes sent sparkling tears down her sunken cheeks, stabbing my heart without mercy. "I'll find a place we can both live. Give me some time."

"How much time? Every day with Madame Dupont gets worse. Yesterday she spilled scalding water on my hand." She showed me a red welt on her thumb. "I think she did it on purpose, though she claimed it was an accident."

Anger burned within. I had to get Justice away from this evil woman without delay. "Give me two days. Then I'll come for you. I promise."

"Thank you, Justin. I can survive that long." Her smile chased away the stabbing daggers. "I almost forgot to tell you. I have been having good dreams lately. In most of them, I am with Father. I am a little girl, and I can see. It's so wonderful to talk to him again and enjoy our walks together."

I slid out my pocket watch and looked at the face in the light of the waning sun. We had kept the carriage driver waiting far too long. "That's wonderful. At least you have good memories to help you wake up happy."

Her smile wilted. "I miss him so much. I still don't believe the horrid story about him. It can't be true."

I put the watch away and brushed a tear from her cheek. "Just keep dreaming about him. Remember him for the good man he was."

She nodded. "I love you, Justin."

"I love you, too."

I closed the door and extended the fare money to the driver, but he shook his head and brushed his own tears from his aged face. "No charge. Going to Montreuil anyway."

"Thank you, Monsieur. Thank you."

When Justice's carriage rolled down the street, the clouds gave way. Rain fell in sheets. A splash turned my attention to an alley entry. A little girl, perhaps seven years old, had fallen into a puddle. Propped by hands and knees, expression forlorn, she stared at me, her coat splattered with mud. Raindrops pelted her uncovered head, plastering dark curls against her pale cheeks.

She seemed familiar, but in the blowing rain, I couldn't be sure. One truth was certain. No one was coming to her aid.

The moment I took a step toward her, a wheel on a swiftly moving carriage hit a puddle and sent a spray of muddy water my way. I spun and dodged in time to avoid getting hit. When I turned again toward the alley, the girl was gone.

I ran to the spot and looked around. She was nowhere in sight. How could she have run away so quickly? In any case, there was no sense conducting a search. I would soon become soaked.

As I hurried toward my building, the girl's face stayed on my mind like a haunting specter. Somehow I knew her from a time long ago, perhaps my childhood, but that would have been before she was born.

Shaking off my ponderings, I rushed into my building and bounded up the stairs to my flat. The room was empty. Marc had not yet returned from the law office.

Today, his absence was fortunate. For the past week he had been goading me into attending a party this very night, and during

4

the morning he had chattered like a little boy, announcing that the masquerade ball in the old schoolhouse was upon us.

After removing my cloak, I sat heavily in my chair, lifted the fountain pen donated by my publisher for translation work, and opened the book I had been working on. Considering the promise I had made to Justice, I couldn't afford to halt my work. In fact, I had to work harder, faster, even on a holiday like today. Le Jour des Morts they call it, All Souls' Day, a morbid holiday in my view. With the heavy rain giving us an encore from yesterday's performance, the street was again turning to mud, the slimy sort that brings horses to an untimely end. If it continued, flooding was sure to follow.

I stared out our window at a two-horse fiacre splashing through turbid water and imagined my own tumble in the mire and a painful journey to the physician, something I could ill afford, especially now. Yet, even that would be tolerable compared to dressing up in whatever ghastly costume Marc had in mind for me. With his imagination, I doubted that I would survive the shame.

After I had worked on the book for a few minutes, Marc entered with a quick stride and brushed water from his cloak, his ever-present smile widening his full cheeks. Lacking facial hair, he often looked like an exuberant child. "The rain is heavy, but my spirits are high. We're going to a ball tonight."

I fidgeted on my tattered seat pad, my knees under my desk. "*You're* going to a ball. I have work to do."

Marc shook his head hard and slung water from his short, dark hair. In his wet state, he reminded me of a bear who had waded in from a swim. Stocky, muscular, and grinning like he had just caught a fish, he was ready to celebrate. "You can't back out, Justin. My mother purchased your disguise, and refunds are not allowed. Besides, the music will be grand. The evening is guaranteed to be festive and fun."

Awkward and embarrassing were closer to the truth, but I held my tongue. I wrote something forgettable about the Renaissance era translated from the tedious history book. I needed to appear busy—disconnected from Marc's make-believe world of romance, a world in which people lived happily ever after. I knew better.

"Marc, I need to finish this. You know how it works. No money until I deliver the final product."

He tiptoed close as if sneaking up on prey. "Will you go if I offer you an advance?"

I stared at him. "An advance? You mean in full?"

He shed his cloak and draped it over his arm. "Payment in full for the book. You can reimburse me when you deliver it."

"But that will take weeks."

"I know." Marc looked at his nails in a nonchalant manner. "What do you say? Are you going?"

"Give me a moment to think." I set the pen down and closed my eyes. Maybe Marc's offer was my opportunity to get a place for Justice and me. With that much money, I could rent a decent flat for at least three months. Of course, I would have no income until I finished the book, but if her confidence in her weaving abilities was justified, we might be able to eke out a living.

Besides that, the frequent rain had kept Marc and me inside for too many hours and sometimes at each other's throats. The morning's rehearsal had been canceled due to our director's sudden illness, the wretched fever that had stricken so many who had reached her advanced age. At least this malady wasn't as deadly as the cholera that broke out soon after Justice and I, a pair of frightened twins, arrived in France at the age of seven. When the disease struck our adoptive parents, we had to lean on each other to survive, thereby sealing our unbreakable bond.

The combination of my passion to help Justice and my need to break away from this tedious text overwhelmed my distaste for social gatherings. Yet, before I agreed to go, I could use my pretended hesitance as leverage to gain more information.

I opened my eyes, picked up the pen, and began writing again. "Why a masquerade party on a night that we're supposed to pray for the souls of the dead?"

"My mother's idea." Marc laid his cloak over the back of his desk chair. "People dress up in your homeland for All Hallows' Eve, do they not?"

"They do, but your mother has no English or Celtic roots. Or does she?"

"Indeed she does, on her paternal grandmother's side, but costumes are not uncommon here on any holiday, including prayerful ones." Marc sat on his chair and pulled off his wet shoes. "You need not worry, though. We'll have the traditional chrysanthemums, candles, and prayers for the dead. You can add something yourself, if you want, maybe a Gaelic prayer. That would impress everyone."

"I'll think about it, but why the old schoolhouse?"

"Our dear Monsieur Haussmann plans to destroy it during the next renovation phase. Mother wishes to preserve it as a museum and a venue for social gatherings, so she decorated it and invited all her aristocratic friends, including Monsieur Haussmann himself. Maybe he will join us and see the building's potential."

"That's all fine for your mother and you, but give me one good reason why *I* should go."

"Besides the money?"

"Yes, otherwise you will think me a mercenary."

Marc lit a lantern and turned up the wick. "Francine will be there." His voice was low and sultry, as if he were playing a scripted role.

My pen paused over a misshapen letter *R*. His mention of Francine raised a shiver that I am not sure I hid from him. She never failed to make my heart race. Her beauty, her wit, her generosity, combined to create an angel on earth, though a sharp-tongued one. And I, probably along with a dozen other men, was in love with her. "What difference does that make? I am far from deserving a spot on her list of potential suitors."

"So little you know." Marc plucked away my pen. "I keep singing the praises of my brilliant roommate."

"Brilliant enough to stay home on a night like this." I nodded at the droplets pecking at the window panes. "You don't need my gloomy face spoiling the fun."

"You're an actor. You can put on any face you choose." Marc patted me on the back. "Close that stuffy old book and get ready. I won't take no for an answer."

I rose, pushed my hands into my empty pockets, and pulled the insides out, palming the carriage fare to keep it out of view. "Your mother would never approve of me courting Francine."

He waved a hand. "Now, don't go speaking ill of my mother again. Ever since Papa died she's trusted my judgment in these matters. Potential trumps poverty, and she knows I wouldn't guide my own sister toward a scoundrel. And you are no scoundrel."

Marc was right. I was hopelessly virtuous, but mostly because women scared me to death, especially Francine. Every time I looked at her, those bright blue eyes made my legs shake. "Is Francine going in costume?"

"Of course. She's been looking forward to this for weeks."

"Let me guess. Joan of Arc."

Marc nodded. "In full military battledress, a copy she made of the museum piece. We are descendants from the family line. She is quite enamored with her heroine."

"So Francine is a seamstress extraordinaire and a war general. A study in contrasts."

"It will take a strong man to tame her." Marc thrust at me with a pretend sword. "Just stay at the safe end of her blade, if you know what I mean."

"All too well." I let my gaze drift back to the window, though a curtain of darkness had fallen. Marc knew of a past spat between Francine and me, a minor dispute about politics that ended in laughter. He seemed not to know, however, about a more recent, harsher skirmish that left me fearful of reentering her presence.

That topic, dear Mother, I will address at the proper time when I hope to dispel any thought that Francine is a hot-headed shrew. It was my own foolish tongue that invited the lashing I received.

"I'll go on one condition. If Francine spurns me, you'll help me invent an excuse to leave on socially acceptable terms."

"Of course, of course. I'll simply say that you took a stroll in the library on the second floor. I'll explain how bookish you are."

"A fair plan, but I hope you'll invent a better word. Bookish is not what I would call a masculine trait."

"Adventurous, then." Marc withdrew a tailcoat from a trunk next to his bed. "Have you seen the library? It is fabulous, filled with ancient books and maps, perfect for your escape should you need one." He held the coat up to my chest. "You'll be a navy captain. I have a hat to go with it and a mask."

I touched one of the coat's brass buttons. "So if Francine turns against me, I can embark on a voyage to the island of books."

"Exactly." Marc laid the coat and a pair of white breeches in my arms. "Get dressed. We have to catch our ride at the carriage house in half an hour."

The getting dressed part proved to be easy. The coat and breeches fit perfectly. In fact, if our mirror reflected truth, I looked rather dashing … relatively speaking, of course. I knew better than to swallow the forbidden fruit of self-admiration.

Marc, now wearing a priest's cassock, set a simple black mask around my eyes and began tying it behind my head. "I know this mask won't hide your identity. The idea is to be recognizable while playing along with the masquerade."

"You want Francine to know who I am."

"Correct, and my mother wants us all to be easy to identify while still playing the game." He tightened the knot, set a cocked Napoleon hat on my head, and stood in front of me, scanning me as if I were a painting. "Perfect. Cuffed, creased, and pressed. Not to mention handsome. You're sure to catch her eye."

"Not her tongue, I hope."

"That will be up to you." He tied on a mask of his own. "Let's go."

After donning our boots and hooded cloaks, we sloshed through rainwater trenches and muddy streets while intermittent gas lamps illuminated a winding path that led us past squalid habitations. The rain kept the prostitutes inside, and the street children had run for cover, allowing for unaccosted travel, though the usual stench worsened. Urine, feces, and an occasional rat carcass saw to that.

Perhaps someday Monsieur Haussmann's renovations would reach our section of the arrondissement, but until then, we had to endure the sad estate of crippling poverty as well as winding narrow roads, missing cobblestones, and dilapidated buildings.

Throughout the journey, I kept watching for the pitiful little girl who had taken a spill at the alley, though surely she wouldn't be wandering alone at this hour. She was safe somewhere, warm and dry. Yet, her haunting ways continued. At the moment I could have helped her, I was more worried about soiling my cloak than rushing to her aid. Guilt rode my shoulders without mercy.

We arrived at the carriage house and caught a covered fiacre that took us to the outskirts of the city. Along the way Marc chattered about his mother's obsession with his decision to live in humble circumstances and pursue acting instead of banking. Her latest diatribe included a threat to remove him from her will, but he shook it off with a laugh. She had many years left to live, plenty of time for him to prove that he had made the right decision.

A rattle interrupted Marc's monologue. Horse hooves and carriage wheels clattered across a wooden bridge that spanned a brook, now swollen by the frequent rains. If the current storm failed to break soon, the brook might transform into a raging river.

As the fiacre drew within a stone's throw of the Seine, the schoolhouse came into view. Long abandoned, the school could easily pass for a museum—stone construction without, arched entries leading to a covered breezeway on the ground floor, tall windows lining the walls on the second, and tiny peek-through windows on the third.

Candlelight shone through one of the first-floor windows, providing a view of minglers inside who were about the business of evaluating each other's upper-crust costumes while sipping blood-red wine from Bordeaux glasses. I had pretended to be rich in a recent theater production, so being in costume felt natural. I could play this role.

After leaving the fiacre, we entered the main door, strolled into a parlor-like anteroom, and took off our wet raingear. Potted chrysanthemums of yellow, white, and purple lined the floor along a path toward an assembly room to the right, a friendly gesture to

10

most people, though to me it felt like the path of a death march. My social ineptitude saw to that.

From somewhere inside, a violin played Mozart in the midst of ambiguous conversation. Warm air flowed, carrying the aroma of perfume, tea, and wine. "I know everyone here," Marc said as he passed our cloaks to an attendant. "Stay close to me for introductions. Then you'll be on your own."

The moment we entered the assembly room, dozens of eyes turned toward us. The display of costumes was dizzying—kings and queens, knights, clowns, animals, and even a wrapped gift box.

Yet, one little girl wore only a simple white dress with a black sash tied in a bow at the back. Her dark curls and piercing eyes were unmistakable. She was the very girl who had fallen at the alley. Now that I had a moment, I studied her features more closely, allowing me to solve the haunting familiarity. She looked like my sister when she was that age. The resemblance was striking.

My conscience relieved, I breathed a sigh and smiled at her, but she just stared without smiling in return. Maybe she was angry at me or simply curious. No matter. She was safe and warm. I could be at peace.

I broke eye contact and looked around. The room itself spanned sixty feet in length and width. Portraits and landscape paintings hung on the walls, separated by lanterns mounted on brackets that provided plenty of light. A violinist dressed in medieval garb stood on the left side, blissfully stroking his bow across the strings. Near the back, a spiral staircase wound through a gap in the ceiling, perhaps the path to the library Marc had mentioned earlier.

Francine separated from a clutch of ladies and approached in full Joan-of-Arc array—boot-leather trousers and an armor-plated vest. A thin mask surrounded her eyes, and makeup hid her telltale freckles, a shade that made her look sun baked, a natural tone for a hard-working peasant girl who had transitioned to a soldier.

The makeup also covered a distinctive birthmark on her neck, an oval spot that she usually didn't mind showing. She also wore a dark wig that resembled the style of an English pageboy, concealing her long, ginger hair. Yet, no one could mistake her for anyone but Francine Noël.

She smiled at Marc. "Bishop Cauchon, so good of you to come in peace, especially considering your animosity toward me at other venues."

Marc bowed. "Joan, it is a time for song and dance. Far be it from me to spoil this occasion by burning you at the stake."

"That would be unpleasant." Francine shifted her gaze to me and tilted her head in a comely fashion. "And who is this young captain of the seas?"

"Joan, Maid of Orléans," Marc said with a formal air, "allow me to introduce to you Captain William Ashford ... Captain, Joan."

I kissed her hand. "I'm pleased to meet you."

"Ah. An Englishman. And polite as well." Francine touched an insignia on my coat. "How did such a young man become a captain?"

I smiled, though I felt the urge to retreat. "How did such a young woman become a general?"

Her own smile brightened. "Well struck, Captain. Well struck." She turned to Marc. "Bishop, if it is all the same to you, I would like to take this officer around to meet the other guests. We want to make sure he feels at home among our countrymen."

Marc gave her another bow. "He's all yours."

"Come along, then." She curled her arm around mine and led me deeper into the room. Her touch sent tingles up my arm, but I stayed calm. She seemed to be at ease with me. I needed to be the same. Maybe she and I could be a couple after all, at least for the evening.

Although the violin continued playing, no one danced. Perhaps they would change their minds later when the wine had taken effect and numbed the participants into thinking dancing was actually fun.

"Tell me, Captain," Francine said, "how long have you been in France?"

12

"I immigrated here with my adoptive parents fifteen years ago."

She halted and turned to me. "Justin ..." Her tone was gentle but firm. "My mother requested that we stay in character the first hour. It's a parlor game, of sorts, and she wishes to play it to the hilt. I assume Marc failed to inform you."

Warmth flooded my face and spread to my ears. "He alluded to it, but I didn't catch on."

"I see." She cast a glance Marc's way. He was chatting with two young ladies dressed as cats, apparently twin sisters vying for his attention.

I had a brief desire to learn how the cats would stay in character, but I brushed it aside. "If we play this game, aren't introductions rather counterproductive?"

"You are the only stranger here. After I introduce you to someone, I will whisper that person's real name to you. The last thing I want to do is get a tongue lashing from my mother."

I nodded. "I want to avoid sharp tongues as well."

"Then stay on my good side tonight." Again guiding me by the arm, she took me to a female court jester dressed in full motley, including a multi-colored hat with dangling bells. "Captain William Ashford, this is the court's designated fool, Astaude du Puy." She then turned to me and lowered her voice. "Jacqueline Noël, my mother."

I gave Madame Noël a head bow. "Pleased to meet you."

She laughed. "An English captain has come to dock his ship in a foreign harbor."

"Well, not exactly. I have been—"

"How many harbors have you visited, Captain?" She scanned me from head to toe. "A man with your decorations has certainly been around the world."

"Decorations?"

She set her fingertips on my cheek. "Dark, curly hair, stunning brown eyes, a firm jaw. Surely you have dropped your anchor in many a port."

Francine hissed, "Mother, you're going a little too far."

13

"Nonsense." Drawing back, Madame Noël shook her head, making the bells jingle. "It is impossible for a fool to go too far." She looked me over and winked. "Then again, maybe I would like to try."

"Mother!" Francine balled a fist. "How much wine have you had?"

"Not a drop, Joan. And why are you calling me Mother?" She waved a hand. "Be off with you now. Show the captain a good time. That is, if a woman wearing trousers and armor is able to do so."

Francine's cheeks turned crimson. Maybe this was my chance to take a permanent place on her good side. I offered Madame Noël another bow. "A woman wearing trousers is much to be preferred over a fool who flaunts her loose skirts."

Madame Noël slapped my face. "Get out."

The bluntness of her words overwhelmed the sting of her slap. "Get out?"

"You heard me." Her lips tight, she pointed toward the door. "Leave. Now."

"Very well." I tugged at my coat to straighten it. "It seems the game playing is quite one-sided."

Francine grabbed my arm and ushered me toward the door. "Justin Trotter, you said you wanted to avoid sharp tongues, so I will keep mine sheathed." When we arrived, she took a deep breath and looked me in the eye. "Did you really think insulting my mother was the best way to endear yourself?"

Blood rushed to my cheeks, inflaming them, but I managed to keep my voice low. "She was playing the fool, so I went along. You said she wanted to play the game to the hilt."

"I know. I know." She blew out a sigh. "Like you said, it's one-sided."

I spread my hands. "So what do I do now? She wants me to leave. It's her party."

Francine looked out the window. Windswept rain continued falling in sheets. Lightning flashed, followed by a thunderclap

14

that shook the building and rattled glass. "It would be inhumane to send you out in this weather."

"May I offer assistance?" Marc asked as he approached, hands pressed together in a priestly fashion. "No need to tell me what happened. The story is already a gossip windstorm, and it's growing into a capital crime."

I nodded. "Yes. Help. What can I do to salvage this disaster?"

Marc patted me on the back. "Go upstairs to the library while I smooth things over with my mother. Take a candelabrum. Read a book. One of us will come to see about you when the time is right."

"Yes, yes," Francine said. "That will do fine."

Although Marc and I had envisioned such an escape, now it felt like a coward's retreat. Still, it couldn't be helped. "Very well. I will go."

After Francine fetched a candelabrum with five tapers—four surrounding a higher one at the center—she escorted me to the spiral staircase while Marc distracted their mother. When I set a foot on the first step, I turned back and gave Francine a thankful nod. "I hope to see you soon."

"You will." She shooed me away. "Now, go."

With one hand on the stairway's central pole and the other clutching the candelabrum, I climbed the stone steps. As I ascended into darkness, the flickering flames created an undulating aura around me that prompted an even darker memory.

Mother, I refer to our last hour together, the fateful night we walked single file up our own spiral staircase, the night we heard the crash and Father's shout. You limped, as usual, and I slowed my pace so you could keep up, though I wanted to rush ahead and learn the reason for the noise. My sense of dread then was the same as I felt now, though not because of the darkness above but because of the darkness below. I had caused pain, and I left others to suffer in its shadow.

Chapter Two

When I reached the top of the stairs, I extended my light and pivoted slowly. Bookshelves towered into the darkness. Arranged in rows and columns, the shelves zigzagged here and about, creating a veritable maze of dusty wood, steep ladders, and tattered book spines. Perhaps the keeper of this assemblage understood the logic of the shelf placements, but with no labels to indicate order, the reasons escaped my perception.

I walked between two rows and slid a finger along an array of books. The candles combined with lightning flashes at the windows to provide enough light. A stroke of luck had put me in English literature—Shakespeare, to be precise. When I came upon Hamlet, I drew the book and tucked it under my arm. On a stormy night like this, trapped for time unknown in an abandoned library, a ghost story seemed appropriate.

After finding a bench near a window and removing the mask, I set it, the candelabrum, and the captain's hat at my side and sat with my back to the storm. The moment I opened the book to page one, lightning flashed, sending a burst of light across the text— ACT I SCENE I: Elsinore. A platform before the castle.

Of course I was intimately familiar with the content, having played the role of Polonius in a production that lasted a fortnight. In this environment, however, maybe familiarity would drown in a sea of mystery. Imagination could come to life in the shifting shadows and rumbling thunder. Yes, let the ghosts come forth and speak their minds. I was ready to be entertained by their gloomy fantasies.

As I read, the frequent thunder and pelting of raindrops on glass, along with the ongoing violin from below, played a hypnotizing concerto. Whether or not I dozed, I cannot say, but a particularly loud thunderclap snapped me to full wakefulness.

From that moment onward, anxiety about the possibility of flooded roads kept me from slumber.

Soon after reading that something was rotten in the state of Denmark, a dull thump shook my attention toward a place unseen beyond the boundaries of the candlelight. A draft ensued and extinguished all but the central taper. Perhaps a window blew open, which could usher in rain, or wet air at the least. Books in that section would not fare well.

I set Hamlet on the bench and walked with the candelabrum toward the source of the sound. With my light only one fifth of its former strength, making the floor ahead a dim mystery, I shuffled my feet to avoid tripping. At the same time, I reached for the lit candle, hoping to reignite the others, but its flame fell prey to another breeze.

Darkness enveloped me. If not for the frequent lightning, I would be lost in a sea of shelves. With each flash, I took note of the distance to a shelf or corner, walked to it, and waited for the next bolt, taking care to make my way toward the mysterious thump.

A new sound arose, a sort of mewing. Perhaps a cat had found its way to the open window and taken advantage of its good fortune—a dry place to spend the night.

Now tracking the cat's cries, I strode with more confidence that I had found the right path. Yet, as I drew closer, the cries took on a new character, more like human whimpering than a cat's lament.

A bright flash lit the room. Two paces away, a small boy sat with his back to a shelf, sobbing with his hands over his eyes. When darkness again veiled him, I imagined the son of a party guest becoming weary of the inane conversations. He had wandered upstairs to seek adventure and become lost in the maze of shelves.

Not wanting to startle him with a call, I whistled a nursery-rhyme tune, though I no longer remember its name.

Words blended in with his sobs. "Who's out there?"

A new flash provided another momentary view. The boy was looking straight at me, trembling, tear tracks evident on his cheeks. How he could see me in the dark was a mystery. Perhaps he was catlike after all.

I attempted a cheery tone. "I apologize for disturbing you, young man. I heard a noise in this direction and wondered if perhaps a window had blown open. I feared for the well-being of the books."

He said nothing. Total darkness blanketed everything.

Of course, suggesting that he was lost or afraid of the dark might injure his pride, so I thought it best to allow him to confess his own fears. "I heard your travail. Are you hurt? May I help you in any way?"

"I've lost my primer." His whimpering restarted. "If I don't find it, my master will beat me."

"Your master? You mean a schoolmaster? Your teacher?"

A lightning flash provided a glimpse of his tearful nod.

I took a step closer, knelt within reach, and set the candelabrum down. "Well, we'll just have to find it, won't we? I will go downstairs and relight my candles. Then I'll come back, and we'll look for your primer together."

When I imagined leaving this poor, weeping boy alone in the dark, I decided against it. "Better yet, why don't you come with me?" I reached for his hand but touched only air. Lightning flashed. The boy was gone. Vanished.

I shot to my feet, stumbled back, and fell against the opposite shelf, my heart racing. Yet again lightning flashed, revealing a small book where the boy once sat.

My hands trembling, I picked up the dust-covered volume and walked toward my reading bench, taking small steps to avoid tripping in the darkness. How could the boy disappear without a sound? No child could get up and run that quickly, could he? Perhaps the lightning pulses had disoriented my sense of time, and thunder masked the boy's sounds.

Bryan Davis

Having convinced myself of that idea, I settled my nerves. The boy had to be around somewhere. I thought to call out to him, but not knowing his name gave me pause. A glow appeared in the midst of the darkness, drawing closer. Perhaps Marc or Francine had arrived to escort me back to the party. I slid the book into a pocket in my breeches, picked up my candelabrum, and walked toward the glow. With no new lightning strokes brightening my path, I was glad for the radiant guide.

As I neared the newcomer, five candles distinguished themselves, similar in arrangement to my own. The flames illuminated an unfamiliar man, slender and sporting a pointed beard. Dressed in what appeared to be a scholar's robe from centuries past, he was obviously a party guest, though he wore no mask. Perhaps the first hour's masquerade had ended.

When we came within a few steps of each other, I stopped and gave him a nod. "Greetings, friend. Will you do me the favor of allowing me to light my candles?"

"With pleasure." He extended his candelabrum.

As I lit mine, I spoke in a casual manner. "What brings you to this dusty book jungle?"

He glanced around. "I am looking for a boy. He seems to have run off."

"I saw a boy, but he also ran from me. I lost him in the darkness." When I lit the final candle, I looked him in the eye. "Are you his father?"

The man offered a thin smile. "No, no. I am Michael, his teacher."

"His schoolmaster?"

"A reasonable synonym, though I prefer teacher. I am master to no one."

I studied his face, the contours of his nose and chin. He appeared to lack the typical lines of the local Parisians, and his skin, darker than most, also gave evidence of foreign heritage, though he might have been wearing makeup. "If you don't mind my asking, where are you from?"

"I hail from Spain, but I have been in France for quite a long time."

"Which explains your perfect French."

"I certainly have had plenty of time to practice it." Michael looked me over. "And I assume you're an Englishman, a military man of some sort."

"From London, sir, but the uniform is merely a disguise for the festivities. My name is Justin." I slid the book from my pocket and held it under the light—an old Latin primer. Had the boy been sitting on it the entire time? "When your student ran away, he left this book behind. Do you recognize it?"

Michael took the primer and sighed. "Yes, this is Jean's."

I gave him a disarming laugh. "He feared that you would beat him if you knew he lost it."

"Beat him? Nonsense. I have never laid a hand on that boy." Michael's brow bent. "If Jean had it with him before he ran, why did he fear punishment for losing it?"

"I think he was sitting on it. He didn't realize it was underneath him."

"No, he is never absentminded. He was playing a game, a mean one." Michael looked past me. "Which way did he go?"

"I don't know. I reached for him to guide him downstairs, and he was gone in a flash. I was startled, but boys can be quick, I suppose."

Michael gazed at me in a quizzical manner for a moment before nodding. "Ah. I understand now."

"Understand what?"

"Your confusion. Jean is, indeed, quick to disappear, especially under the cover of darkness. You are not the first to be startled by his antics. He enjoys such pranks."

I lifted my candelabrum. "I'll be glad to help you search for him."

Michael shook his head. "It would be better if you stay away from him."

"Stay away? Why?"

"He has a violent streak."

I laughed. "He's just a boy."

"An unpredictable boy. Even a rogue. I am thankful that you escaped unharmed."

"Escaped unharmed?" I gave him a doubtful stare. "He's no older than seven. What could he possibly—"

"I have already said too much." He patted my shoulder. "Perhaps you should get back to your festivities while I look for Jean."

"*My* festivities? Aren't you also one of the guests?"

"I am a guest, to be sure, but that is neither here nor there. The people on the ground floor are the reason I am looking for Jean. He is likely to give them a fright ... or worse."

"Is he ..." I searched for the right words. "Mentally unstable?"

Michael cleared his throat. "He is ... recovering ... I hope."

"If he is unstable, then why are you here in this abandoned school?"

His tone turned condescending. "Perhaps the building is not as abandoned as you assume."

"Then is it ... an asylum?"

"In a manner of speaking." He nodded toward the spiral staircase and clipped his words. "I suggest that you go. Now. Leave Jean to me. Your presence here will serve only to agitate him."

I looked at the stairs. As before, the darkness below seemed terrifying. Apparently Marc and Francine had not yet succeeded in mollifying Madame Noël. "I prefer to stay. I am more comfortable with books than I am with people."

"I cannot force compliance, but you must be careful lest something evil befall you." Michael's dark eyes seemed penetrating as he altered to a warning tone. "If you see Jean, stay away from him and call out to me. I am the only one who is able to handle him." He walked away in the direction I had seen Jean.

As he faded into the darkness, I sat on the bench, set the candelabrum down, and picked up Hamlet. I stared blankly at the pages and listened to the violin downstairs. The new mysteries stirred in my mind. What an odd place to house an asylum, especially since Monsieur Haussmann planned to destroy it. Did Michael know of the demolition plans? And how could that boy harm anyone?

Mother, the confusion raised reminders of what we discovered in the attic. Father looked like a stranger. Blood dripped from his hands, a man who had never harmed a fly. I will never forget his face, a mask of rage as you screamed for me to run. Although I wanted to know the identity of the woman who hung from the rafters, I obeyed. I ran and never stopped running.

If such a man as my father could do harm, then maybe a boy could devise a harmful scheme. A prank, perhaps? A trip line that causes a stumble? Who could tell what evils a lunatic boy might conceive?

Then a counter idea dawned on me. Could it be that Jean was the victim, and Michael, the unassuming teacher, was actually a predator? Was his story a lie? Had I betrayed Jean by giving his approximate whereabouts to a vindictive schoolmaster? Certainly I owed it to Jean to find out.

I dropped the book, snatched the candelabrum, and walked toward the area where I had met Jean. Again a breeze threatened to snuff the flames, prompting me to cup my hand in front of the candles as I hurried on.

After meandering around various shelves, I found the open window and shut it, stifling the breeze. I held the candelabrum high. Nothing but shelves and books met my view, certainly no sign of Jean or Michael.

"Captain?"

I turned toward the voice. A woman holding a lantern walked toward me, my costume's hat in her other hand. As my eyes adjusted to her lantern's brighter glow, she came into focus. Francine had finally come for me, still dressed in her Joan of Arc costume, though now without a mask. "Francine, I'm so glad you're here."

She walked to a point just out of reach and stopped, her expression blank. "My name is Joan."

I narrowed my eyes. For some reason, she looked more gaunt than usual. "If the masquerade game is still going on, why did you remove your mask?"

"Mask?" She tilted her head. "Why would I wear a mask?"

"Ah. Right. No one can see you while you're up here."

When she gave me the hat, her expression hardened. "Captain, you should go now."

I put the hat on. "Has your mother's anger subsided?"

She blinked in a confused manner. "My mother is no longer with us."

"Did she fall ill?"

"No, she is not ill." She curled her arm around mine. "Come. I will lead you out."

I resisted her pull. "Francine ... I mean, Joan. I saw a boy here. Scared. Crying. He feared his schoolmaster. I'm concerned for his safety."

She shook her head. "Michael is not a danger to Jean."

"You know them?" I nodded. "Of course you know them. You know everyone here. Then why is Jean so frightened of Michael?"

"It is a ruse, I assure you." She pulled again. "Come. You must leave at once."

This time I walked with her, matching her hurried gait. "Where is Marc ... I mean, Bishop Cauchon? Is he behaving himself tonight?"

"No better than usual." She halted near the spiral staircase and squinted at me. "Have you seen him?"

"Not since I came up here."

"Good. I told him to stay out of sight." She lifted the lantern and let the glow seep into every crevice in the walls and bookshelves. "I will search for Jean. If he is here, my lantern will find him."

A woman's scream pierced the air, coming from the first floor. Another followed, along with a third, then silence. Even the violin hushed.

Francine set a hand on my back. "Go. Hurry."

With the candelabrum still in hand, I ran down the spiraling steps while blowing out the tapers. On the first floor a group of about ten party guests crowded an interior door near a far back corner of the assembly hall. Marc stood high within the inner room, perhaps perched on a chair. With a knife in hand, he sawed a taut rope as his cassock sleeve swayed with the effort.

I squeezed through the crowd until I made my way into the room, apparently a small lounge where more guests stood shoulder to shoulder. A woman dressed in a jester's costume dangled limply at the rope's end, a noose around her neck.

I dropped the candelabrum. Madame Noël?

When the rope severed, Marc and another man guided the woman to the floor. Then Marc straightened and waved an arm, shouting, "Get back, everyone. Give her room."

As the guests pulled away, murmurs and whispers buzzed in my ears.

"Is she dead?"

"Did anyone see what happened?"

"She wasn't feeling well. She excused herself to sit here for a while."

I again pushed past guests and broke through to the inner circle. Madame Noël lay on the floor with Marc's helper kneeling next to her, setting a hand on her neck and another on her chest.

I grasped Marc's arm. "Is she ..." I couldn't speak the word.

Marc heaved quick, shallow breaths. "I don't know, Justin. Dr. Cousineau will tell us."

The doctor, dressed as a gendarme, poked and prodded. His long nose twitched, raising an image of a sniffing hound searching for a scent. The bald spot atop his middle-aged head, however, brushed the image away.

He looked up. "She is dead. Her neck is intact. I assume she strangled to death."

The news spread across the room like a fanned wildfire.

"Suicide?" a man called from the crowd.

"Murder?" a woman asked.

24

Marc stood on tiptoes and scanned the room. "Has anyone seen—"

Footsteps clattered from the assembly room staircase. The party guests divided. Francine ran into the room, holding a lit candelabrum. When she saw her mother's corpse, she staggered toward Marc, gasping, "Marc? Marc? She's alive. Tell me she's alive."

"Sister ..." He took her candelabrum, handed it to a nearby woman, and wrapped Francine in his arms. "She's dead."

"No, no, no!" Francine buried her face in Marc's cassock and let out a wordless wail.

While others wept with her, Dr. Cousineau rose and looked into the crowd. "Who found Madame Noël?"

One of the cat sisters raised her hand. "About an hour ago she said she wasn't feeling well. When she didn't return to the party, I came here to check on her."

The doctor pointed at the chair. "Was this here?"

She shook her head. "Marc dragged it over."

"Then suicide seems unlikely. We should call an inspector."

A woman dressed as a pirate spoke with a shrill voice. "If we have a murderer in the building, shouldn't we leave? One of us could be the next victim."

"We all have to stay here," Marc said. "The bridge over the brook washed out, and the Seine is flooding. Travel is unsafe. We will have to conduct an investigation ourselves."

Dr. Cousineau scanned the room. "Did anyone see anything peculiar? A stranger in our midst, perhaps?"

The cat sister pointed at me. "He's the only person I don't know. He insulted Jacqueline, so she told him to leave. I thought he was gone, but here he is."

"Now, Sabina," Dr. Cousineau said, "let's not jump to conclusions. I'm sure the storm prevented his departure." He turned toward me with an arched bushy brow that seemed friendly enough. "Where have you been, young man?"

"Upstairs. Reading." My voice trembled. "Marc's suggestion."

"It's true," Marc said. "Francine and I told him to go."

"And I was there the entire time," I added. "I ran down when I heard the screams."

Still supporting Francine with one arm, Marc grasped my wrist. "Did you see anyone up there? A stranger?"

"Marc, everyone here is a stranger to me, but I did see two people, a man and a boy. Michael and Jean."

"Can you describe the man?"

I ran my hand along an imagined beard. "He has a beard that tapered to a point. Dressed in a scholar's robes. Dark. A Spaniard, he said. He claimed to be the boy's schoolmaster."

Marc shook his head. "He doesn't sound familiar."

"Francine knows him." I pointed. "Ask her."

She brushed tears from her cheeks, her voice fractured by sobs. "I don't ... know of any guest named ... Michael. And no children ... are here."

"No children?" The little girl who looked like Justice came to mind, but I decided not to contradict Francine. "You were in the library with me only a moment ago. We were together at the top of the staircase when we heard the screams."

"Justin ..." Francine took a deep breath, which seemed to settle her spasms. "Justin, I went up there to bring you back to the party. When I heard the first scream, I was at the far side of the library. I had to run through a dark maze of bookshelves before I could get to the stairs."

As I gazed at her, confusion swirled. How could she lie without a hint of guilt? And why? While upstairs, she had been mysterious, even macabre when she said, *My mother is no longer with us.* Francine knew Madame Noël was dead. Could she have committed the murder? If so, why did she go upstairs and tell me about her mother's death? Nothing made sense.

"Justin," Marc said, breaking into my dark reverie, "you appear to be spellbound. Were you going to say something else?"

"I ... uh ..." I averted my gaze. "Nothing at the moment. Apparently my memory is failing. I feel as if I have taken a blow to the head."

26

"As we all feel, I'm sure." Marc stared at me as did everyone else in the room. Their eyes felt like daggers, pointing fingers. I had to help them find the killer as quickly as possible.

I looked at the ceiling a few yards above. The rope appeared to run through a gap between two broken boards. "The murderer must have fastened the rope to something in the library. Some of us should search for clues up there."

"I will go," Dr. Cousineau said.

"And I." Marc retrieved Francine's candelabrum and vaulted onto the chair. He swung toward the assembled group and spoke with an authoritative voice. "The three of us will go upstairs to see what we can learn. Everyone else stay together. No one is to go anywhere without escort."

He jumped down to the floor, kissed Francine, and strode into the assembly room while I followed and the doctor trailed. As we ascended the stairs, the candles cast a familiar glow. When we reached the library, Marc lifted the candelabrum high. Light poured into the gaps between the shelves, though not as brightly or with as much depth as the lantern had.

I stared at the candelabrum. Francine had it with her when she descended the stairs. Yet, when I met her here, she was carrying a lantern, the one she claimed she could use to find Jean, which meant that it was still somewhere in the library. Why would Francine switch from one to the other?

Dr. Cousineau pointed toward the area where I had found Jean. "The rope's fastening point has to be in that direction."

Marc led the way again, now with more deliberation. Taking uneasy steps, he shifted the candelabrum from side to side and peered between shelves. As when I walked along this same path, lightning flashes added to the illumination. I watched for any glimpse of movement, whether from Jean or Michael. Of course, calling out their names would be foolish. After contradicting Francine in front of her friends even while she suffered wretched grief, I, the stranger in their midst, was likely already a prime suspect, or at least considered insane. Why confirm either suspicion by calling for people who, according to Francine's most recent words, weren't here?

When we reached the farthest corner, Marc's light passed across a rope that ran from the floor upward into darkness.

"We should get a ladder," Dr. Cousineau said. "A knot can provide a clue to who tied it."

Marc nodded. "A sailor's hitch, for example."

I hoped my captain's uniform wasn't the reason for Marc's suggestion. I decided against asking. "There are ladders leaning against some of the shelves."

Dr. Cousineau looked at Marc. "I saw one a few rows back. Perhaps the two of us should get it."

"No," I said. "We should stay together."

The doctor gave me an icy stare. "I prefer that Marc and I conduct this investigation from this point on. Without you."

"Without me? What exactly are you saying?"

"I am saying that it would be better for you to be ignorant of our findings."

"But ..." My retort died. He probably already considered me guilty of the crime. How could I insist on anything?

Marc patted Dr. Cousineau's back. "Please give me a moment with Justin."

"Very well." The doctor plucked a taper from the candelabrum. "I'll find the ladder. Call me when you're finished."

As Dr. Cousineau walked away, Marc looked at me, the glow of the four remaining candles highlighting tears in his eyes. "Justin, I ..." His lips trembling, he looked away.

"Marc, I'm your friend. What are your thoughts?"

He heaved a deep sigh. "My thoughts are a jumble. I barely know which way is up. My mother is dead and ..." His voice pinched. "And my last conversation with her was an argument, just an hour before she died."

"I'm sorry to hear that. Very sorry." I dared to probe further. "What did you argue about?"

His voice became a hammer. "About you, Justin." The words bounced off the walls in echoed shouts. After a moment of silence, he whispered, "I apologize."

"No need. These are tragic moments. I understand the pain."

"As well you should." A flash of lightning highlighted Marc's sympathetic expression. "Justin, how old were you when the police arrested your father?"

"Seven. A month past my birthday."

"And they never found your mother." He averted his eyes again. "You suffered two tragedies in one night."

I didn't bother to claim once again that my mother was still alive somewhere. He had heard my attestations many times before, calling them questionable theories at best. "I have had time to heal. Your tragedy is fresh and raw. Don't hold back. Say what's on your mind."

He lifted his brow in a skeptical manner. "Really, Justin? Do you really want me to say what's on my mind?"

The pain in his voice gave me pause, but I couldn't retract my offer of solace. "Yes. Yes, I do."

"Well, I'm thinking what Francine is likely thinking. What everyone at the party is likely thinking."

As he took in a deep breath, his pause swelled, ready to explode. "And that is?" I prompted.

He followed with a longer, louder sigh. "That you killed my mother."

My own voice rose. "What? Marc, are you serious? You know I could never hurt anyone."

"You asked me to say what's on my mind. It's madness, of course, and the better part of me doesn't believe it, but my thoughts are barking dogs that refuse to stay quiet. And judging the way the other guests looked at you, I'm certain they have already found you guilty. Dr. Cousineau has as well, which is why he doesn't want you to help us investigate."

"Because I'm the stranger in their midst."

"And because you insulted the victim. Because you were out of sight and had plenty of time to conceive and execute the murder. No one else had motive or opportunity."

A foolish thought entered my mind—to mention Francine's statement about her mother no longer being with us—but I thought better of it. "You're right, Marc. I am the obvious suspect, but I assure you—"

"No need. I know you're innocent. We just have to find the real culprit. I merely wanted a moment to explain Dr. Cousineau's hesitance."

"Speaking of which," I said, "we have left him alone too long."

"Yes, you're right." Marc turned toward the shelves and called out, "Dr. Cousineau? Can you hear me?"

Only a distant rumble of thunder replied.

Marc sniffed. "Do you smell smoke?"

I inhaled, detecting a waxy odor. "Candle fumes?"

"No. It's more than that." Light erupted from beyond a nearby shelf—a fire.

30

Chapter Three

We ran toward the fire, past two sets of shelves and into a gap between two others. A heap of books burned in wild, crackling flames. Something moved underneath.

I whipped my coat off and beat the flames with it while kicking books. Marc set the candelabrum down, stripped off his cassock, and used it to smother the fire. Soon, we extinguished it except for a few scattered embers.

Dr. Cousineau, his clothes burned away and his body blackened, moaned. Marc and I knelt next to him, one on each side. "Dr. Cousineau," Marc said, coughing in the midst of thick smoke. "What happened? Who did this?"

The doctor's mouth opened, though his melted lips clung to each other by thin strands. "A boy. P … Pierre."

"Pierre?" I looked at Marc, clearer now as the smoke lifted toward the ceiling. "Remember I mentioned Michael and Jean? Michael is Jean's schoolmaster. Maybe he has another student named Pierre."

"My sincerest apologies for doubting you." Marc grasped the doctor's ankles. "Let's get him downstairs."

I wrapped my hands around the doctor's hot, sticky wrists. The moment we lifted, something thudded nearby. The sound repeated again and again. Then the bookshelf to my left toppled, slammed into the shelf to my right, and knocked us down. Loud cracks erupted as the fragile wood snapped over my back.

I lay sprawled over the doctor. A pile of books and the fractured shelf pressed me down. I called, "Marc, are you all right?"

No one answered.

Setting one hand on each side of the doctor, I pushed against the floor. The shelf cracked further, and books slid off my back. As I straightened, I rose until I stood upright.

Unable to see through the darkness, I reached down and felt Dr. Cousineau's wrist. I detected no pulse. The smoky odors choked me. "Marc?" I pushed forward, breaking shelves with my feet and fists and tossing books aside until I found him. I felt along his body and found his wrist. His pulse throbbed, fast and even.

Now heaving quick breaths, I cleared the debris away, grabbed Marc under his arms, and dragged him to a clear part of the floor, guided by helpful flashes of lightning. After laying him on his back, I knelt at his side and patted his cheek. "Marc, can you hear me?"

He offered no response.

I felt for broken bones but found none. I ran my fingers across his scalp and came upon a gash, perhaps five inches in length, though it was impossible to tell how deep. Blood matted his hair, warm and wet. "I have to get you downstairs. You probably need sutures."

The moment I slid my hands under his arms again, a light glowed in the distance, coming closer at a rapid pace. Within seconds, Francine appeared, running while holding a lantern. When she arrived, she set the lantern down, knelt next to me, and looked Marc over. "He is breathing." She was calm, strangely calm, as she ran her fingers through his hair. "He has a severe cut on his head."

"Yes, the bookshelves fell over."

"I can see that." Her terse reply added to her unusual demeanor. "I smell smoke."

"Someone set Dr. Cousineau on fire. Before he died, he said a boy named Pierre did it."

Francine swung her head toward me, her eyes aflame. "Pierre set a man on fire?"

I nodded. "Do you know him?"

"I do, indeed. He is my student."

"Student? I knew you teach sewing, but to a boy?"

She returned her gaze to Marc. "I have taught many men how to sew. Now you must learn if you want to save his life."

"I'll be glad to. But why can't *you* stitch his wound?"

"I must search for Pierre while you stitch." She peered at Marc's cut again. "The bleeding is profuse. We should cauterize the vessel."

"Cauterize? Do you know how to do that?"

"Of course." She picked up the lantern and hurried away, calling back, "Use your hand to put pressure on the wound. I will return in a moment with what we need."

As the light faded, I sat on the floor and pressed a trembling hand against Marc's head. Hot and sticky, his scalp seemed feverish next to my cold skin. In contrast to my shaking limbs, Francine seemed calm, miraculously calm, in spite of her brother's dangerous wound and her mother's tragic death. Perhaps some sort of survival mechanism had taken control, an instinct implanted by God Almighty for such a time as this.

Soon, a bobbing light appeared. Francine ran into view, carrying a small wicker basket. When she arrived, she set the lantern and basket on the floor, removed the lantern's glass enclosure, and withdrew a long metal nail from the basket. She wrapped a black cloth around the nail's head and placed the point in the wick's flame. When the nail reddened, she passed it and the cloth to me and continued talking while threading a needle. "Now do exactly what I tell you. First, lift your hand from the wound."

I did so, staring at Francine's steady countenance. I had never seen such a commanding aspect in her personality before. When she finished with the needle and set it down, she slid the lantern close to Marc's head, picked up a white cloth and scissors from the basket, and cleared hair and blood from around the wound. "Do you see where the bleeding is heavy?"

"At the middle of the cut?"

She nodded. "When I finish cleaning the wound, apply the hot nail. I will show you how. Then I will guide you through the first few stitches. After that, I must find Pierre."

Other than the initial sizzle of the cauterization and the renewed stench of burnt flesh, I remember little of the actual surgery. Perhaps my own survival mechanism came upon me, and stress and urgency wiped the details away. Still, Francine must have taught me well. My senses returned as I was tying the final stitch. The bleeding had stopped, and the gash had become a line of black, knotted threads.

When I finished, I put the nail and thread in my pocket, pushed the needle into my shoe leather, and used the cloth to absorb the remaining blood, then looked around. Francine was gone.

After finding the cassock and making it into a pillow for Marc, I rose to my feet, picked up the lantern, and lifted it high. The bright light washed over the toppled shelves. Five had fallen, the last of which leaned against an upright shelf that stood ninety degrees askew from the others. The mysterious arrangement had kept the remaining shelves from toppling.

A small human shape moved beyond the upright shelf. I took a step closer and extended the lantern as far as my arm would reach. Francine had said something about the lantern being able to find Jean. Maybe his mental illness caused him to be drawn to its light.

I called, "Jean? Is that you?"

A pair of eyes glowed in the midst of the darkness, but the child, whoever he was, stayed quiet. Yet human eyes don't glow in the dark. Light had to be casting a ray upon them from somewhere.

Still, the haunting visage sent shivers across my skin. Perhaps a murderer stared at me from the shadows. I shook off the feeling and ventured another call. "Pierre?"

"Who are you?" The reply was soft, timid, definitely the voice of a boy.

"I am Justin Trotter. And you?"

"Pierre Cauchon."

The name raised memories from my history studies. Pierre Cauchon was the bishop who persecuted Joan of Arc. Why would this boy claim that name? Considering Francine's and Marc's disguises, the coincidence was too incredible to believe. "Pierre, I know you set a man on fire."

34

"He deserved to die. He lied to me." Pierre walked into the light. Dressed in a long, white shirt and black hose and shoes, he appeared to be the same age as Jean, perhaps six or seven. His piercing eyes added a sinister element. Not wanting to give him access to Marc, I stayed in place. "I heard that Francine is your teacher."

He shook his head but offered no explanation.

"Come now. She told me herself that she's your teacher."

"Then she lies." His face reddened as he spat out, "I hate lies."

I shuddered. Pierre's venom removed all doubt that he, indeed, murdered Dr. Cousineau.

"Pierre?" Francine appeared from the shadows behind Pierre and grabbed his wrist. "I have searched everywhere for you." He tried to pull away, but she held tight.

Still extending the lantern, I took a step closer. "We should call the police. The little demon is a murderer."

"He *is* a demon and a murderer." Francine pulled him toward me, forcing him to stumble along. When they came within a few paces, she stopped. "Yet there is no need to call the police. We must make sure the people downstairs leave at once."

Francine's manner of speech once again struck me as odd. Her usual diction had changed. And why would she call her guests *the people downstairs*? "Didn't you hear that the bridge washed out? Travel is dangerous."

"Remaining here is also dangerous, likely more so than leaving."

"Because this is an asylum for the criminally insane?"

Pierre tried to run, but Francine jerked him back to her side. "That is not quite accurate, but if using that label will help you chase the people away, then so be it."

I shook my head. "I don't understand. If you knew this place is dangerous, why did you have a party here? And Pierre said you're not his teacher. What's going on?"

She narrowed her eyes. "Pierre said that? It is not like him to lie."

Pierre tried to pull away again. "I didn't lie. He said someone named Francine is my teacher."

"Francine?" She cast a hard stare at me. "Who is this Francine? You mentioned her earlier."

The strangeness of her words added to my confusion, a stormy nightmare that wouldn't end. For some reason she had decided to play a role, to continue the game, perhaps for her dead mother's sake. Who was I to object to her means of coping with grief? I could play along. "I apologize, Joan. You look very much like a Francine I know."

"I accept your apology, but apologies are not going to protect your friends downstairs. Jean is still missing, and he is unpredictable."

"Did he hang Madame Noël?"

"It is possible, though using fire is more common for both him and Pierre."

Again her words fomented turmoil. How could she be so intimately acquainted with these murderously insane boys? "Will you help me carry Marc downstairs? Since the people are your guests, you have to be the one to dismiss them."

"You are mistaken. They are not my guests."

"What?" I shook my head. "You're not making sense."

"Marc?" A woman who sounded like Francine called from the direction of the staircase. "Justin? Are you up here?"

My hands trembled. "Yes," I called in return. "Who are you?"

"Francine. Are Marc and Dr. Cousineau with you?"

I stared at the woman and boy in my company. Who were they? Were they both mad? Lunatics in an asylum? Yet, how could this Joan of Arc impersonator look exactly like Francine?

"You should answer your friend," Joan said. "With Jean lurking, she could be in danger."

I called out, "Francine, we've had an accident. Bring some men to help me carry Marc. He's alive but unconscious."

"Unconscious?" Her voice spiked with alarm. "Yes. Right away."

36

Again I stared at the woman. She returned the stare—patient, emotionless. I whispered, "Who are you, really?"

Michael stepped out from behind a nearby shelf. "Joan, we have already risked too much exposure."

She looked at him. "This man deserves an explanation. I sense integrity in him."

"Few of us receive what we deserve." He extended a hand toward her. "Help me find Jean. We must all return to the catacombs before investigators arrive."

She let out a sigh and turned back to me. "I hope you are in a state of grace, Justin. I fear that your trials have only begun." She took the lantern from me, and the three of them walked out of sight behind a shelf. The light from Joan's lantern slowly faded.

Now in darkness, I searched in vain for Marc's candelabrum. New lights appeared, approaching at a rapid pace. Three men hurried toward me, one carrying a candelabrum. When they arrived, Francine appeared behind them, also carrying a light. Two men lifted Marc by his wrists and ankles and, without a word, began carrying him away, guided by the third.

Francine stayed and swept her light across the fallen shelves. "Is this the accident you mentioned?"

I nodded. "One of the shelves struck Marc. I stitched a cut on his head."

"*You* stitched it?"

"He was bleeding to death." I showed her my bloodstained hand.

"So you saved his life." She scanned the floor and spied t̶ basket. "Where did you get the supplies?"

Of course I ached to tell her everything, but surely she wᵈld think that *I* was a lunatic in an asylum. "I found it here in the library."

"You found the basket and stitched Marc without a light?"

"I had a light. It's a long story."

"Very well." She again guided her light across the shelves, sniffing. "What is that odor?"

My throat caught. "I ... I hesitate to tell you."

Her brow knitted tightly. "Where is Dr. Cousineau?"

"Dead. Under the bookshelves."

She gasped. "Dead?"

I nodded. "As I said, it's a long story."

Trembling, she backed away. "I ... I must see to my brother."

"Are you afraid of me?"

"Terrified."

"Francine, it was an accident. You can see for yourself that the shelves toppled. And if I were a killer, I wouldn't have sewn Marc's cut."

She halted and swallowed hard. "This is true."

"Something strange is afoot. I think the murderer is lurking here in the library."

Her eyes darted. "Then we'd better go. Now."

"Should I? Your friends already think I murdered your mother."

"You decide for yourself." She removed a burning candle and gave it to me. "As I said, I must see to my brother. I will send someone for Dr. Cousineau soon, that is, if anyone is brave enough to come." She turned and strode toward the staircase. Seconds later, she disappeared from sight.

I stood alone, holding a single white taper.

It is impossible to relate the many feelings that flooded my mind, but I will attempt to explain a few. In the midst of turmoil and shivering fear, I doubted my own sanity. And why wouldn't I? The other options were too strange to believe. Either this old library housed four deranged people, or I had encountered ghosts who could walk in physical form. In either case, the boys had apparently committed two murders and had the potential to commit more.

Not only this, but why was the martyr, Joan of Arc, acting as a teacher for a young version of her persecutor? Could the other pair, Michael and Jean, have a similar relationship? If so, who were they?

I determined to investigate the matter, but with danger all around, both in the library and below on the ground floor, this was not the time, even though the thousands of books could lend a hand in research. Now I had to decide how to explain myself to Francine's suspicious friends.

Hoping to relax, I inhaled deeply. The odor of smoke and burnt flesh returned, now with more intensity. With the candle extended, I walked toward Dr. Cousineau's resting place. A flame flickered. Smoke rose in a thin curl of gray. At any moment, these old books could erupt in an inferno.

I pushed through the toppled debris again. When I reached the doctor's body, I grasped his gendarme coat with my free hand and rolled him toward me. The moment he moved, flames shot up and spread like fiery locusts, devouring shredded books and splintered shelves.

I stumbled back through the debris. "Michael," I shouted. "Joan. Are you in here?"

The growing fire roared and crackled, dashing any hopes that they could hear me. Maybe they had already left the building as Michael had indicated. I prayed for their safety and continued trudging through piles of books to escape the flames.

Once in the clear, I ran toward the staircase and hurried down the dizzying spiral. When I reached bottom, I shouted, "The library's on fire," but found no one in the assembly room.

The front door banged open. A wet breeze poured in. The chrysanthemum pots were scattered, some tipped over, as if a herd had stampeded into the storm.

Breathing heavily, I scanned the room again. Whatever incited the escape must have been more frightening than lightning and floods. Perhaps another murder?

I ran to the door and looked outside. Dozens of people hurried away on the carriage path, their heads low. Near the back, two men dragged something on a tablecloth, perhaps bodies. Covered by a cloak, it was impossible to tell who lay there, perhaps Marc and his mother. A man held a lantern at the front and another did the same at the rear, both constantly looking around as if ready to ward off a potential attack.

Since they left me behind, they must have concluded that I was the murderer. They had to carry Marc to a physician, of course, but that mission of mercy required only a few capable men. And since they went on foot instead of carriages, they fled knowing the roads were washed out. They simply wanted to escape a greater danger by braving a lesser one.

I sighed. Francine didn't bother to come for me or even shout her intentions. She must have agreed with the others that I was the culprit, and the only person who knew otherwise lay unconscious on a makeshift litter.

When the group had moved nearly out of sight, I retrieved my raingear, walked out of the school, and ventured into the storm. Although it rained heavily, the lightning had subsided. The only peril might be a stumble into a rainwater ditch.

Cupping my hand over the candle, I slogged behind the others while keeping my distance. As long as I stayed in their path, I could watch their progress and avoid high water.

To my rear, flames sprouted through the roof and sizzled on contact with the downpour, a battle between the fire and the storm. With so much fuel inside, the fire would likely win the clash, and the entire building would soon be engulfed.

Maybe this result was a blessing. Surely the party guests could see the conflagration. Francine was sure to tell them that she left me behind. If I disappeared from society, everyone might assume that I perished in the blaze. The supposed murderer received his just deserts.

Then again, my life would be ruined in a different way. No home. No job. No money. And worst of all, no way to rescue Justice from her travail.

Somehow I had to survive, maybe take on a new identity and work for a different publisher. Since practically no one at the party knew me, maybe the police wouldn't be able to track me down. If I revealed my new identity to Francine and Marc, maybe they would stay quiet for my sake. Their help would make my task easier, but I couldn't count on their help or anyone else's.

As the rain eased, I trudged on. My only hope was for Marc to wake up and tell Francine of my innocence and how Dr. Cousineau died at the hands of Pierre. If I could stay out of sight until he recovered, perhaps all would be well.

Chapter Four

After walking a few miles to find a safe passage over the brook and later spending a chilly night in a barn under a horse blanket, I awoke to sunshine peeking through a hayloft window. A new day had dawned. The storm was finally over. I rose, stretched my stiff limbs, and returned the blanket to the horse stall. Now I had to emerge from my hiding place and learn whether or not I was a hunted man.

I left the barn and walked the muddy path toward the city center, thankful for the boots and cloak that had kept me relatively dry. With a sun-warmed breeze flowing through my clothes and hair, I would be as good as new by the time I arrived at my flat.

When I drew close, I lowered my head and slowed my pace. In weeks past, I had always been glad of the commissary in the building's first floor. Its presence meant police protection. Who would burglarize our flat with a law-enforcement office in the way?

Yet, now the office was my obstacle. If Francine or one of the guests reported me as a murder suspect, surely this office would be the first to be contacted by police headquarters. One or more officers might be happy to track down a penniless immigrant from England and throw him in jail.

After passing the office without being accosted, I climbed the stairs and checked my pocket for the key. It lay next to the candle stub that had guided my way last night. I quietly unlocked the door and entered. Inside, Marc reclined on his bed and Francine on mine, both uncovered and still in costume, as if they had collapsed from exhaustion.

I crept close to Marc and listened. He breathed easily, and his color was good. A quick check on Francine yielded the same observations. The wig now removed, her ginger hair spread across the bed, and the makeup that had discolored her face had been washed away, revealing her fair, freckled skin, including the oval birthmark on the side of her neck. No more the hardened soldier, she had transformed back into the feisty socialite.

Why she and Marc came here instead of her house or a hospital, I could only guess, and I couldn't stay to learn the reason. I had to pack my essentials and leave as quickly as possible.

Moving without a sound, I withdrew a carpetbag from under my bed and filled it with my clothes and other personal items, though I omitted the book I was translating. Once I finished, I tiptoed toward the door.

"Justin Trotter," Francine said in a calm tone.

I pivoted. She sat on the bed with her bare feet on the floor next to her shoes. Her expression was stoic, unreadable. "Yes?"

"Where are you going?"

I glanced at my bag. "I haven't decided yet."

"I spoke to the officer in charge downstairs. I suggested that he allow you to come home. Staying here would indicate innocence. Fleeing would indicate guilt. If you leave, he will arrest you the moment you reach the street."

I set the bag down. "Why are you warning me?"

Her voice and facial expression stayed perfectly calm. "Because I believe you are innocent."

"Then who reported the crime to the police?"

"I did, Justin. She was my mother."

"Of course. I apologize." I pulled my desk chair over and sat in front of her. "I hoped to stay out of sight until Marc wakes up. He was with me when someone set Dr. Cousineau on fire. He knows I'm innocent."

Her eyes sparkled with tears. "The fact that you stitched Marc's cut is proof enough for me, but the police might think otherwise."

"Who do you think killed your mother?"

She averted her eyes. "I hesitate to tell you."

"Why? I have no ties to any of your party guests."

When she returned her gaze to me, a tear rolled down her cheek. "You have ties to my brother."

My mouth dropped open unbidden. I looked at Marc, then back at Francine. "No." I shook my head. "Just ... no. Marc would never do that. His own mother? Francine, how could you—"

"You don't know Marc as well as you think." She leaned close and lowered her voice to a whisper. "Marc and Mother have had terrible fights in recent weeks. She kept threatening to remove him from her will if he didn't alter his course in life."

I whispered in return. "Marc told me of their disagreements, including the disinheritance threats."

"Disagreements?" Francine laughed under her breath. "Justin, once she flew into a drunken rage and tried to stab Marc. On another occasion, she tried to poison him."

"Poison him? With what? How did he avoid it?"

"Arsenic, I assume. Mother keeps it in the house for rats. One evening, she was drunk and kept insisting that he eat his soup. He threw it outside without considering that Mother's new puppy was nearby, eager to eat any castaway food."

I imagined the scenario, including the unfortunate pup. "Did she confess?"

Francine shook her head. "She swore she had no idea, but I knew better. She bought a supply of rat poison only two days earlier."

"Is it possible that she has offended others with her recent ill behavior?"

"Possible, yes, but she tried to kill her own son. He had a clear motive."

"Revenge?"

She nodded. "And survival, not to mention his inheritance."

"Marc is strong, but how could he have hanged her by himself?"

"I have a theory." Francine glanced around as if wary of ears in the walls. "Dr. Cousineau had a recent surgery mishap that resulted in death, and many of his patients are now going to other doctors. Rumors say he became an opium addict and needed money to maintain his habit."

"Do you think Marc promised him part of his inheritance?"

"Maybe." Tears welled in her eyes. "Oh, Justin, I feel like a traitor for even mentioning this, but what are the chances that Marc and Dr. Cousineau would be the first men at the scene with a knife ready to cut her down? And no one else examined her body. How do we know they didn't kill her in an easier way and then hanged her so it would look like someone upstairs was to blame?"

"Are you suggesting that Marc wanted to implicate me? That would be treachery."

A second tear rolled down her cheek. "I'm sorry, Justin. It's a terrible theory, I know, but it has more than crossed my mind. It has taken up residence there, and I can't get it out of my head."

"Let me think a minute." I closed my eyes. Images of the previous night streamed past. The idea that Jean could hang Madame Noël seemed ridiculous now. Here, in the light of day, the existence of a little boy living in a library asylum was absurd. Had I imagined it all? Michael, Joan, Pierre, and Jean? Was I losing my mind?

Not only that, now Francine was more than hinting that her own brother murdered their mother. Did she expect me to agree with such a shocking assertion? Marc had been my friend for three years, and, besides a few snide remarks, he never showed any animosity toward his mother, certainly never an attitude of revenge or a threat of violence.

I buried my face in my hands. "This is too much to take in."

"I know." She touched my knee. "Let me change the subject for a moment and tell you why we're here in your flat. I had Marc carried in because the way to my house was flooded. Then I sent for our physician, and he was able to make his way here and attended Marc during the night. Although he is worried about Marc staying unconscious ever since the party, the head wound doesn't appear to be life threatening, and he should awaken after sufficient rest, which will allow the swelling to diminish."

"That's a comfort." I looked out the window. The water in our own street had abated. "The flood is receding. Will you go home now?"

"I will see if the road is clear. If so, I will arrange for Marc to come home with me. But first I will speak to the officer and tell him that you're staying, that there is no need to arrest you."

"But a murder has taken place, the killing of a wealthy woman. You know how Paris reacts to stories like this. Tomorrow's papers will set fire to kindling. The police will be pressured to arrest someone for the crime as soon as possible, and your party guests will point their fingers directly at me."

Francine let out a deep sigh, as if trying to summon the courage to say something difficult. "Justin, you claimed that we were together in the library right before the screams. I will gladly confirm that alibi if it will keep you from losing your head. I doubt if anyone will remember that I said otherwise."

"The two of us together? Do you mean …" I cleared my throat. "What of your reputation?"

She bit her lip before replying. "That is a risk I am willing to take. Scandal is not as destructive as execution. I will recover."

New heat burned my ears. "I can't let you do that, Francine. You can't lie for my sake. The truth will come out."

"Let's hope so, but I am still willing to be seen as your lover in order to save your life." She gave me a coy smile. "Being matched with me wouldn't be so bad, would it?"

"No. Of course not. I wouldn't mind that at all. It's just that I don't want any shadow of scandal to fall on you. You don't deserve it."

"I am thankful for your chivalry." She grasped my hand. "Let's do this. We can portray ourselves as courting. We'll say that was the reason you came to the party, so I could introduce my suitor to my friends. Then if the tide turns against you, and it appears that you will be condemned, I will reveal our tryst in the library. That way, the revelation won't come out of the blue."

Her coy smile returned. "Truth be told, I have admired you for quite some time. I need a man who speaks his mind, a man who isn't afraid of my sharp tongue. It won't take much for me to convince people of my affection toward you. And since you're an actor, you won't have any trouble either."

"Francine ..." I enclosed her hand in both of mine. "Showing affection toward you won't be an act. Be sure of that."

"Oh ... I see." Her cheeks reddening, she withdrew her hand. "I didn't know."

"Does my confession spoil your plan?"

"No, no. You just took me by surprise. After all, we have had some ... shall we say ... intense conversations."

"True. Your surprise is warranted."

"In any case, as I told everyone last night, I went upstairs to bring you back to the party. I never denied seeing you there, so I won't be contradicting myself when I confirm that you were in the library at the time of the murder."

"A lie?"

"A white lie. To protect the innocent."

I looked at Marc. "And what of the guilty?"

"Yes. Marc." Francine withdrew a handkerchief from an insert in her costume and dabbed her eyes. "All we can do is allow the investigation to take its course. Mother had a few guests who hated her, so you won't be the only suspect."

"Will Marc be a suspect? Will you tell the police what you know?"

She slid her feet into her shoes, simple black leather, nothing ornamental, perfect for Joan of Arc. "Only if the investigation leads to pointed questions."

"For example, if an inspector learns of your mother's recent rat poison purchase."

She nodded. "Or our dog's untimely death."

"Yes, I suppose that's a reasonable lead to follow."

"I had better go." She rose and kissed me on both cheeks. "Au revoir, my newly discovered admirer. As I said, I will speak to the officer and send someone for Marc." Without another word, she walked out and closed the door.

I stared at the wall, my muscles flaccid. Were Francine and I now a couple? It seemed so. One of my dreams was coming true. I just had to survive the investigation.

Mother, I hope you can understand my perspective at that time. I saw many fine qualities in Francine. Of course you would not approve of her lies, no matter the shade, but in my view, perhaps colored at the moment by emotion, her motivations were pure. It would have been easy for her to blame me for Madame Noël's death, absolve her brother, and share the inheritance with him. She could have turned on me that very day and used her wealth against me. A few Napoléons in a judge's pocket weigh far more than a peasant's plaintive cries for mercy.

My legs weak, I rose and picked up my carpetbag. Obviously I couldn't leave now, but what if an inspector decided that I was the most likely suspect after all? Maybe he wouldn't believe my alibi. The danger was not yet over. It would be better to keep my bag packed and be ready to leave at a moment's notice.

After changing to my travel clothes, I sat on Marc's bed near his bare feet. Since sunshine infused our room with a healthy dose of warmth, he would be comfortable uncovered.

I whispered, "Marc, can you hear me?"

He stirred, and his eyes shifted under their lids, but he stayed quiet.

Warmth and silence opened the gateway to exhaustion. Since I had slept so little, it would be best to try to recover. Sleep would be a welcome retreat from my worries.

I took off my shoes and lay on my bed. As I drifted toward sleep, images of the previous night again swam through my thoughts. Jean, Michael, Joan, and Pierre were so real. How could they have been figments? Even Dr. Cousineau had seen Pierre. If the boys really were the murderers, then Marc and the doctor, of course, were innocent. But how could I find the truth, or, even more difficult, prove it?

My respite proved to be short lived. After less than an hour, a police officer arrived accompanied by two large, muscular men. While the men lifted and carried Marc out, the officer glared at me, his thick eyebrows dipping low and his mustache twitching as if incited by suspicious thoughts.

He glanced at my carpetbag, still sitting near the door. Although he said nothing about it, he likely came to the conclusion that I was planning to leave. At that moment, fear insisted that I run for my life, and in the same breath it demanded that I stay put. The second command won out, mainly because my legs refused to budge.

When the men left, I lay down again, this time unable to sleep. After a few moments, my door swung open, but no one stood in the stairway. Perhaps the officer had left the door ajar, and a breeze from downstairs pushed it open.

The moment I sat up to close it, Francine, wearing the pageboy wig once again, peeked around the jamb. "The men are gone?"

I rose to my feet and nodded. "Come in."

When she walked in, her shoes drew my attention, made of thick leather, earth tones instead of black. My gaze shifted to her face, darker and void of freckles. A shudder ran through my body. "Joan?"

"Yes, of course." She pivoted and looked at the stairwell. "Don't be scared. He won't hurt you."

Pierre walked in and took Joan's hand. Today the boy seemed much less sinister. In fact, he appeared childlike as he looked around with wide eyes.

The idea of two ghosts entering my flat affected me in a peculiar way. I felt no terror as I might have expected, though my legs quivered as I stared at these two apparitions, or whatever they might have been. Yet, even the tremors seemed void of fear. Their source seemed to be excitement, perhaps even familiarity.

"To what do I owe the pleasure of your visit?" I asked.

Joan touched the boy's head. "Pierre wishes to tell you something."

"By all means." I gestured toward my chair. Joan took that seat while Pierre sat cross-legged on the floor. I rested on my bed, folded my hands, and gave him a nod. "What do you want to tell me?"

He looked me in the eye. "I didn't set the fire. I didn't kill that man."

His quiet yet firm voice helped settle my tremors. "That man is Dr. Cousineau. He said that you did do it."

"I scared him but not on purpose. I only told him my name. He fell, and his candles dropped on some books. Then when he tried to get up, he pulled more books down on himself. I think maybe he broke a bone. That's why he couldn't get up."

Pierre's story seemed unlikely. Although the books were old and falling apart, how could they catch so quickly without the addition of a flammable fuel? And who thwarted our rescue efforts?

I gave the boy a hard stare. "How did the shelves tip over?"

He shrugged. "Maybe the wind? I don't know."

"No, I closed the window before it happened." I looked at Joan. "Have you questioned Jean about this?"

She shook her head. "I have little to do with Jean and know only what Michael tells me."

"Could such a small boy have pushed the bookshelf over? Or climbed the rafters to fasten a hangman's rope?"

Her expression turned sorrowful. "Jean is capable of almost anything. His heart is still quite dark and filled with malice."

"Joan ..." My hands began shaking, though again I felt no fear. I refolded them tightly and set them on my lap. "I need to know who you really are."

She touched her chest. "I am Joan, the Maid of Orléans, daughter of Jacques and Isabelle from the village of Domrémy. In my time, I was in command of the army of France."

"What I mean is, what are you now? You died centuries ago."

She smiled. "You are asking how I rose from the dead and came to be in charge of Pierre."

"Yes. Are you able to spare the time to tell me?"

"Only a little. Pierre gets anxious if he is in the company of strangers for too long."

"I understand. Feel free to leave whenever you must."

50

Chapter Five

As if copying my pose, Joan folded her hands on her lap and looked at me with attentive eyes. "Pierre Cauchon was the primary instigator of my persecution and the main reason I was burned at the stake. He was cold and calculating. He longed for my death. In his eyes, I was a witch, a sorceress. How could any woman, an untrained peasant, hear directly from God, especially one who wore the garments of a man? At first I thought he was simply protecting the clergy and his office of bishop, but his obsession with my trousers convinced me of his insanity.

"In any case, I resurrected in my nineteen-year-old body, while Pierre resurrected as a child. I am teaching him how to love and not hate, how to see beyond his blinders, to understand that God is not a respecter of educational status or wealth or clothing. God can speak to a king or a peasant, to a scholar or a knave, whether they wear finery or rags. He even used an ass to deliver a message to a prophet, so choosing a woman in trousers as his message bearer should be no surprise. Surely we are of greater nobility than an ass."

I stared at her while processing her nearly inconceivable explanation. Many questions rushed through my mind. I asked the one that seemed the most obvious. "What is the purpose? If Pierre heeds your teaching and reforms, what then?"

"I do not know. I am merely carrying out what I have been called upon to do. I have ventured guesses, of course. Perhaps he will be given another chance at life, become a true shepherd of souls, wielding a gentle crook instead of a harsh whip. And perhaps I will find better rest in heaven knowing that I played a part in his reformation. Yet, there is no way to be sure. Since Pierre is so stubborn, he might never reform. Maybe this exercise is simply a way to show him that he deserves the punishment reserved for hypocrites like him."

"Did one of your angels tell you to teach him?"

She nodded. "Saint Michael the Archangel."

Her answer reminded me of the events on the night of the murder. Although I steeled myself for more shakes, they failed to come. It seemed that I was growing accustomed to being in fellowship with ghosts. "Is the Michael I saw in the library doing the same as you are? Teaching Jean, I mean."

"He is. We have been teaching together since we started, first in the catacombs, then in the school. He thought the library would be a better environment, especially because of the easy access to books."

"Was Jean an adult who persecuted someone?"

"He was." Joan cocked her head. "Did you hear something?"

"No. Nothing."

"Someone is coming. I must leave." She rose from the chair and reached for Pierre's hand. He got up quickly and took it.

"Wait," I said. "What kind of being are you? Since Jean disappeared suddenly, I thought he might be a ghost, but you and Michael are both able to manipulate physical objects."

She glanced at the door, her eyes wary. "Ghost is an inadequate term, but since we are able to shed our physicality, it is reasonable for you to use it. I have no other word to give you."

"If you can shed physicality, why the rush to avoid being seen?"

"There is too much light to shift without being noticed during our transparent stage." She walked toward the door. "Good-bye, Justin. When I find Jean, I will take him to the catacombs. If you have further questions, you may seek us there." They walked out.

Two sets of rapid footsteps descended the stairs, replaced moments later by a heavier pair, ascending at a casual pace. I hurried to the door and looked down. A thirtyish man with a full mustache approached. Wearing a top hat, pressed trousers, and a double-buttoned vest under a frock coat, he appeared to be a gentleman.

When he saw me, he offered a nod. "I am Inspector Paul Fortier. May I ask you a few questions?"

"Of course." I gestured with a hand. "Come in."

As he entered, he unbuttoned his coat and took off his hat, revealing neatly combed short hair. "It's warmer today than I expected."

"Yes, it seems the rain ushered in a warm spell. But I don't think you came here to discuss the weather."

"No, I did not." The inspector tossed his hat to Marc's bed. "I am investigating the murder of Jacqueline Noël."

I touched my desk chair. "Sit. Please." As he shed his coat and seated himself, I pulled Marc's chair over and sat in front of him. "What are your questions?"

"First, let's dispense with formalities and friendliness. I hope we can be straightforward with each other."

I nodded. "Very well. I appreciate frankness."

"Good." The inspector laid his coat in his lap and gave me a hard stare. "What brought a young rosbif like you to Paris?"

I ignored the mild insult and, in the spirit of frankness, gave him a direct answer. "My father was accused of murder and sent to prison, and my mother went missing. My mother's sister and her husband took my sister and me in and became our adoptive parents. When his London business failed, they moved here because he had a brother in Versailles. My adoptive parents died of cholera when my sister and I were ten, at which time—"

"So you and your sister are twins."

"Yes. As I was saying, when our adoptive parents died, we were put in an orphanage. My sister contracted smallpox and went blind. No one, of course, wanted to adopt a blind girl, and I refused to be adopted without her. When we came of age, we left the orphanage, and I found employment and paid for my sister's keep at various homes that would take her in."

"What is your employment?"

"I work as a translator for a publisher. I am fluent in English, Gaelic, and French."

"Interesting. So you are an educated peasant. I assume, however, that your sister is little more than rabble, worthless for anything useful."

53

Although my hands ached to curl into fists, I inhaled deeply and kept my voice calm. "Inspector, I said I appreciate frankness, but base insults are a different—"

"Monsieur Trotter," he said, waving a hand, "please take no offense. I was merely testing your temper. I heard how Madame Noël treated you, and I wanted to see how you comport yourself."

"I see." I straightened in my chair. "And?"

He laughed. "You passed. Most Englishmen I know would have socked me in the nose."

"Well, good." I sat more at ease. "So the question about coming to Paris was a ruse."

"No. Actually I am quite interested." He laid the coat on my bed, easily within reach. "I learned about your birth parents from an interview with Francine Noël. That prompted me to send a telegraph message to Scotland Yard requesting more information, which should arrive soon. Fortunately, like you, I am fluent in English, so it won't require translation. But to save even more time, perhaps you can tell me what you remember about the tragic circumstances in your homeland."

"I don't remember much. Images, mostly. I heard a noise in our attic, so Mother and I went upstairs. We found my father standing next to a woman who was hanging by a rope from the rafters."

The inspector's brow lifted. "Hanging, you say?"

I nodded. "My father had blood on his hands. I don't know how it got there."

"Go on."

"Mother told me to run, so I did. I called for help. When a police officer came, I told him what I saw. After that, everything is a blur. I never went home again. My adoptive parents told me the rest, that the police arrested my father, and my mother was nowhere to be found."

The inspector's eyes locked on me. "That must have been a terrifying experience."

"It was. I still have nightmares."

Bryan Davis

"Then why did you copy your father by hanging Madame Noël?"

"What?"

"Like father, like son. I've seen it before. A son is haunted by his father's ways, but deep inside the son knows he will follow in his father's footsteps. It's only a matter of time. It is ingrained. A demon seed waiting to sprout."

I shook my head hard. "No, no. That's not true. I had nothing to do with Madame Noël's death. Nothing."

The inspector's brow dipped. "You were the only one in the library, the only one with access to the rope's fastening point. And you were the last to see Dr. Cousineau alive."

My heart raced, and my tongue tripped over my words. "Marc was with me. When he recovers, he'll tell you."

"Tell me what?"

"That I didn't kill Dr. Cousineau. He was already burning when we found him."

The inspector narrowed his eyes. "Already burning?"

I nodded. "Buried under a pile of burning books."

"Buried, you say. How do you think he managed to get into that position?"

"Someone else was in the library. Dr. Cousineau told me his name."

"And?"

"Pierre. That's all I know. Marc was there. He heard the doctor."

"And this Pierre, presumably, is the man who murdered Madame Noël."

"That I don't know. All I know is that I didn't kill anyone, and there was someone else in the library."

"Well, as they say in your home country, that is a horse of a different color."

A sense of relief filtered in. "So, you believe me."

The inspector again looked me in the eye. "Monsieur Trotter, I interviewed five other guests, and their statements were identical.

No one mentioned anyone named Pierre, and no Pierre appeared on the list of guests Francine provided. Not only that, the only body we found in the rubble was that of Dr. Cousineau." He huffed in a haughty way. "I don't believe you in the slightest."

"Then why the idiom? The horse of a different color. And the test. You said I passed."

"Regarding the test, experience tells me that murders related to passion and hot tempers are usually carried out with pounding fists or slashing knives. This murder required a calculating mind, a deliberative strategy, and a steady hand. A man with a bad temper could never have carried it out. Regarding the horse of a different color, I assumed you would have no alibi whatsoever, but now you have claimed Marc Noël as a witness, which means that I must wait for him to recover before I finish this investigation. In any case, it seems that your friend is your only hope for escaping prison … or the guillotine."

My neck tingled. I had seen the blade's work at the La Grand Roquette prison. The public executions there left an indelible mark. My only hope now lay with Francine's willingness to falsify her testimony. "When did you interview Francine?"

"Late last night. Why do you ask?"

"Did she tell you she was upstairs with me when Madame Noël was found?"

"She told me she went upstairs looking for you. She did not mention finding you."

"Then ask her. You'll see. We were together when Madame Noël was murdered."

Inspector Fortier gave me a tight-lipped smile. "I see how it is. And I can't say I blame you. She is quite attractive."

"Exactly what are you saying, Inspector?"

"I am saying that you hope your lover will protect you, which means that I will have to interview her again, that is, before you have a chance to corrupt her testimony." He rose and gestured toward the door. "Will you come peacefully, or must I call the commissaire?"

"Where do you want me to go?"

"To prison where you will await trial for the murders of Jacqueline Noël and Victor Cousineau."

Chapter Six

The hairs on my neck stood on end. The urge to escape, to run away like a frightened dog seemed overwhelming, but then I would look more guilty than ever. "I will come peacefully." I nodded toward my carpetbag. "May I bring anything along?"

"You may, but the prison officers will likely take it from you."

I picked up my bag, exited with the inspector, and, after securing the door, walked to street level. "Which way?" I asked.

He pointed toward the east. "To Rue de la Roquette."

"La Grande prison?"

"That depends. How old are you?"

"Twenty-two."

"Too old for La Petite." He gestured with his head. "Come along. I have a fiacre waiting for us."

We walked abreast, taking a different course than Marc and I had the night before. Since our section of the arrondissement still lacked Monsieur Haussmann's vision of checkerboard perfection, the road took us on a meandering path that eventually wound back toward the carriage house. Along the way, the inspector stepped aside and spoke to a commissaire out of range of my hearing, most likely the officer who would have apprehended me had I refused to cooperate. Since the officer went on his way, I assumed the inspector told him his services were no longer needed.

Soon, we boarded a single-horse, uncovered fiacre, and I set my bag at my feet. Normally I would have enjoyed a ride like this. Warm sunlight dried the cobblestones, allowing children to romp on this holiday weekend, but now the delights seemed like cruel reminders that today might be my last to savor freedom.

Along the way, Inspector Fortier said nothing as he stared straight ahead. Perhaps he was preoccupied with the details of our recent conversation, or perhaps he was watching me out of the corner of his eye, wary of any move I might make to escape.

Of course, thoughts of escape dominated my mind, but where would I run? Where could I hide? I would be caught, and a visit to the guillotine would be assured. Only a guilty man would take such a risk.

The driver, on the other hand, asked a string of questions, which I felt obliged to answer. He learned that I was a translator, a student, and an actor, that I traveled here when I was seven, and that I enjoyed French cuisine much more than English, to which he responded with a cheerful recollection of his days as a chef.

At a pause, I said, "I haven't had a chance to read the papers today. Have you?"

"Yes, but I saw nothing of interest. Politics, fashion, social events, the weather. It's always the same."

I gave the inspector a glance. He showed no reaction to the driver's summary. Either the murders occurred too late for the reporters to write about them, or the police had kept them quiet, at least for now.

After a few minutes, a boy darted into our path. The horse veered sharply to the side. Our carriage tipped over, and the inspector and I flew from our seats to the road. His head struck a stone, and I landed on top of him, cushioning my own impact. The driver also fell and slid to the edge of the road.

As several men and women hurried toward us, I climbed to my feet. My ribs ached and the city spun. While one man steadied the horse, wet and dirty from its tumble, another checked on the inspector and driver as they lay motionless on the cobblestones two steps away. "Are they dead?" I asked.

A thin man kneeling over the inspector shook his head. "Unconscious."

I looked at the street but found no sign of the boy who had startled the horse. "And the boy?"

"What boy?" The man opened the inspector's shirt down to his waist and grimaced. "He's bleeding badly. Clarice, go for a doctor. Hurry."

"Yes, Father." A young woman dressed in a calf-length skirt ran down the street.

Now less dizzy, I knelt at the inspector's other side. A deep cut below his ribcage spurted blood. At that rate, he would be dead in minutes. "We need to cauterize the wound."

The man gave me a puzzled stare. "What will that do?"

"Keep him alive." I withdrew the nail and thread from my pocket and plucked the needle from my shoe. "I need a flame. A lantern or a candle."

An older woman wearing an apron and a coif called out, "I'll get a lantern."

While I waited for her to return, I pressed a hand over the cut. The warm, sticky sensation raised memories of Marc as he lay bleeding under my cold, trembling hand. Yet, now my hand was steady, my confidence elevated. Still, with so many eyes aimed my way, the scrutiny threatened to fracture my poise. I had to distract myself. "How is the driver?"

"He took a blow to the head," the man said, "but no broken bones, I think. He responded to my questions."

"Good. Good." I looked at the street once more, still strewn with puddles in the low areas. The children had scattered. Whoever the boy was, he must have dodged the fiacre.

"Here is the lantern." The woman set it next to me, lifted the glass, and blocked the breeze with a hand. "Is there anything else you need?"

"Not yet. Thank you." I inserted the nail into the flame. As it reddened, the metal heated in my grip. I had forgotten to shield my skin with a cloth. Since I hoped to instill the onlookers with confidence in my meager skills, I endured the pain and held on until the tip became bright.

Mother, as you often taught, urgency empowers instinct while character is revealed by contemplation. At the time, I had no thought that trying to save this man's life threatened my own, that I might be acting against my own best interests. Letting Inspector Fortier die meant freedom for me, at least for long enough to seek refuge until Marc recovered. Granting him life, on the other hand, increased my chances of visiting Madame La Guillotine, a deadly lady I hoped to avoid at all costs.

My impulses told me to help the man. If I had contemplated the matter, would I have done the same? I truly do not know, which is why my life-saving efforts added no luster to my character. At the moment, I was nothing more than a creature of instinct.

When I touched the hot metal to the wound, a sizzle erupted. The inspector's muscles tightened. A few onlookers gasped. But when the bleeding slowed, they whispered cheery words among themselves, which heightened my confidence.

Unlike during my previous surgery, my mind stayed clear during the stitching portion. Each time I pierced the inspector's skin with the needle, I flinched, though with less intensity as the procedure continued. The inch-by-inch closing of the wound buoyed my hopes and settled my nerves. I was saving this man's life.

A moment after I tied the final stitch, the doctor arrived, and, with the help of three other men, put the inspector and the driver back in the fiacre and hauled them away. My carpetbag now sat on the street, most likely tossed there by the spill or to make room for the ailing passengers.

As the clatter of the horse's hooves faded, I stood at the side of the street, staring blankly at the retreating carriage. The first man who had cared for the inspector patted me on the back, whispered something that failed to register, and walked away with the others.

When I picked up my bag, a small hand slid into mine. "I'm glad I found you." A boy with a familiar face stood at my side, looking up at me.

"Jean?" I asked.

He nodded. "I'm sorry the men got hurt. I was just trying to stop the horse so I could tell you something."

"Then you're the boy who ran in front of the carriage."

He nodded again.

"What do you want to tell me?"

"That I didn't kill the woman. The one who was hanged. Joan told me you thought I did it."

LET THE GHOSTS SPEAK

I looked at our clasped hands. Blood oozed from mine to his, but he seemed not to care. And again I felt completely comfortable in the company of a ghost. "Do you have any idea who killed her?"

"No, but Joan does. She said if you come to the catacombs, she'll tell you."

Chapter Seven

Although Jean spoke in a normal tone, *catacombs* invaded my mind like a haunting specter. Millions of corpses lay in those underground chambers, a maze of quarries, many filled with bones. Michael had mentioned the place, and Joan had confirmed it, but now that I was actually invited there, the thought incited a fresh shudder. "Where do I enter?"

"At the burned schoolhouse. It has a secret door." He pulled my hand. "I'll show you."

Still carrying my bag, I gave in to his pull. The road led us around a curve and toward the Seine. "How did you find me?"

He looked up at me with a friendly smile. "Joan guessed where they would take you, so I found the street that goes there."

"Why do you care if I think you're guilty or not?"

"You tried to help me, and I want to make sure you don't get punished."

"I see." As we walked, our earlier encounter came to mind. Jean seemed so different now, confident and carefree. "Speaking of punishment, why did you say your master would beat you? I met him, and he said he has never hurt you."

"I was playing a trick. But then I heard that you got in trouble." He pulled again. "Let's go faster before someone tries to catch you."

I looked back. The scene of the accident was now out of view. Indeed, if the inspector recovered quickly, he might send someone to apprehend me and escort me to prison. What else was I to do but escape?

Jean and I walked at a brisk pace toward the schoolhouse. Along the way, I washed my hands in a discarded mop bucket and straightened my hair and clothes. I hoped to make us look like a pair of brothers out for a romp on this sunny Saturday. Bloody hands would surely draw stares.

After about half an hour, we crossed the brook, still swollen by the storm. At the deepest point, the chilly water rose to my chest, and Jean had to swim. When I reached to help him, he jerked his hand away, saying that he had already crossed it once. He could do it again. Trying to keep the shivering in check, I waded to the edge and trudged to dry land. After wringing as much water as possible out of my clothes, we hurried on, though the cool air incited more shivers.

Soon, we arrived at the schoolhouse, now a burnt shell. The upper two stories had collapsed into piles of ashes at the center, leaving only a surrounding wall of blackened bricks, head high in most places, a bit higher or lower in others.

Jean led me through an open arch that used to be the doorway. We meandered around piles of broken beams, bricks, and charred books. Smoke rising from the debris provided a variety of odors, most of them noxious.

Near the farthest corner, close to the area where Madame Noël drew her final breath, Jean pulled on a short rope that lay on the floor and lifted a trapdoor. The wooden square stood upright, held in place by a pair of hinges. "It was hidden under a rug," Jean said.

I peered into the darkness below. Wooden slats had been attached to a wall on a side of a square pit, not much wider than a man's shoulders. "How far down does it go?"

"I'm not sure. I didn't count those wooden things. More than sixty, I'd guess. Could be a hundred."

"Then it's quite far to the bottom." I set my bag down, knelt, and touched one of the slats. "I assume they're strong enough to support me. I am no bigger than Michael."

"I think so, but some are loose. Since we're wet, we have to be careful." Jean scrambled into the hole and lowered himself until only his head remained above floor level. "I'll tell you which ones are loose on the way down." He then descended out of sight, calling, "Close the door over you."

I looked at my carpetbag. Carrying it that far would be difficult at best. I could leave it here, at least for now. I grabbed the edge of the trapdoor, stepped onto the highest slat, and, bracing with my other hand, lowered myself one careful step at a time. When the hole's lid dropped into place, darkness filled the narrow chamber. A shiver swept across my wet legs, though the air seemed no colder here than in the open. Ever since the night I ascended those foreboding stairs to discover the truth about my murderous father, dark, tight places had been the theme of every nightmare.

"Keep going." Jean said. "I think a loose one is coming up."

With no need to see anything, I closed my eyes and concentrated on the slats, imagining my hands and feet applying pressure to them. Jean guided me with precision throughout the ordeal. Once I grew accustomed to the effort, I opened my eyes and looked down, yet nothing but blackness appeared.

Jean called, "I'm at the bottom. Just a few more. The rest are solid."

Seconds later, my foot touched an uneven surface that moved and crunched beneath my feet. "Do you have a source of light down here?"

"I'll get it." More crunching sounds followed, slowly diminishing as Jean walked away.

Soon, a wavering yellow glow appeared, giving light to my surroundings. I stood with my head still in the vertical passage I had descended, the rest of my body in a tunnel-like chamber. I lowered my head and looked around. Carrying a lantern, Jean walked on a carpet of bones and skulls that stretched as far as the lantern cast its light.

I looked past the boy. "Where is your teacher?"

"In our room, the last I saw him. He'll be back soon." He walked along the corridor, his clothes now drier than seemed possible. "This way."

My head still low, I followed at his pace, though the bones provided an uneven foundation that forced me to set a hand on a side wall to keep my balance. After about twenty steps, Jean led me through an opening in the wall on the right that led to a larger chamber with a higher ceiling and a floor free of bones.

A cross constructed with two long bones, perhaps an arm and a leg, and tied at the center with a ragged cloth, leaned against the wall on the left. Spiny brambles encircled the cross's top, a fair representation of a crown of thorns. On all four walls, multicolored French words had been painted on nearly every open space, at least the spaces within reach by a diminutive teacher.

I read a few phrases, apparently from the gospels, if I remembered my childhood lessons well enough.

Jean set the lantern next to an unlit lantern on the floor and turned up the wick, then remained standing. Joan and Pierre sat in opposing chairs with a small worktable between them. A book lay open in front of Pierre, though he stared at us rather than the book, likely because Jean had taken his light source.

"Welcome," Joan said. "I'm glad Jean was able to find you."

Pierre rose and bowed. "Sit in my chair."

Joan smiled. "Yes. Please do. It has taken me months to teach Pierre the simplest manners."

"As you wish." I sat in the chair, a wooden straight-backed one that creaked under my weight. My damp clothes would probably leave a wet spot, but maybe it wouldn't matter.

As I looked at Joan, her visage seemed different in this lair of death. Her unkempt hair, shorn for battle, and her sun-bronzed skin made her look like a ragged fugitive hiding in a cave, though her youthful face and shining eyes countered that visage. "Where is Michael?"

"He is conducting"—Joan glanced upward as if searching for a word—"an investigation."

"May I ask what he is investigating?"

"The hanging of the woman at the party."

"Ah. Jean said if I came to the catacombs you would tell me who you think the culprit is."

Joan cast a scolding glance at Jean. "Then he has said too much. He often takes liberty with words and uses them to manipulate others to do his will. I suspect that he has taken a liking to you and wishes to be in your company."

Jean averted his eyes but stayed quiet.

I leaned close to Joan and whispered, "So you have no idea who did it?"

Joan whispered in reply. "Unless Pierre is a suspect, I have no reason to speculate. The same is true regarding Michael and Jean. Although Jean has denied all wrongdoing, Michael wishes to verify his claims. It is crucial that we make sure our students are trustworthy and do no harm."

"Does Michael believe Jean?"

"Yes." Joan resumed a normal tone of voice. "Although Jean is unusually precocious and is capable of hanging a woman from a rope tied in the rafters, Michael thinks it is highly unlikely that he killed anyone."

"Well, he is precocious, to be sure." I gave her a summary of the carriage accident and thanked her for teaching me the skills necessary to save the inspector's life. "Where did Michael go to investigate?"

"I don't know. He is a scientist who is skilled in analysis. I trust that he will find the answers he seeks."

"A scientist, you say? Which field of science?"

"Biology, I believe. He knows much about how the human body functions."

"As do you."

She looked away, a flush in her cheeks. "I learned on the battlefield. When bodies were split open for all to see, my education accelerated far too quickly." She returned her gaze to me. "Yet, Michael's knowledge dwarfs my own. He is also a philosopher and a theologian."

"You mentioned that Pierre was your persecutor. Did Jean persecute Michael when they were alive?"

"It is not my place to tell another person's story. Perhaps when Michael returns he will answer your questions." She nodded toward Jean. "Or you could ask his ward."

When I turned toward Jean, he lowered his head, his chin nearly touching his chest. It seemed that my conversation with Joan had cast a dark shadow over his mood. "Jean, could you tell me—"

"I'm leaving." Jean pivoted and walked out of the room.

"Jean," Joan called. "You must not leave again. Michael would oppose it."

Jean's voice filtered in like a dying echo. "Tell him I'm going to help him find the murderer."

Chapter Eight

Silence followed. I looked at Joan and Pierre. They both stared at me. The stillness felt stifling.

I tugged at my collar. "Should I go with him?"

"If you wish, but you would risk capture, thereby undoing Jean's efforts to save you." Joan's smile took on a peaceful aspect. "Fear not. Michael knows how to find Jean. They will return together in due time."

"Then may I watch you teach Pierre? Perhaps I will learn something."

"I trust that you will, as do I with each session. Sometimes I wonder who is the teacher and who is the student."

I rose and gestured for Pierre to sit. When he did, I lifted the lantern to the table and sat on the floor against a wall.

The scene that followed is impossible to describe in mere words, but I will make an attempt. Imagine if you can, two actors on a stage. Why actors? Because these two people could not possibly be who they claimed to be. Yet, they believed themselves to be with all their hearts. And their ardor convinced me, as well. At that moment and in this place, they could be no one else.

Imagine also that the script had been written by Shakespeare himself. No, someone greater than Shakespeare. An angelic majesty. A muse without equal. A goddess who wields a flaming quill.

Finally, imagine emotions unleashed—heartfelt, unbridled, unashamed—two combatants sitting eye to eye engaging in verbal jousts, stabbing each other with anger, passion, and, yes, even love.

An earthquake sometimes begins with a tremble. For a time, Joan and Pierre discussed politics in the fifteenth century, and both agreed that corruption at every level nurtured dissatisfaction and grumbling within the lower and middle classes. They conversed as friends—Joan spoke with the natural wisdom of a rural farmer combined with the experience of a seasoned general, yet with the sweet lilt of a girl. Pierre spoke with the gravity of a bishop who took seriously his responsibility of caring for a needy flock, yet with the juvenile tenor of a child. The combination proved to be mesmerizing.

Peace reigned, that is, until the topic turned to religious issues. A veritable sword severed their harmony.

"You will confess," Joan said with utter calmness, "that the church hierarchy is filled with men who are more concerned with outward appearances than with inward purity. They are whitewashed tombs that carry dead men's bones."

"No, indeed." For the first time, Pierre's voice sounded older, no longer like a child's. "Unlike the political sea of filth, the clergy are remarkably unstained. Only a few have soiled their garments, which is why the Church should always have its hand in the political processes. We must maintain a purifying influence."

"Purifying?" Joan let out a huff. "As sewage purifies a latrine. You would have me drinking bilge water."

Pierre's brow dipped low as he growled through his words. "There was a day when you would have thanked me for bilge water."

"Only because you set fire to my tongue." Joan braced her elbows on the table and glared at him, the lantern's flame flickering in her eyes. "Because of you, I cried for relief, and now you mock my agony. Yes, I pleaded for water. I begged for a merciful quenching, but you gave me none. Not even a drop. When I begged for relief, you offered only a scornful smirk."

Pierre shook his head. "You suffered only for a moment."

"You lie." Her teeth set on edge, she pressed a fist on the table, as if aching to pound it. "You blinded yourself to my torment. Even now you hope to excuse the brutal torture of an innocent woman, but you cannot blind God. Until you realize your guilt, until you confess your sins, you will be forever imprisoned. No man can be set free from chains he refuses to see."

Pierre's voice deepened further. "I prosecuted a heretic, a peasant woman who foolishly heeded the voices of demons, a Jezebel who dressed like a man, a siren who gathered followers by means of dark arts."

"Pierre." Joan reached across the table and grabbed his shirt, her eyes aflame. "Come back to me, Pierre. Reject the cynical blinders placed upon you by sweeping robes and kissed rings. You are to be a child, not a judge. A servant, not a king."

His face twisted in rage as he bellowed, "I am a bishop of the Most High God who has appointed me as a judge over blasphemers. A servant cannot carry out this duty, nor can a child. Only fire can purge the blackness in the heart of a heretic."

"No, Pierre. You are wrong." Joan marched around the table and drew Pierre into her arms. As she stroked his head, she whispered, "Kindness begets compassion. Compassion begets love. And only love can purge the blackness in a soul."

Pierre raged on, fighting to break free from Joan's embrace, but, like the warrior she is, she held on. Slowly, ever so slowly, his masculine shouts transformed into quiet whimpers. After a moment of silence, she released him and kissed his forehead. "Are you all right now?"

He nodded and added a sniffle. "I'm sorry."

"All is well. Your eruptions have been less frequent of late, and they last only a few moments." She smiled and tousled his hair. "But your timing was likely divinely appointed to allow our guest to see what our sessions are sometimes like. The path from darkness to light is often fraught with setbacks."

Pierre looked at me, tears in his eyes. "I'm sorry I acted that way."

"Oh." I climbed to my feet and dusted off my trousers. "That's quite all right."

Joan tilted her head and stared at me as if prompting for more, but I had no idea what she hoped for, so I just added a genial nod.

"What Justin means," Joan said to Pierre, "is that he was not offended by your bad behavior, but surely he doesn't think it was all right. That is a figure of speech, not literal truth."

I nodded again. "Yes. Yes, of course." Warmth coursed through my cheeks. It seemed that my ability to say the right thing was crippled even in the land of the dead. "Joan is correct. Your behavior was not all right, but I was not harmed by it."

"While Pierre reads his lessons, let us have a private conversation." Joan took my arm and led me into the corridor. The bones under our feet emitted their now-familiar crunch. As we walked toward the exit hole, the light from the teaching chamber dimmed. Soon, she stopped and faced me, looking up from her shorter stature. Her eyes, still visible in the low light, sparkled with tears. "I have a terrible dilemma, Justin Trotter. May I ask your opinion about it?"

"Yes. By all means."

She glanced at the chamber. "Did you see Pierre's eyes when he raged at me?"

I nodded once more. "Terrifying."

"Indeed. He displayed the same look while I was being tied to the stake. He lusted for my death. Oh, as surely as a ravenous dog hungers for meat, Pierre Cauchon hungered to see me burn."

"And he wanted to murder you again? Just now?"

"That's what his eyes told me."

"What is your dilemma?"

"Michael is of the opinion that Jean could not have killed that poor woman, but Jean has eruptions similar to Pierre's. While in that state, his strength surges. He is capable of hanging a woman, or worse."

"But you seemed to agree with Michael that it's unlikely."

"Unlikely, but not impossible. During the minutes Pierre was raging, my doubts returned. If you could have felt his strength as I held him, you would understand. If not for my training and his respect for my authority, he might have broken free and unleashed a violent attack. Jean is no different."

"I see. Then may I assume that Pierre could set a man on fire and knock bookshelves over in an attempt to crush people? Do you doubt his word that he is innocent?"

72

Her lips firm, she nodded. "He claims to hate lies, but he is not so condemning with regard to his own falsehoods."

"So is your dilemma whether or not to challenge Michael's opinion?"

"Yes. He is a wise man, and I have willingly submitted to his opinions in the past. As you might know, I am not shy about asserting opinions of my own."

"What are your options? If you decide that Jean and Pierre are murderers, what would you do about it?"

She trembled as she spoke. "Abandon them." Her words echoed in the corridor, as if spoken by the dead souls entombed within. "As I mentioned to you before, Pierre and I have been put together so that he can learn love. Yet, I am not certain of the reason for this trial or what would happen to him if our sessions are successful. I do know, however, what will happen if they fail. Pierre will be banished to everlasting fire, and I have the option to end the trial if I decide that he is too recalcitrant or dangerous to continue."

"In which case," I said, "I assume he would be banished immediately. Since it seems that he might have hurt others, it could be your duty to walk away while he is delivered to the fire."

"Yes." Her chest heaved as she wept through her words. "Can you see the dilemma? I, who suffered flames myself, one who knows the torture of burning flesh, have the responsibility to decide whether or not to abandon another soul to such flames, not for moments, but for eternity."

She wrapped her arms around me and laid her head on my shoulder as she sobbed. "I who was judged must become a judge. I who was executed must choose whether or not to execute. I who burned to ashes must decide if ... if a boy, mind you ... if a boy should be banished to the flames of perdition, not to become ashes, but to suffer torture for years without end, scream for succor without deliverance, beg for death without the mercy of annihilation."

Spasms now overwhelming her words, she wept bitter tears while her entire body shook.

I patted her on the back. "But if you abandon him, it's because of his own actions. You aren't really the one casting him into the fire. You're giving him over to the true judge. What happens to Pierre at that point is up to God, isn't it?"

She spoke into my shirt, muffling her voice. "You're right, but the judgment I have to make is still almost too heavy to bear."

After a few moments of silence, I whispered, "My guess is that Michael sympathizes with your dilemma. He also has doubts, which is why he's investigating. We need to learn the truth. If Jean and Pierre are innocent, then all is well. If they are not, then we can address the consequences at the proper time."

After a final spasm and an echoing shudder, she drew back and brushed tears from her cheeks. "You're right, of course. I apologize for my outburst."

"No need. As you said to Pierre, compassion begets love. And love can purge the blackness in any soul. Your love for Pierre will work wonders. You'll see."

"Again, you're right." She took a deep breath and straightened her shoulders. "If I don't believe in him, who will?"

I spoke with an upbeat tone. "I'll go to the Noëls' home and do some investigating myself. Maybe Marc has awakened. Maybe my danger has already passed. Then I could search for clues freely."

"What would you look for?"

"I'm not sure. Perhaps Madame Noël's enemies, anyone who hated her enough to kill her. She had a number of business interests. It could be that someone wanted to get her out of the way."

"Then Godspeed to you." She set a hand on my arm. "And if you are so inclined, return to me with news of your efforts. If you find that Pierre is not the culprit, I will be greatly relieved."

Chapter Nine

I found the makeshift ladder and began climbing. Without Jean as a guide, I took more care to test each slat, which greatly slowed my progress. Of course, battling gravity further added to the difficulty, forcing me to rest from time to time. When I finally reached the top, I pushed the door open an inch and peered out. A woman's dress swept past, hiked up to avoid the debris, thereby exposing thin ankles and flat shoes. She walked away, revealing more of her svelte frame, accentuated by a gray, form-fitting house dress. Even from the back I had no trouble recognizing Francine Noël, especially since her reddish tresses had escaped the costume wig. Her mode of dress violated the usual mourning etiquette, but challenging customs was certainly not unusual for her.

Moving as quietly as possible, I climbed out and set the door back in place. Francine picked through the rubble with a pair of fireplace tongs, unaware of my presence.

I cleared my throat.

She spun, gasping, then laid a hand on her chest and exhaled. "Justin. You frightened me."

"I apologize." I spread my hands. "In a place like this there is no sure way to approach someone without inciting a scare."

"I suppose that's true." She pointed toward my carpetbag, still near the trapdoor. "I thought you might be close by, so I shouldn't have been so surprised. But I heard you were arrested and then escaped. There's talk about a fiacre accident."

"All true." I gestured with my thumb toward the brook. "An Inspector Fortier was escorting me to prison, and the horse took a fright. The carriage spilled, and the inspector was rendered unconscious. I had no idea what to do, so after making sure the inspector and driver were taken care of, I left."

"It's a good thing you left when you did. A manhunt is underway. The police are searching everywhere for you." Francine tapped a finger on her chin. "And I know this inspector you mentioned. He questioned me about my mother's murder."

"Did he talk to Marc? Is he well enough to answer questions?"

She shook her head. "He murmurs now and then. And he says my name when I speak to him. A good sign, I think."

"May I visit him? Maybe he will respond to me."

"Yes. That might be exactly the medicine he needs."

"Let's hope so, but I will have to come in without being seen, perhaps through your back door."

"Of course. You have to avoid the manhunt." She glanced from side to side. "Why did you choose this as your hiding place? It's the scene of the crime."

"What place is less likely?"

"The home of the murder victim is less likely." She looked across the brook toward the city center. "When you come, go to the back door. If you find it ajar, then it's safe to enter."

"Safe? Why wouldn't it be safe?"

"When I spoke to Inspector Fortier, he said he would come to my house this evening for a more thorough interview. Now that he has been injured, maybe he won't come."

"Did you mention our, shall we say, romantic relationship?"

She laughed as she replied. "Justin, it's hardly a relationship. We aired our interest in each other only this morning. My conversation with him took place before we agreed to pose as lovers, but I already had the idea, so I dropped a hint. I'm sure he took note."

"Then it won't be out of line for me to call on you tonight."

"Not out of line, but still dangerous for a wanted man." She touched my arm. "Our neighbors are inquisitive. Be sure to stay in darkness."

"I will. Thank you."

She used the tongs to lift a blackened book. "Although you didn't ask, I'll tell you that I have been searching for a brooch my mother wore to the party. Not on her jester's costume, mind you.

On the dress she wore underneath. I took no thought of it until the undertaker asked me about her burial attire. When I looked at her body, she wasn't wearing the brooch. How she could have lost it is a mystery."

"Her burial. I forgot about that. When is it?"

"Monday morning. Nine o'clock. At Père Lachaise. We will have mass at the cathedral an hour before."

"Then I will be there."

"Even as a fugitive?"

"I will come in stealth. No one will recognize me."

"As you wish." She let out a sigh. "I have nearly lost hope trying to find the brooch. I had no idea there would be so much rubbish here. If I can't find it, she will be buried without it."

"What does it look like?"

She formed an oval with her thumb and finger. "It's about this size with gold trim. It has a pearl-like surface on the front, and it opens on a hinge. It looks like a beetle. Mother kept a key inside, a key to a box of other heirlooms."

"Well, at least you could break the box open if necessary." I reached for the tongs. "May I?"

"Certainly." After handing them to me, she looked at the trapdoor. "Do you know where that leads? I looked down but saw only darkness."

"It leads to the catacombs."

Fear and delight crossed her face. "Did you go down there?"

"I did. It is far, far down, and the way is narrow. The floor is covered with bones."

"How do you know?" She glanced around. "I see no lantern."

"I felt them under my feet. Long and short bones. Even skulls."

Mother, I know what you're thinking. Truth can be a lie if it is intended to deceive. Although I did, indeed, feel the bones under my feet, I also saw them with light from a source not my own. I wanted Francine to think that I was alone down there. Therefore, I lied to her, though indirectly.

I often wonder why I always found it difficult to tell a bold lie but easy to tell a deceptive half truth. Yet, every time I tried to deceive, a pitchfork stabbed my heart. I never seemed to learn how to avoid the scolding of my conscience.

I slid a hand into my pocket as if searching for my dwindling soul. "It's a morbid place. I don't recommend going there."

"Don't worry. I'll stay right here." She stepped on the door and looked around as if orienting herself. "Might the real killer have escaped this way? Isn't this where the room was, the place he hanged my mother?"

"I believe it is."

"Then we should notify the police. He might be hiding down there at this moment."

"Francine, the catacombs run for many miles with dozens of ways to get in and out. It would be a hopeless search."

"I suppose you're right." She tapped her foot on the door. "Were you planning on sleeping down there?"

"Among all the bones?" I laughed. "No. And carrying my bag down there would be a chore I want to avoid."

"Then let's do this." She walked over and picked up the bag. "I will take your bag, go home, and ask Marguerite to prepare a lovely meal for us while you search for the brooch. I'm sure you're hungry."

At that moment, my stomach rumbled. "Yes. Very much so."

"Good. It will be dark in a couple of hours. You can come then." She glanced toward the brook. "Do you remember how to get there?"

I nodded. "But that's a long way to walk with the bag. Let me take it."

"I came by carriage. The bridge is out, so we had to cross the next bridge some miles upstream. My driver is waiting for me around the forest bend."

"Why not closer?"

"The grass is thicker there. For the horse." She patted me on the chest. "Feel free to get dirty while searching. You can wash at my house. Marc's clothes fit you if I remember correctly."

"They're not too small, if that's what you mean. But I brought clothes with me."

She looked at the bag. "Yes. Of course." During the ensuing pause, she stared at me. Her eyes probed mine as if asking me a question. As usual, I felt awkward. What was I supposed to say? After a few seconds of silence, she drew close and kissed me. Her lips were hot and dry, but they felt like heaven. I luxuriated in the touch and ran a hand along her silky hair, hoping to communicate that I wanted the moment to last.

She eased back, her lips still pursed. "I'm glad you escaped, Justin. An innocent man should never suffer in a locked cage, much less face the guillotine."

She turned toward the road and walked away. Sooty streaks on her dress became apparent, evidence that she had been searching with diligence, not caring how dirty she made herself. Her mother's brooch was precious to her.

The kiss provided a surge of energy. I took to the task immediately, tongs in hand, concentrating on the murder scene before moving to places where party guests likely danced. One of the livelier dances might have shaken the brooch free, and it could have been kicked without anyone noticing.

As expected, I became saturated with sweat and smeared with grime during my search, but I found nothing but broken wine glasses, burnt books, and other scorched items. The only real oddity was a military boot with no mate, perhaps from Dr. Cousineau's gendarme costume, though it was not as blackened as everything else in the ruins.

When daylight gave way to twilight, I left the ruins and walked toward the city. I waded across the brook again, this time enjoying the coolness of the water. As I crossed, I washed my face and hands. I could bathe more thoroughly at the Noëls' house, perhaps in warm water.

Now under the cover of evening shade, I hurried toward the house, a reasonable walking distance from the school. All the while, the terrors and wonders of recent hours stalked my mind.

Only a day ago, I would have thought it madness to believe the real Joan of Arc had returned to Paris, not to rally soldiers in battle, but to teach love to a young version of her persecutor. But

79

I could not deny what I saw on that macabre stage—two ghostly performers revisiting an ancient nightmare, the hunted now in control of the hunter.

And what of Michael and Jean? They seemed to be impossible phantoms as well, another young persecutor and his prey whose identities I had not yet divined.

As Joan indicated, Jean was unstable, perhaps ready to strangle or burn another victim. Yet, Michael allowed Jean to go where he wished, apparently unfettered by restraints. Who could tell when the boy might revert to a murderous monster?

And thoughts of Justice returned. My fugitive status threatened my plans to rescue her from Madame Dupont. How could I meet my dear sister without exposing myself to public scrutiny and possible recognition? If I were to be captured and sent to prison, what would become of her? With no more payments coming in, Madame Dupont would throw her out. Then where would she go? She didn't know Marc and Francine well at all and, even if she did, she wouldn't be able to find them. With no friends or family, how could she possibly sustain herself?

I shook the nagging questions away and hurried on.

When I reached the house, a one-story townhome in a traditionally bourgeoisie section of the city, I skulked to the rear and climbed three stairs to the door, which stood ajar, a signal for safe entry.

I pushed it open and looked inside. Although I had visited the Noëls several times, I had never entered this way. The door led to a dingy scullery where linens lay folded on a table and washed dishes had been piled in neat stacks, illuminated by light coming from somewhere beyond.

A young girl on hands and knees scrubbed the floor with a bristle brush. Since she wore a tattered peasant's dress, she was likely a temporary hire. Marc had told me that Francine sometimes offered work to beggars in exchange for food.

Not bothering to give me a glance, the girl pushed hard to clean a dark spot and added her fingernails to the effort as if her life depended on pleasing her employer. Considering her thin frame and bony hands, maybe it did. She likely hadn't enjoyed a decent meal in a long time.

Voices filtered in from the direction of the front sitting room—Francine's and that of a man I did not recognize, though it seemed familiar.

After closing the door in perfect silence, I tiptoed past the girl and into the hallway leading toward the front. When I drew near, I peeked around a corner in view of the sitting room. Now wearing a more presentable black dress, Francine sat on a sofa adjacent to an upholstered chair occupied by Inspector Fortier, dressed in the same clothes as when he arrested me, a hole in one elbow giving evidence of his tumble. His hat lay on the sofa next to Francine.

A small flame crackled in the fireplace, adding a hint of wood-smoke odor to the room. A poker leaned against the wall, its pointed end on the hearth, still smoking from recent use.

I stepped back. Why had Francine left the door ajar? Perhaps the inspector had shown up only moments ago, and she had no opportunity to alter the signal. Or maybe she had already provided my alibi, making it safe for me to enter. But how could I be sure? I could wait for him to leave, perhaps check on Marc who probably lay in his room down the hall. That option would be safer.

Yet, even if she had not spoken about my alibi, she would do so if the inspector chose to try to arrest me. It would be better to end the law's pursuit here and now instead of hiding.

I walked in and bowed my head toward each of them. "Francine. Inspector."

The inspector rose from his chair. He winced, his wound likely still excruciating. "Well, Monsieur Trotter, I must say that you are the last person I expected to see here."

"Francine invited me. The back door was open." I gestured toward a second chair that stood opposite his. "May I sit? The journey has been tiring."

Francine gave the inspector an odd glance before nodding. "Of course, Justin."

I lowered myself, but when I remembered how wet and dirty I was, I straightened. "Maybe after I bathe."

The inspector also remained standing. "First," he said with a polite nod, "thank you for saving my life. The eyewitnesses cheered your efforts to no end. They called you a hero."

"You're welcome, Inspector. I couldn't leave a bleeding man to die. That would be the act of a scoundrel."

"Yes ... I suppose it would." He picked up his hat and worried the brim with both hands. "Second, although it would have benefitted you to allow me to die, and although you risked your life to save mine, I cannot allow your actions to dissuade me from pursuing justice in the matter of the death of Madame Noël."

His words appeared to be leading to a bad conclusion, but I stayed calm. "As I would expect from an honorable servant of the law."

"Then you will understand why I must arrest you again and take you to prison."

I gave Francine a pleading glance, but her expression was blank, giving me no sign of help. "No, I don't understand. I did not kill Madame Noël. Ask Francine. She'll tell you. We were together at the time of the murder."

The inspector turned to her. "Were you?"

Francine's cheeks flushed. "I ... I didn't believe he was the murderer, so I told him I would say that to protect him, but the situation has changed."

Her words drove into me like a charging bull. I couldn't speak or even move, as if fastened to the floor.

Francine rose and picked up my carpetbag from behind her chair. "I lost a precious heirloom last night, so I went to the school to search for it. After an hour or so, Justin came and volunteered to continue my search. Since I was tired and dirty, I gladly accepted his offer and invited him home to visit Marc once it was too dark to search. I also took Justin's bag in my carriage so he wouldn't have to carry it on foot. When I arrived here, I decided to see if his clothes needed laundering." She pushed her hand into the bag and withdrew a brooch. "And I found the heirloom. My mother was wearing it the night of her death."

The inspector took the brooch and looked it over. "Interesting. It looks like a scarab."

Although dizziness made me sway, my voice returned. "I have no idea how it got in my bag. I have never seen it before in my life."

"Yes you have, Justin." Marc hobbled into the room. Wearing a thin, silken nightshirt over his trousers, he appeared pale and gaunt. "My mother was wearing it when you first met her."

"Marc?" Francine rushed to him and guided him to the sofa.

When they sat, Marc looked at the inspector. "Justin did not kill my mother. He and I were together in the library when someone set fire to Dr. Cousineau. As the good doctor lay dying, he told us that someone named Pierre was the culprit. Then a bookshelf fell over us. Justin was with me at that moment as well. And from what I gathered during my semiconscious periods, he rescued me and repaired a cut on my head." Marc took in a deep breath and let it out slowly. "Inspector, these are not the actions of a murderer."

The inspector touched his shirt over his own wound site. "No, they are not." He returned the brooch to Francine. "And a murderer would not give his bag to the victim's daughter knowing that evidence against him lay inside."

Marc nodded. "Nor would he continue a search for something that he knew wasn't there."

The inspector scanned me from head to toe. "Your filthy state is testimony to the doggedness of your search."

I smiled. It seemed that a heavy weight lifted from my shoulders. My innocence had been exposed to the light.

The inspector kept his gaze on me. "Monsieur Trotter, was the bag ever out of your sight after you left your flat?"

"Yes. The school has a trapdoor, and curiosity led me to investigate. I found a primitive ladder leading down into darkness, but the way was too narrow to take my bag, so I left it behind. It was out of my sight for quite some time."

"What did you find?"

"Bones, Inspector. The ladder led to the catacombs."

"The catacombs? Why did you stay there for, as you said, quite some time? I would have left as quickly as possible."

"It was a long way down, perhaps a hundred rungs. I rested at the bottom and took several rests on the way back up."

The pitchfork stabbed again. My half truths were multiplying, inviting more punishment.

"I see." The inspector stroked his chin. "You say you saw bones. Did you see anything else?"

More deception begged to be dispensed. It was time for a bold lie. Hang the pitchfork. "No. Nothing. It was dark. I only felt the bones. I didn't see them."

"Did you hear anything? Perhaps footsteps or other noises? Any sign of a living human? Criminals have been known to hide in those old quarries."

"Only my own footsteps."

"Therefore," Marc said, "the murderer took Mother's brooch, decided that it had no monetary value, and put it in Justin's bag, hoping to make him look guilty, thereby throwing the investigation off the trail."

Inspector Fortier shook his head. "Nonsense. That would be true only if the murderer knew that someone other than Justin would find the brooch, which is a wild guess to say the least."

"The carriage driver?" Marc turned toward Francine. "Who drove you to the schoolhouse?"

"Denis. As always."

"Did he drive you and Mother to the party?"

"Of course. But he didn't stay. He had instructions to return later. That's why we had to walk in the rainstorm."

"Did Denis and your mother ever argue?" the inspector asked.

Marc and Francine glanced at each other. "A quarrel or two," Marc said. "Nothing unusual."

Francine nodded. "Mother was not the most agreeable person. She had quarrels with everyone we know."

"Including everyone at the party?" the inspector asked.

Marc sighed. "Unfortunately … yes. But there were no guests named Pierre. It's possible, however, that I misheard Dr. Cousineau.

His lips were badly damaged." He turned toward me. "True, Justin?"

Although Marc likely wanted confirmation that Dr. Cousineau's speech had been garbled, I opted to mention the only truth I could confirm. "His lips had nearly melted. It was truly awful."

The inspector stroked his chin. "Then that name is not a trustworthy clue." He looked at Francine. "Was this Denis fellow the only person who had access to the bag?"

"As far as I know," she said. "Besides me, of course."

Inspector Fortier gave her a clumsy smile. "Mademoiselle, if not for the fact that you lack the strength to subdue your mother and hoist her by a rope, you would be my primary suspect."

She blinked. "Why so?"

"Your inheritance. You must have guessed that I would look into the amount of money you and your brother will receive. It is much more than substantial. Madame Noël saved and invested wisely."

"Really?" Francine said with a tone of naïveté. "I haven't been privy to her business affairs."

"I have," Marc said. "Francine and I will both be quite wealthy, which raised a concern in my mind that *I* would be a suspect."

"Until I solve the murder, Monsieur Noël, everyone at the party is a suspect, especially any man who has motivation, opportunity, and no substantiated alibi." The inspector set his hat on his head. "I am expecting a report to arrive tonight, information from Scotland Yard about Monsieur Trotter's family records. If it does, I will return to discuss it in the morning." He nodded to each of us in turn. "Good evening. I will let myself out."

Chapter Ten

When the inspector left, Marc exhaled and looked at me. "Well, Justin, it seems that we're both high on the list of suspects."

I nodded. "Since we provided an alibi for each other, maybe he thinks we conspired to kill your mother."

Marc touched the stitches on his scalp. "And I intentionally cut my head as a diversion."

"Gentlemen," Francine said, "there is no profit in speculating. The inspector seems to be a careful, honest man. Since we are innocent, we have nothing to fear."

"Do *you* have any suspects?" I asked. "What about Denis?"

Francine huffed. "Denis is eighty-five years old. He can barely step up into our carriage, much less overpower and hang my mother. When the inspector questions him, he'll drop from the list."

"Which men at the party might have enough animosity toward—"

"No one," Marc said with a sharp tone. "I said everyone had quarrels with Mother, but this crime was pure insanity. Only a madman would hang Mother in a public place. A sane killer would commit the crime in stealth, maybe poison her."

"Yet," I countered, "even in public, the murder happened without any witnesses, without any real suspects."

"Besides the three of us," Francine said.

Marc let out a loud sigh. "I can't blame the inspector for suspecting us. Like I said, you and I will both inherit a lot of money."

"I care nothing about money." Francine rose. "Come to the dining room. Marguerite is preparing a soufflé, and we'll have some wine. I'm sure both of you are hungry."

"Thank you," I said. "That would be wonderful."

She fanned the air with a hand. "A bath for you first. You smell like a pig. By the time you finish, the soufflé should be ready."

"Excellent." Marc rose to his feet and balanced himself as if dizzy. "Is Marguerite staying overnight again?"

Francine nodded. "A few more nights until we're used to Mother's absence."

"Even so, she's busy with dinner. I'll draw Justin's bath."

"Nonsense. You can barely stand, much less carry water without spilling it."

I raised a hand. "I can do it myself. I know my way around."

"Just be sure to find my soap," Francine said. "You need a new aroma."

"I will."

After I enjoyed a warm bath, complete with Francine's perfumed soap, I put on the last remaining set of clean clothes from my bag and transferred the carriage fare from the soiled trousers to the new set. I then reconvened with Francine and Marc in the dining room, where the three of us sat at the formal table, Marc at the head and Francine and me adjacent to him, one at each side. Although the place settings were humble, lacking real silver or china, the lacy tablecloth spilled over every edge and nearly touched the floor—a handsome decoration.

Marc warned us not to discuss the murder during the meal or else we might suffer indigestion. We chose instead to talk about our hopes for the next theater production, Francine's tutoring, anything to get our minds off the lurking shadow of death.

Marguerite, a woman in her forties, lithe and lovely for her age and wearing a black dress that molded to her feminine form, served us with professional aloofness, though she watched me with a nervous eye from time to time.

When she set a pastry before us as the final course, she looked at Francine. "Will you need anything else?" Her tone was pleasant though guarded as her eyes kept wandering toward me.

"No, Marguerite," Francine said. "Thank you. The meal was marvelous. Feel free to retire." She gestured toward an empty chair. "Or you may join us for conversation."

Marguerite glanced at the chair, then at me before looking again at Francine. Her wavy blonde locks shifted over one eye. "I'll retire, but may I ask if your guest is staying the night as well?"

"Justin?" Francine tilted her head. "Yes, he is. Why do you ask?"

Marguerite shuddered. "I want to be aware of who is here at night so I won't be taken by surprise. A murder suspect under the same roof is—"

"Marguerite," Marc said with a rebuking tone, "Justin did not kill my mother. You have no reason to fear him."

Francine nodded toward the front door. "No one is making this house your prison. Your nighttime service has always been voluntary."

"It's too late to go home now," Marguerite said, her eyes moistening. "I will stay."

Francine's tone remained firm. "The door to your bedroom has a lock. Use it if it will make you feel safer."

"Thank you." Marguerite turned and walked away with long, quick strides.

"Well …" Marc dabbed his lips with a napkin. "That was … awkward."

Francine glared in the direction Marguerite had exited, her teeth set as she spoke through them. "She should know better than to insult a guest."

"It's all right," I said, waving a hand. "After all, I am the prime suspect."

Marc picked up a bottle of wine from the table. "May I suggest an extra glass to take the edge off our anxieties?"

"By all means." I slid my glass toward him. "I need a good night's sleep."

After we finished the pastry and drank enough wine to settle our nerves, Marc leaned back in his chair. "I saw on the calendar that we have a funeral in the offing."

Francine nodded. "Monday morning. This is Saturday evening, in case you didn't know."

"Then I don't need to get up early." Marc turned to me. "If you're not too tired, we can talk."

Francine gave Marc a questioning look but said nothing. She rose, bade us both goodnight, and walked out.

Marc and I returned to the sitting room. He reclined on the sofa, his head propped by a pillow, while I chose the chair closest to him.

He folded his hands over his chest and looked straight at me. "Justin ..." His pained expression dragged through the pause. "Justin, I apologize for my part in drawing you into this mess. You didn't want to come to the party, but I insisted."

"You did, but I still had the option to refuse. Part of me wanted to come."

"The part that wishes to court Francine."

Warmth flooded my cheeks, but in the dim lantern light, Marc probably didn't notice. It wouldn't be right to mention that Francine and I had already agreed to see each other. She needed to be present for that announcement. "I do admire her qualities. She has an impressive strength of spirit."

"Indeed she does. She is taking Mother's death remarkably well." Marc glanced toward the hallway for a brief moment. "Justin ..." His voice grew quieter. "The murders are puzzling. I could count people who hated my mother all day long. Those who had a motive are aplenty, but no one had the opportunity. Mother was mingling as she always does, constantly in the company of multiple people." He set a hand over his wound and winced. "At least as far as I can remember."

"One of the cat girls said your mother wasn't feeling well and went to the lounge."

"Right. Sabina. I remember now. So the opportunity was there."

I lowered my tone. "Did you notice if anyone in particular stayed close to your mother?"

"Only Francine. But, as the inspector said, she's not strong enough to commit the crime."

The fact that Marc mentioned Francine and then defended her in the same breath gave me pause. Did he secretly suspect her while doubting his own suspicions? Of course, asking him directly might be offensive. I had to draw his thoughts out. "I suppose no woman could do it alone."

Marc raised a finger. "A valid point. But a woman could do it with help. Perhaps two women, or a woman and a man."

"Especially if your mother was first incapacitated with a drug of some sort."

Marc gave me a weak smile. "You said that because I mentioned poison, didn't you?"

"Francine told me about your mother trying to poison you with arsenic. It was on my mind."

"You should be the inspector's assistant. You have more ideas than he has."

I couldn't help but smile myself. "I'm sure he's considering all the possibilities. If he really suspects Francine conspired with someone, he wouldn't tell her so."

"True. But since he was ready to arrest you, he must believe you are the murderer."

"A ruse, maybe? An arrest to make the real murderer less wary?"

"Only the inspector knows." Marc's countenance darkened. He looked away, staring at nothing that I could discern.

"What's troubling you?" I asked.

He returned his gaze to me. "Justin, I've always been able to confide in you before …" His voice trailed off.

"And you may continue confiding in me." I slid my chair closer. "What's on your mind?"

His pained expression returned. "Ever since Mother tried to poison me, Francine has acted strangely. Moody. Argumentative. Even pugilistic. You have experienced one of her bouts yourself."

"A mere spat, Marc. A disagreement over politics."

He wagged a finger at me. "You think I don't know about the fight you two had after mass that day. But I know. She ranted to me long after your verbal fisticuffs."

"Did she tell you what I said that made her so angry?"
He nodded. "Four times."
"Four times?" I slumped in my chair. "I was an idiot."
Marc's smile reappeared. "She said that as well."
"I hoped my note of apology would help, but I suppose it didn't."
"Oh, it helped. She threw it away, but she stopped cursing your name. In fact, it was her idea to invite you to the party. And she was genial to you there, at least as far as I could tell."
"She was. Much friendlier than I expected."
"Then her vendetta was temporary. She has a short fuse, but her explosions last only a few days." Marc's expression turned somber again. "Still, the row you two had proves my point. She can be volatile."

We both drifted into silent contemplation, for how long, I don't remember.

Now is a good time, Mother, to return to a topic I mentioned earlier, that I would dispel notions that Francine was a bad-tempered woman, in spite of Marc's accusation.

The altercation came about one Sunday when I attended mass with the Noëls. The cathedral was magnificent—a towering steeple, marble columns, lovely stained glass, and much more. Most of the parishioners were dressed in finery that made my only suit appear impoverished by comparison, but Marc gave assurances that no one would look down on me.

Once inside, I sat between Marc and Francine with their mother to Francine's left, farther from the aisle. Although the singing was grand, the homily was surprisingly harsh—a diatribe from the bishop against the Protestant reformers. No member of that clan escaped his sharp tongue. According to his polemic, Hus, Luther, and Calvin were all spawns of the devil, demonic characters charged with conspiring to destroy the holy institution that Christ built upon the rock, Saint Peter himself.

Furtive glances at Francine revealed her approval of this character assassination. I was appalled at her stern countenance, punctuated by nods at the bishop's most damning pronouncements.

Mother, although you raised me in the Church of England, I later held no special affinity toward it. My adoptive parents never attended services and spoke little about religion, so any love that I had for the Church or its founder had grown cold by this time. I found it nearly unbearable to listen to a frocked clergyman who, I assume, espoused the golden rule, rip these men and their cause to shreds. They were dead and could not defend themselves. Would this bishop have wanted one of his polemical targets to speak of him in such a manner?

Although I endured to the end, the storming condemnations continued assaulting my mind, and I maintained silence as we left the church and walked toward the Noëls' carriage, me next to Francine, and Marc and their mother a few steps in front. I hoped no one would ask my opinion of the message, but that hope was quickly dashed.

"What did you think of the homily?" Francine said.

I cringed inwardly but kept a calm expression intact as I whispered, "This is a topic that is better discussed in private."

"Very well." She grasped my arm, pulled me to a stop, and called ahead. "Mother. Marc. Justin and I will join you in a moment."

"Take your time," Marc said, glancing back. "Mother wants to talk to her banker."

When they walked away, Francine turned toward me and raised an eyebrow. "Well?"

I shifted my weight from foot to foot. "He has a forceful delivery, to be sure."

Francine nodded, gaily unaware of my cheerless tone. "The holy church has been assaulted by these pretenders for centuries. I'm glad to hear someone putting them in their place."

"What is their place?"

"Damnation. The eternal flames."

"Flames? That's quite harsh, isn't it?"

"Indeed not. No one should be forgiven for blaspheming Christ's church. Ever."

"Like Joan of Arc?"

Francine tilted her head. "Why do you mention her?"

"She was consigned to flames for blasphemy. Was Joan a pretender? Did she assault the holy church?"

"That was different. She loved the Church. She never spoke against it."

"But it spoke against her. How can a church be called holy if it would kill one of its most devoted daughters?"

Her face turned stony. "A group of men made an error, a murderous error. Men are fallible."

"They are, and you are right to criticize them. Yet, you are ready to burn others who criticize men of the Church who, at least in the eyes of the critics, have also made mistakes." Then my tongue seemed to come unhinged as I committed the foolish blunder I regretted ever since. "Doesn't your own murderous desire against these reformers make you a hypocrite? Maybe you deserve burning at the stake yourself."

She raised a hand as if to slap me. Her fingers curled into a tight fist, but the blow never came, at least not a physical one.

"Justin Trotter ..." She spoke through clenched teeth. "When I was little, we lived on a farm. At the age of seven, I learned how to castrate a horse. Trust me. My gelding blade is still sharp."

She lowered her arm to her side, turned, and stalked toward the carriage.

Not knowing what else to do, I followed. With every step, I cursed my unbridled tongue. Perhaps my statement bore some truth, but my words were foul, uncalled for, not in keeping with proper manners or chivalry.

We rode to the Noëls' home in awkward silence. From there, I excused myself and walked to the flat. Marc joined me in the evening but mentioned nothing about my altercation with Francine, so I assumed he was ignorant of it at the time.

Now you understand, Mother. Francine's fiery tongue was unleashed by my own. I set the spark to the fuel. At all other times, she was kind and thoughtful, as you have learned from my story to this point.

After our moments of quiet reflection, Marc spoke up. "You look tired."

"I am. The last twenty-four hours have been a nightmare."

"Which is why we should retire for the night." He slid his hands behind his head. "Take my room. I'll sleep here. That will save me some effort."

"Thank you." I picked up the lantern. "Will you need a light?"

"The moon is sufficient. It's nearly full."

"Very well." I gave him a nod. "I'll see you in the morning."

Guided by the lantern, I walked to his room, which was situated next to Francine's. Beyond hers lay their mother's room and the spare bedroom, now occupied by Marguerite. Since my clothes were clean and comfortable, I kept them on, blew out the lantern, and slid into Marc's bed and under the covers.

While I lay there, my eyes adjusted to the darkness. As Marc had indicated, moonlight coming through the room's window illuminated my surroundings enough to see a closet and a dresser. Although he lived in our flat most of the time, he kept a second home here. Now I knew another reason for his home away from home. Who would want to live with a woman who tried to kill you?

Numbed by wine and exhausted, I fell asleep in mere moments. I dreamed about wandering lost through the catacombs. Demons chased me, wielding bones as clubs. Whenever one caught me and struck me with a bone, I awakened with a start, then slept again, only to return to the same troubling dream.

After several such cycles, I awakened to see Michael standing at the side of my bed, holding a short black candle. When I gasped and tried to rise, he set a hand on my shoulder, gentle yet firm.

"I am looking for Jean. Have you seen him?"

Battling a narrowed throat, I whispered, "Not since yesterday afternoon. He led me to the catacombs, then he left without me."

Michael nodded, his face tight. "Joan told me about his latest escapade."

"She said Jean is ... well ... volatile. He has episodes of violent behavior."

"*Violent* is an understatement, which is why I need to find him."

"If he has episodes like that, why were you separated in the first place? Shouldn't you stay with him constantly?"

He laughed under his breath. "If only it were so easy. Jean despises his lessons. He is not one who enjoys being corrected, and he is elusive."

"Do you have any idea where he is?"

"I suspect he has been following you. For some reason I have not yet discovered, he has taken a liking to you and is keenly interested in your well-being. He knows you are innocent, and I suspect that he is angered by the investigation. And any anger can cause him to act in an irrational manner, which is why I must find him as soon as possible."

"If I see him, should I try to catch him? Hold him?"

"No, no. Definitely not. If he is in a rage, he might hurt you."

"A little boy?"

Michael sighed. "He has hurt many people."

"You mean in the past? When he was alive?"

"Yes, but he is still capable of harming people now."

"Who is he? Or rather, who *was* he? And who are you?"

Michael's face hardened. "He was a scoundrel. A villain. As a pastor, he was a wolf in sheep's clothing. A wretched—" He shook his head and took in a deep breath. "I apologize. Memories of torture broke down my guard."

"Jean tortured you?"

"By proxy. I burned at the stake while wearing a crown of straw infused with sulfur. Jean's minions used green wood to prolong my suffering." He looked toward the bedroom door. "I have no time to tell you more. I must search for Jean. If you see him, please notify me."

"How? Should I go to the catacombs?"

"No." He blew out the candle and extended it. "Light this, and I will come."

LET THE GHOSTS SPEAK

I took the candle, still visible in the moonlight. About four inches long, it fit in the palm of my hand. "Is this some sort of magic?"

Michael smiled. "Not at all. I have a spiritual connection to it. When the candle is fully consumed, my time here and Jean's will be finished. I feel it burning, as if my own life is dwindling, and I am drawn to it. Joan has the same connection with the lantern she carries. When it runs out of oil, her time will come to an end."

"I see. That's why she had two lanterns in the catacombs. One stayed dark while I was there."

"Yes, it would be foolish for her to burn her remaining time unnecessarily."

"Then why were you burning your candle just now?"

"The light seeks for Jean. It led me to this house."

"So he might still be near."

"That is my hope."

I scanned the room. If Jean were hiding somewhere within, Michael would probably have found him. "Joan said you're investigating the murder. Have you discovered anything yet?"

"Besides the fact that Madame Noël was a cruel, vindictive woman? Nothing of substance, but ..." He lowered his voice to a whisper. "A shadow of evil lurks here. I can feel it. Perhaps I sense only the echoes of the victim's cruelty, but, in any case, be wary, my friend. Watch with wide-open eyes."

I fought off a cold shiver. "I will."

"Since you are here, I assume you are currently safe from prosecution. I will suspend my investigation and leave it up to you. I must find Jean."

"Won't you need your candle?"

"I have already burned too much time. My remaining days with Jean are precious. For both of us." He walked from the room and faded from view.

I slipped out of bed and pushed the candle into my pocket. Since I might see Jean most anywhere, I would have to find matches to carry with me. And if my search led me outside, I would also need my shoes.

96

Bryan Davis

With moonlight allowing a view of my path, I walked on tiptoes through the kitchen to the scullery, where I found my shoes and stockings on the floor as well as a box of matches on a shelf. After sliding the matchbox into my pocket, I made my way to the sitting room where Marc slept. His deep, steady breathing indicated restful sleep.

Just as I sat in one of the chairs and began putting on my stockings, a flickering glow appeared from the corridor leading to the bedrooms. I lowered myself to all fours and crawled behind the chair.

The glow vanished. At the room's intersection to the hallway, a shadowy figure appeared, a female adult judging by the shape. When she turned toward me, moonlight shone on her face and long hair—Francine. She walked in, stopped at the foot of the sofa, and leaned close to Marc. Apparently satisfied that he was asleep, she retreated on tiptoes toward the kitchen. Dressed in her Joan of Arc trousers and a man's work shirt, she appeared ready for rough duty, perhaps primitive travel.

Seconds later, the back door opened and closed. I put my shoes on and followed. When I exited, I searched the alleyway. Perhaps three blocks to the left, Francine walked at a rapid pace toward the main street on that side.

Keeping my footfalls quiet, I jogged in pursuit. As I closed in, an unlit lantern in her hand came into view. With moonlight so bright and gas streetlamps not far away, the lantern's need was not yet clear. When I drew within half a block, I slowed to her pace, again careful to maintain silence.

Upon reaching the street, she turned left and accelerated. Again I followed but allowed a greater distance between us in case my presence had already raised an alarm.

Soon, she walked to a cemetery gate. I ducked behind a bush and peeked around the edge. When she opened the gate, she looked back with darting eyes. After another moment, she entered the grounds.

Once again I followed, now on a winding path that led us past tombstones, monuments, and various mausolea. An owl hooted,

97

giving me cause to duck behind a tombstone when Francine stopped and looked around. Twice more I had to hide as various noises incited halts and nervous scans of the graveyard. Yet, she kept the lantern dark, perhaps to make herself as invisible as possible.

After a few minutes, she stopped at a mausoleum—a relatively unornamented stone structure with only a pair of columns framing a head-high entry. She grasped an iron ring on the door and pulled, but it held fast. She plucked something from her shirt and looked at it. Standing perhaps fifteen feet away, I could tell that it was an ornament of some kind, likely the brooch she had so desperately searched for at the school's ruins.

She opened the brooch, withdrew a small key, and inserted it into the mausoleum's door. When it turned, she again pulled the ring. As the hefty door shifted, she leaned back and gritted her teeth. Inch by inch, the rectangular block dragged outward, making a grinding noise. The moment the gap grew large enough for entry, she stopped, struck a match, lit her lantern, and slipped inside.

I leaped from behind the bush and ran to the door. Slowly, ever so slowly, I eased my head around the door's edge and peeked inside. Francine knelt with her back to me and leaned over a white sarcophagus—a small stone coffin, perhaps a child's.

She set the lantern on the floor and turned up the wick, shedding more light in the cubical room. The walls were plain, without carvings or ornaments. Wispy cobwebs, long abandoned, dangled at upper corners, swaying in a drowsy dance aroused by renewed air.

Francine set her hands on the coffin's lid and slid it toward the side. As another grinding noise ensued, I crept in and stood against a wall, behind her and to her left.

When she set the lid down, she looked inside the coffin. I dared a step closer and peered in. A child lay on dark velvet. Long, blonde hair and a lacy white dress indicated a girl, about six to eight years old, judging by her size. From my vantage point, her withered face seemed mostly intact, though dark splotches, perhaps mold, marred her cheek and forehead. Since I had no idea whether or not she had been embalmed, I couldn't guess how long she had been in this crypt.

Francine unpinned a brooch from the girl's dress and hooked it back to back with the one she already had. She then withdrew a small book from her dress's pocket and laid it on the edge of the coffin. As she held the book open with one hand, she waved the combined brooches over the dead girl's face while reading out loud in Gaelic.

Mother, I had not heard your native tongue spoken since your lullabies caressed me to sleep too many years ago. You sang with ardor and passion that is birthed by experience, years of life on the green island. In contrast, Francine sang as one ignorant of the language, simply reciting words on a page, even mispronouncing some, though she managed to stumble through the verses with a modicum of meter.

Unfortunately, as I translate here, I am unable to reproduce the author's rhyme and meter scheme. Yet, here it is, reproduced to the best of my memory with an added dash of syllabic orientation and rhyme of my own.

Child of mayhem
Born in chaos
Destroyed by cruel hands
Shed your nightglow
On the moonstones
Reveal your secret plans

When she finished, the combined ornaments emanated a greenish glow that provided a view of her hands and face. She smiled in a childlike way, fascinated, mesmerized. The juvenile aspect seemed eerie, as if she had taken on the dead child's expression—chilling, to say the least.

A whisper entered my ear. "She's a witch."

Chapter Eleven

I looked to my side. Jean stood next to me, his stare locked on Francine.

As if startled by the whisper, she disconnected the brooches, slid them and the book into her pocket, and reached for the coffin lid.

I grasped Jean's hand and hurried outside. We rushed around the corner of the mausoleum and set our backs against the wall. I peeked at the door. Francine emerged, the lantern again dark. She pushed the door closed, pulled the key from its lock, and jogged down the path in the direction we had come.

I crouched next to Jean. Moonlight illuminated his cherubic face. "What are you doing here?"

"I followed you. I don't trust her."

"You don't trust her? Do you mean you're trying to protect me from her?"

"Yes. Witches are dangerous."

"She's not a witch," I said, though her actions seemed to contradict my words. "I have to hurry back to the house before Francine gets there. She might lock me out."

"I know a shorter way." He took off in a trot.

I followed at the same pace. When we reached a fork in the path, he led me on the narrower of the two options, a trail covered by vines that, in the shifting shadows, raised images of crawling vipers. I trained my stare on Jean and ran, driven by fear, not of snakes but that Francine might be drawn into some sort of dark arts that could endanger her well-being.

Michael's warning returned to mind. A shadow of evil lurked in Francine's home. And I was a guest there, a vulnerable spectator who had to feign ignorance of her secrets.

When Jean and I arrived at the house well ahead of Francine, we crept past Marc and into my room. I closed the door with a quiet click and listened. A few minutes later, footsteps approached, light and quick. They halted at my door.

As silent as death, I slid into bed, pulled Jean with me, and covered our bodies, including Jean's head. I kept my face uncovered and closed my eyes, though I allowed a slit to remain open.

A light appeared at the door, Francine carrying the lantern, now relit. She walked in, set the lantern on the floor, and withdrew the brooches, again combined. The green aura shone more eerily than ever—ghostly, demonic.

As she set the brooches close to my face, a sound filtered into my ears, the distant wailing of a frightened little girl, perhaps lost or grief stricken.

I steeled myself to keep from trembling. Francine's eyes moved from side to side, her expression nervous, anxious. After a moment, she breathed a relieved sigh and returned the brooches to her pocket, dousing the ghastly glow and silencing the forlorn child. Then she rushed out of the room and closed the door.

Again in near darkness, I threw the covers back and climbed out of bed with Jean. My hands trembling, I withdrew Michael's black candle and the matches from my pocket and lit the wick. The flame sputtered before rising tall and burning brightly.

"My master's candle," Jean whispered as he stared. "Why do you have it?"

I bypassed the whole truth, that I was summoning Michael, and whispered in return, "He lent it to me."

"You'll shorten our lives." Jean blew out the flame. When my vision readjusted to the renewed darkness, his sincere countenance returned to view. His eyes brimmed with tears. "I'm not ready yet."

"Not ready? What do you mean?"

"Like my master tells me, I still have darkness in my heart. I want to kill people. Like Francine."

"Because you think she's a witch?"

His eyes narrowed. "Of course she's a witch. You saw what she did. You heard the dead girl's cries, didn't you?"

"I heard, and I'm not sure what it all means, but I intend to find out." I set a hand on his shoulder. "Will you help me?"

He nodded. "But I wonder what she was doing with that light. Will her witchcraft affect you?"

"I suffered no ill effects, I assure you. Besides the odd sounds, it was merely a light."

"A witch's victims sometimes never know, especially when she is hoping to addle their minds."

"Nonsense. If anything, the frightening experience has fully cleared my mind." I lifted my hand. "In any case, if memory serves, Madame Noël has a family tree diagram hanging on her bedroom wall. I would like to examine it without Francine knowing. She probably went to bed, so I don't expect her to interrupt, but you can help me watch and listen for her."

Jean nodded again. "I can do that."

"Then follow without a sound." I found the room's candlestick and lit its nearly spent candle. Guided by its bare glow, I opened the door and padded toward the house's master bedroom with Jean at my heels. As I had hoped, he made no noise at all, perhaps because he was really a ghost, a fact I had pushed from my thoughts until this moment. His deathly quiet presence added to a chill that rode across my skin.

When we arrived, I found the door ajar and pushed it open. The aroma of scented wax wafted past, as if someone had burned perfumed candles in recent days. After pushing the door to its original position, I walked to the adjacent wall on the left and lifted the candle close to a framed drawing—the Noël family tree.

Printed names, as well as dates of birth and death, ran along a tree-like shape. It took only a moment to find Marc and Francine near the top. A quick trace down the tree revealed their father, Henri, their paternal grandfather, Adolphe, and his wife, Claire— born in Killarney, Ireland, and died in Marseille, France. Adolphe died at the age of forty-seven, making Claire a widow a month before her forty-second birthday.

I scanned other names, searching for a girl who died young. Retracing up the branches revealed a third child of Jacqueline

Noël—Siobhan, an older sister to Marc and Francine. She died at the age of seven, a year before Marc was born. Maybe she was the girl in the crypt.

I read the birth years again—Siobhan in 1830, Marc in 1838, and Francine in 1840—an eight-year gap between the first and second child. Their father died in 1849, a fact I already knew. He had been a victim of that year's cholera epidemic. Yet, my recollections told me that he and Madame Noël had been married twelve years when he died, placing their wedding in 1837, the same year Siobhan died. Had Madame Noël been married before? If so, the tree gave no such indication.

And Siobhan was an Irish name. Why would they choose it?

I held the candle closer to Siobhan's entry. Unlike the connections between the other two children and their parents, no line attached Siobhan to any parentage, as if she were hovering on the tree with no support—an orphan, separated and lost.

A new tingle ran along my skin. The candle's light pulsed, and the sound of shallow respiration reached my ears.

Jean whispered, "I hear someone breathing."

Without a word, I tiptoed to the door and set my ear next to the gap. No sound emanated from the hallway. The breathing was coming from somewhere in the bedroom. I spun and lifted the candle high, shifting it from left to right as I scanned the area from wall to wall. The bed sat with its covers undisturbed, and every piece of furniture, from a tall dresser to a full-length mirror, stood where I had always seen them.

My heart thumped, now much louder than any competing sound. Although no other humans were in sight, someone could easily hide under the bed or in the shadows. I had no desire to search for the mysterious breather. Whoever this person was, living or dead, he or she could stay hidden.

In a rush, I opened the door and, taking Jean by the hand, walked with long, silent steps to my bedroom. When we entered, I closed the door and leaned against it, now heaving shallow breaths myself.

Jean looked up at me. "Are you scared?"

I swallowed and gave him a nod. "Aren't you?"

He shook his head. "What is there to be scared of?"

"The breathing. It sounded like ..." I was about to mention the possibility of a ghostly presence, but his unearthly bright eyes reminded me that I had been accompanied by a ghost all along. "Well, I suppose it felt like a stranger lurked in our midst, and I wasn't certain of his or her intentions."

"I don't think she wanted to hurt us."

"She? A woman?"

"A girl. Maybe my age."

"How do you know?"

"I saw her. Didn't you?"

"No." I pushed away from the door. "Where was she? What was she doing?"

"Standing by the bed, looking at us."

"I didn't see anyone."

"But you heard her breathing, so you know she was there."

"Was she a ghost?"

He nodded. "Like me, I think. Only maybe she hasn't learned how to be visible to you."

"Interesting." I narrowed my eyes. "Do ghosts also have to learn how to manipulate physical objects?"

He blinked. "What do you mean?"

"You have a physical presence. I held your hand. You can move objects. Do you have to learn how to be physical?"

"Not really. When we're visible, we're ... solid. If that's what you mean. Sometimes we can be sort of visible and not solid."

"Transparent?"

He offered another nod.

I stooped and looked him in the eye. "Jean, tell me what you saw the night Madame Noël was hanged. You said you're innocent, but since you can see things I can't, maybe you can tell me more about what happened."

Jean averted his gaze. After a moment of silence, he looked again at me, his eyes awash in tears. "I said I didn't do it, but I really don't know if I did or not."

"You don't know? How could you not know?"

A deeper voice replied. "Because Jean forgets what he does during his bouts of rage." Michael stood at the door, hands folded at his waist, his body semitransparent. "He truly doesn't know if he was involved in the killing."

I touched my chest. "Why does he believe that *I* am not the murderer?"

"Jean is putting his heart into one of his lessons, which is, in the absence of damning evidence, to believe an accused person who claims innocence. To err on the side of mercy."

"I see."

Michael became fully visible and grasped Jean's hand. "You must come with me. We are too close to success and too close to our deadline to abandon your lessons now."

"When is your deadline?" I asked.

"As I told you before, when the candle is spent." He extended his hand. "May I have it, please?"

I withdrew the black candle from my pocket and set it in his palm. "When Jean runs away," I said, "you have to use the candle to search for him. He shortens his own life. That makes no sense."

"True, but people often act in ways that bring about their own demise, do they not?" Michael raised a hand. Like fog rolling along a meadow, glowing mist spread across the floor. People appeared as if formed from the mist—drunken men fighting in a bar while scantily dressed prostitutes looked on, laughing. "Look at these pitiful souls. Are they considering tomorrow? The next day? Where will they end? Although they see the results of their perilous behaviors in cemeteries throughout the city, they carry on as if the evidence has no import. Momentary pleasure outweighs time-tested wisdom, and they rush to their graves as if eager for eternal darkness."

I let out a sigh. "I suppose you're right. People can be blind."

"And yet Jean has no such examples. Although he gives lip service to the dire prophecy about the candle, he has never seen someone perish at the dousing of a flaming wick or at the dripping of a final dram of wax. Experience is not his teacher, so he must rely on words and the integrity of those who speak them."

"Such as yourself."

Michael nodded. "And I taught him in the catacombs, which is far from an ideal learning environment. He sees only death in that place, nothing that promotes the value of life. That's why we moved to the abandoned schoolhouse not long ago. Jean progressed much better there, and his moments of rage diminished substantially."

"Was the same true for Pierre?"

A light knock sounded at the bedroom door. "Justin?" Francine said from the other side. "May I come in?"

I stiffened, unable to come up with a response.

"We will take our leave," Michael whispered as he and Jean faded into transparency.

"Jean," I whispered, "tell Michael about what we saw at the crypt and in the bedroom."

After Jean nodded, they disappeared. My muscles tightened further. I had to clear my throat with great force just to squeak, "Come in."

The door opened. Now wearing a house dress and carrying a lit candelabrum, Francine bustled in and closed the door behind her in hurried motions. After setting the light on the bedside table, she faced me and looked into my eyes. "We're alone," she said in a breathless whisper.

I looked at the closed door. Barely able to breathe myself, I fumbled through my response. "Yes. Of course. Why wouldn't we be?"

"I heard voices." She glanced around. "Yours and someone else's."

"Ah, yes. I wasn't able to sleep, so ..." I couldn't think of a believable lie.

"You were rehearsing. Marc told me you had a play coming up." Smiling, she gave me a playful push. "You shouldn't be embarrassed about that. You sounded wonderful, especially when you used that deeper voice, the one with precise diction."

"Well …" I bowed my head. "Thank you."

"You are quite welcome." Her smile melted as she touched my arm. "Justin, I must speak to you about something important."

"By all means."

She sat on the bed and gestured for me to sit next to her. When I did, she opened a hand, revealing the combined brooches. The greenish glow bathed her palm. "Do you know what this is?"

My eyes felt locked in place, unable to pull away from the scarab's pearl-like surface. "No. What is it?"

"Part of a puzzle. My mother's brooch was half, and a key inside unlocked a door that led to the other half. Now that they are combined, they provide a way to get to the next part of the puzzle."

"The next part? What is it?"

She closed her hand, hiding the eerie light. "I don't know. I was hoping you would help me figure it out."

"How do you know there even *is* a next part?"

"My mother's diary. When she died, I went through her possessions and found it. That's how I learned that her brooch had a mate and where to look for it."

"Where was it hidden?"

She bit her lip and looked down. "I can't tell you, Justin. It's a secret place. A family secret that needs to stay in darkness."

I suppressed a smile. She could have easily lied. The fact that she told the truth increased my desire to help. "If you have to keep the secret, how do you expect me to help you?"

"With your knowledge of languages. According to Mother's diary, the puzzle is connected to a legend about Joan of Arc. She had a ring that gave her protection during the battles. If that's true, it would be a priceless treasure. Imagine, nothing of this world could bring harm to the ring's wearer."

"If the ring protected Joan, then how could she die in the flames?"

Francine twisted a ring on her own finger. "According to legend, her persecutors took her ring, suspecting that it might be a protective device. Although they claimed to be servants of the Church, they feared superstitions."

"So whether or not the ring actually works is based on a legend."

"Yes, but even if the protective power is a myth, the ring would be quite valuable, don't you think?"

"Without a doubt. But if you find it, will it rightfully be yours?"

She nodded. "One of my ancestors purchased it in the sixteenth century. I am certain of the lineage, because Mother kept a diagram of our family's genealogy. According to the diary, my grandmother hid the ring and devised a complex puzzle to keep it safe. Mother's diary says that one step to finding the ring is written in a language she didn't understand. She intended to do more research, but obviously she died before she could find the answer."

"May I see the diary?"

"Well ..." She glanced away. "Much of it is personal." When she focused her eyes on me, she added, "You understand, I'm sure."

"I do, but how can I be of help if you won't let me study the clues?"

"I will show you what is pertinent, the portion written in a foreign language." She withdrew a small book from a dress pocket and turned it to a marked page. As she stepped closer to the candles, she read out loud. "Grandmother Claire's journal says that once the brooches are attached, the next step is to ..." Francine pointed at the page. "Can you read this?"

I blinked at the odd handwriting. As I studied it, the poorly formed letters took familiar shapes. "It's written in Gaelic. It says, roughly speaking, 'The jewels make light that pierce his bones. I set them in the shape of a cross. You will find it near a wall of skulls.'"

"A wall of skulls," Francine repeated in a whisper.

"There are such walls in the catacombs. Actually I hear there are quite a number of them."

"The catacombs?" She looked at me with wide eyes. "I have to search there?"

"It seems so." I read the text again and verified that I had translated it correctly. "Whose bones is she referring to?"

"Maybe Adolphe's. Her husband's. He died long before she did. A fever, I think."

My thoughts drifted to the little girl in the crypt. Maybe this was my chance to learn more about her. "Where is the genealogy diagram you mentioned?"

"Mother used to keep it on a wall in her bedroom, but when I looked for it, it wasn't there."

"Not there? When did you look for it?"

"Just moments ago. Before I came in here."

I tried to hide my shock. "Stolen?"

"I can't imagine who would steal it. It has only sentimental value."

"Why were you looking for it?"

"Mother's diary mentioned that the words you translated were related to someone in the family. I thought the diagram might help, but, as I said, it's missing. That's when I heard you rehearsing."

Another knock came from the door. "Justin?" Marc called. "Francine?"

Francine leaped to the door and opened it. "Marc, how embarrassing that you should find us here with the door closed." She gestured toward me, her smile disarming. "But, as you can see, all is well. I was helping Justin rehearse his lines."

"Is that so?" Marc walked in and glanced around the room. "Where is the script?"

"I have it all memorized," I said. "Even Zara's lines, a role which Francine is remarkably suited for."

"Really?" Marc crossed his arms. "Please continue. This should be entertaining."

Francine grasped Marc's arm. "No need for that. We were passing time waiting for you to wake up. I closed the door so you wouldn't be disturbed."

"It's five in the morning," he said. "Couldn't you sleep?"

Francine shook her head. "The funeral has dominated my thoughts. So much to do, but I didn't want to make any noise. Then I heard Justin rehearsing, so I thought I'd join him."

"Sleeplessness is contagious, I see." Marc let out a sigh. "All right. Fine. But I will not scold myself for thinking that you two might have been rehearsing for your wedding night."

Blushing, Francine looked everywhere but at me. "Marc, I am fond of Justin, and we have discussed possible courtship, but we are far from being lovers."

"Sure. Keep acting. I'll play along." Marc spread an arm toward the doorway. "Shall I brew coffee for us?"

"I'll do it." Francine walked out, not bothering to give me another glance.

Marc looked at me with a bent brow. "Justin, although I approve of you courting my sister—"

"Marc, it was nothing. Trust me. Not even a kiss or an embrace. Our relationship has barely begun."

"Still, it would be better to avoid compromising situations. If *I* had suspicious thoughts, neighbors and strangers will find you guilty without a trial, and you can't afford bad publicity, especially after what the papers are likely to print today." He gestured with his head. "Let's put it behind us and get a cup of coffee. This could be a difficult day for all of us. Marguerite and Francine had to chase away five reporters yesterday. More are sure to come."

As we walked toward the sitting room, questions roared within, demanding answers. Why didn't Francine want Marc to know about her search for the ring? Should I reveal her quest to him? What might she be hiding? Maybe a stealthy conversation would provide the answers.

With coffee in hand, we entered the sitting room where Francine had set a table and slid chairs up to each side. Once we sat and began drinking, I nodded toward Francine. "Marc told me that your paternal grandmother has Celtic roots. That came as quite a surprise."

Francine finished a sip and set her cup down. "Yes, she does, but why the surprise?"

"I thought you were French for many generations." I raised my brow at Marc. "If you were to trace your lineage, where would you find the first Celtic or Irish name?"

"Not far at all," Marc said. "We had a half-sister named Siobhan."

I nodded. "Definitely Irish. I'm not sure I remember what it means."

"God is gracious," Francine said. "It is an Irish form of Joan."

"Joan," I whispered. "How interesting."

"Interesting indeed." Marc sipped his coffee before continuing. Although his casual action appeared nonchalant, a facial tic gave away more than a little anxiety. "Mother grew up poor. Poor as dirt, actually. One of five daughters. According to all accounts, she was desperate to get out of the squalor her family called home, but her father wouldn't let her leave."

He set his cup down, a slight tremor in his hand as well as his voice. "You see, her mother had died, and as a young teenager she was the only daughter old enough to keep house. She also attracted male customers to her father's shop by dressing more provocatively than most and spending time outside close to the door. That led her father to encourage the behavior. As you might expect, eventually one of the customers decided that looking wasn't enough, so he took advantage of her."

Francine gasped and raised a hand over her mouth, though she said nothing. I shifted in my seat, not knowing what to say myself. How does one respond to the rape of a child?

Marc drummed his fingers on his thigh while biting his lip and staring at his cup. After a quiet moment, he looked at us with misty eyes and continued at a slower cadence. "When she became pregnant and could no longer hide the fact, she told her father what happened. It turns out that the attacker was quite wealthy, an Irishman of noble descent, so her father, knowing that an unwed, pregnant daughter wouldn't be able to attract customers or a husband of any worth, demanded that the man give him a sizeable bride price and take her away. Otherwise, he would have the scoundrel arrested."

"A scoundrel, indeed," Francine said. "Beheading was too good for him." Her cheeks suddenly flushing red, she waved a hand. "I apologize, Marc. My emotions got the best of me. Please continue."

"I understand. I can barely contain my own emotions. But I think it's important to realize what our mother suffered." Marc settled back in his seat, appearing more comfortable now as he finished his tale quickly. "Not wanting to soil his reputation, the man acquiesced and took Mother into his home. Although they never married, he supported her, and when the baby was born, she suggested the name Siobhan."

"Because she was obsessed with Joan of Arc," Francine said.

Marc offered a tight smile. "And it seems that she passed along her fascination with Joan to you."

"I suppose she did." Francine tilted her head. "Marc, I have never heard this story before. Why haven't you told me?"

"Because Mother made me swear to secrecy. She said I could tell you after she passed."

Francine gave him a nod. "Go on."

"There isn't much more to tell. I don't even know the man's name. But he died in the eighteen-thirty-two cholera epidemic, just two years after Siobhan was born. A judge awarded her a portion of the man's estate, so Mother was able to live well enough, and by the time she married our father, she had established herself as part of the bourgeoisie."

"How could she do that with a bastard child?" Francine asked.

"I asked her that question in a more delicate way, but she wouldn't answer. I suppose it will remain a mystery."

"How did Siobhan die?" I asked.

"That, too, is a mystery. Mother refused to tell me, but there were no cholera outbreaks that year, though smallpox and consumption are always around. In any case, we don't even know where Siobhan is buried. Mother kept that a secret as well."

I cast a stealthy glance at Francine, wondering if she would mention the mausoleum she had recently visited, but she stayed quiet.

Marc arched a brow. "Speaking of secrets, Mother told me that Grandmother Claire had secrets of her own. Apparently she hid some valuable treasures, and Mother often wondered where they were. Not that she needed the money, of course, but what a shame it would be to lose precious family heirlooms."

"What kind of heirlooms?" Francine asked.

"A ring of some sort." Marc touched the top of his chest. "And a diamond pendant that hung from a necklace. Supposedly it was too valuable to wear openly, so Claire put it away for safekeeping."

Francine touched her own chest as if caressing an invisible pendant. "Were there any clues to its location?"

"None that I know of, but now that Mother is dead ..." Marc rose from his chair slowly, apparently still weakened by the blow to his head. "Now we can search for answers to our questions. Mother has a trunk—"

"I've already gone through it," Francine said. "I found nothing but clothes she hasn't worn in years."

"The family tree, then. She stared at it so often, I'm sure it holds secrets."

Francine set her coffee cup down. "It's missing."

"What?" Marc furrowed his brow. "Missing? Since when?"

"Since last night. It was on the wall then, but this morning it was gone."

"Who could have taken it? It has no value to anyone but us."

"My thoughts exactly."

"Perhaps Marguerite moved it." Marc ambled toward the master bedroom. "I'll be back in a moment."

When he had walked out of earshot, Francine spoke in a low tone. "You raised that topic intentionally, didn't you?"

I nodded. "I suspected that he might know more, since he's older than you and has access to your mother's papers. I thought it might be a good way to learn something without telling him what you're looking for."

She let out a resigned sigh. "Well, we learned quite a lot."

"Why don't you want him to know about your search for the ring?"

"Because if he killed Mother for her money, it wouldn't be right for him to get a share of any heirloom's value."

"And if he didn't?"

"I'll wait for the investigation to complete. If he is innocent, then of course I'll share it with him."

I glanced down the hall. Marc was nowhere in sight. "Speaking of the investigation, do you think the inspector will be at the funeral?"

"I think so. He'll want to interview people who were at the party, which would be impolite to do that day, of course, but he can make appointments."

"It sounds like this could drag on for quite some time."

"Not likely. Publicity will hurry it along. We'll know the truth soon, but until then, let's take care about what we tell Marc and what we keep to ourselves."

I leaned closer to her. "Do you *really* think Marc might be the murderer?"

She leaned as well. "Sound reasoning says no. If he were, why would he help you? It would have been easy for him to deny your alibi. The investigation would be over, he would be free, and you would be facing the guillotine."

My throat tingled. "Trust me. I have thought of that many times."

"Yet, as intelligent as Marc is, perhaps he knew that helping you would cast suspicions away from him."

"I wondered about that possibility as well."

"Here it is." Marc walked in with the document, one hand on each side of the frame. "It was in the spare bedroom."

"The spare bedroom?" Francine asked. "With Marguerite? Wasn't the door locked?"

"No. The door was partially open. That's why I looked there."

"And Marguerite?"

"Asleep, I assume. I didn't check on her."

Francine looked down the hall. "How odd that it would be there."

Marc laid the document flat on the table. As the three of us looked at it, my eyes shifted immediately to Siobhan's place on the tree, but her name as well as Marc's and Francine's had been scratched out by three lines, each colored in red, though the words were still readable.

"Look," I said, pointing. "Is that blood?"

Marc set a finger on one of the abrasions. "It seems so. It's still a bit tacky."

"How could it have happened?" I asked.

"I have no idea. It wasn't like this the last time I saw it."

Francine crossed her arms. "Marguerite must have done it. After all, you found it in her room."

"Or someone hopes we think so," Marc said. "She was scared of Justin, so I'm sure she locked the door."

"True. The open door is curious."

"Mother kept a key to that door on her dresser. Finding it would not be difficult."

"Marc …" Francine curled her arm around his and pulled him close. "Someone is playing pranks, and I don't like it."

"Cruel pranks." Marc looked at me. "Did you see or hear anything unusual last night?"

I attempted a disarming smile. "Would you call rehearsing a play in the middle of night unusual?"

"Normally I would appreciate the levity, but not now." He turned to Francine. "Did you hear anything?"

She shook her head. "Nothing."

I kept my face slack. Of course I failed to tell the whole truth, but so had Francine. Obviously she wasn't ready to trust him yet.

After giving her a long, hard look, Marc grasped her hand. "I think it's time you and I had a talk."

She glanced at the hand clasp, then at him. "About what?"

"Family matters. Private matters."

"Then we should go outside." Francine nodded toward the door. "I want to show you something."

"Very well." Marc looked at me. "Are you comfortable staying here alone?"

"I think so. This prankster could have easily attacked us in our sleep. I doubt that he or she has the courage to face one of us."

"Just in case ..." He looked around the room. "You should have a weapon of some kind."

Francine pointed toward the fireplace. "The poker?"

"Perfect." Marc took the poker and handed it to me. "For your protection."

I gripped the handle and tested its weight. "Thank you. And I'll check on Marguerite as well."

"Find something for breakfast," Francine said. "Or you can wait for Marguerite to get up. She is an early riser."

"You'll be gone that long?"

"It's possible. I need to take Marc out of the neighborhood for a little while."

I nodded. Maybe she was ready to show him the girl in the crypt. "Take your time."

When they left, I returned to my seat next to the table and studied the family tree. The scratches were narrow and well defined, as if they were made by pointed fingernails. But what was the source of the red coloring? Perhaps the prankster's own blood?

A knock at the main door drew my attention. Who would visit so early in the morning? A reporter, maybe?

I rose, walked to the door, and opened it, revealing a petite woman wearing a simple white dress. Carrying a lit lantern by its top handle, she bent her knee in a shallow curtsy. "My name is Siobhan. May I come in?"

Chapter Twelve

I backed away, stuttering. "Y—yes. Of course." As Siobhan entered, I couldn't help but stare. Not only did this visitor bear the name of the mysterious sister, she looked like an adult version of the girl in the crypt. Her hair and the style of her dress were identical.

When I closed the door, she squinted as if examining me. "You are an Englishman, are you not?" Her words carried an Irish flavor.

"I am, and my guess is that you are familiar with the Isles yourself."

She smiled demurely. "Is it that obvious?"

"Probably not to most. Your French is perfect."

"Thank you." She glanced around. "I am looking for someone, and all signs pointed to this house."

"Signs? What signs?"

Her smile stiffened. "It would be impossible to explain. May I search for her?"

"Her? A woman?"

"A girl." She walked toward the hall. "Are the bedrooms this way?"

I strode ahead and blocked her path. "The master and mistress of the house are not here right now. It wouldn't be proper for you to search without their permission."

She lifted the lantern. "If she is here, this light should find her in mere moments. So I ask again, may I search?"

I stared at the lantern. Similar to Joan's light, the flame within leaned on its wick as if pointing down the hall. From that direction, a draft breezed by, cold and fetid.

I coughed, nearly gagging. "Yes. Yes, go and find her."

"Thank you, sir." Siobhan walked down the hall, extending the lantern in front.

The poker in hand, I followed. With every footstep, the air thickened and grew fouler. Breathing felt like drinking sewage. It seemed that the flame called the stench from a festering hole, as if drawing pus from a wound.

Siobhan walked into Marguerite's room. I stopped at the door and peeked inside. At the foot of the bed, a girl dressed in rags sat cross-legged. When she saw the light, she leaped to her feet and backed against a wall. Her eyes wild with terror, she clawed at the air and growled.

My own eyes widened. This was the same girl I had seen scrubbing the scullery floor. Had she sought a place to sleep after finishing her cleaning assignment?

"Fear not, Jacqueline," Siobhan whispered as she eased toward the girl. "I am here to help you."

I withheld a gasp. Jacqueline? Jacqueline Noël?

As Siobhan drew closer to the girl, her voice softened further, forcing me to step into the room to hear.

"I will be your teacher," Siobhan said. "You are safe with me. I will take you away from this scary place, and we'll have many good talks. Would you like that?"

Jacqueline brushed a tear with a fist and nodded. Barely covered by a ratty dress, and her shoulder-length hair in disarray, she looked like one of the street urchins, far from the grand woman Jacqueline Noël had portrayed herself to be, and certainly less pretentious than the fool dressed in motley.

"Then come with me," Siobhan said, extending a hand. "All will be well."

Jacqueline slowly lifted a hand and slid it into Siobhan's.

"Good girl." Siobhan walked with her toward the door. As they passed me, Siobhan gave me a sad sort of smile. "Thank you for allowing me to search."

I breathed a stammering, "You're welcome."

As they walked down the hall, I stared at them, a teacher and a student hand-in-hand, now silhouettes in the lantern's fading glow. Seconds later, they turned a corner, and the sound of the door opening and closing announced their exit.

Scarcely able to breathe, I looked around the spare bedroom as if waking from a dream. With the poker in hand, I felt like a fool holding a weapon out of fear of a frightened little girl. She was barely more than a shadow, a mist reborn, lost and drifting in a strange world.

The first rays of dawn crept through a window, giving light to the room. A lump under the bed covers raised a start. I had forgotten about Marguerite. Although we had stayed relatively quiet, it seemed odd that she had slept through Jacqueline's growls.

My mind filled with dread, I touched her shoulder. "Marguerite?"

She stayed motionless, no sign of breathing.

I shook her. "Marguerite?"

Again, she showed no signs of life. As the room grew brighter, it became clear that she was supine, her face exposed. I pulled her covers down. Blood covered her nightgown, torn to shreds.

I gasped. My heart thumped. Staggering back, I grasped for support but found only air until my hand clutched the side of the doorway. Now steadied, I stared at the brutalized corpse. Who could have committed this terrible crime? Little Jacqueline? But with what? Surely the murderer used a sharp weapon of some kind.

I lifted the poker and stared at it. Free of bloodstains, this could not have been the murder weapon unless someone had cleaned it thoroughly.

The moment I first saw it came to mind, when I walked into the sitting room while the inspector was there. At that time, it was still hot from stirring the fire, and now it carried no hint of ashes or even the odor of smoke.

Indeed, someone *had* cleaned it.

But who? Maybe Marguerite herself had cleaned it as part of her evening duties. Yet, who would routinely clean a fire poker?

My heart still thrumming, I hurried toward the front door. When I drew near, it opened, and Marc and Francine walked in, both with sour expressions. The urge to hide the poker behind my back nearly overwhelmed me, but I resisted.

"You should have told me sooner," Marc said to Francine. "She was our sister."

"I just learned about it yesterday," she replied. "You were unconscious until late evening."

When Marc saw me, he cleared his throat and gave me an uneasy nod. "Well, I see that you are safe and sound."

At that instant, a trance enveloped me. A hush descended, and the three of us stood as statues. A memory resurrected, the moment I saw Father with the hangman's rope in his grasp. He held the instrument of murder. Yet, in my youth and trusting naïveté, I assumed him to be innocent of the crime in spite of the blood coloring his guilty hands. And now I held the poker that likely ended the life of poor Marguerite. Since no blood stained either skin or metal, would my friends give me the benefit of the doubt? Perhaps not. But, being innocent, I had to act innocent, to declare innocence with fervor.

Time restarted. Motion returned. Trying to quell rising bile, I swallowed, but my voice squeaked all the same. "Marc, Francine …" I licked my lips. "Marguerite is dead."

Francine sucked in a gasping breath. Marc's mouth dropped open. He stuttered in reply. "D … dead? How? Who?"

"I don't know who did it." I extended the poker. "But I think this might be the weapon."

They both stared as if caught in another trance. A moment later, Marc took the poker. "Is she in her room?"

I nodded. "Come."

We hurried to the spare bedroom. When Francine saw Marguerite, she crouched and sobbed. Marc examined the body and verified that the wounds appeared to be inflicted by the poker or something similar in size and sharpness. Someone had plunged the point into her chest five times, piercing her heart and lungs. Since she had no blood in her nose or mouth, she likely died in an instant, unable to take another breath.

Marc showed me the point of the poker. "Someone cleaned it."

I nodded. "No ash or odor. And no blood."

"But why clean it? Why not take it and throw it away? Instead, the murderer put it back where it belongs. I think he would be in too much of a hurry."

"You're right. It is odd behavior." The little girl in the scullery came to mind, the way she scrubbed the floor with such meticulous care. Could the resurrected Jacqueline have murdered Marguerite? In her nightmarish state, she might have rushed to hide the instrument of her crime in the only way she knew how.

"Marc," Francine said as she brushed tears from her eyes. "Was it clean when you took it from the fireplace this morning and gave it to Justin?"

"I ... I don't remember." He looked again at the poker's point. "Maybe."

Francine turned to me with an acidic glare. "Justin, you stayed here alone even though we wondered if someone might be stalking us. Now Marguerite is dead, and we found you holding the murder weapon."

I pointed at myself. "Do you think *I* killed her? You know I could never—"

"Of course you couldn't," Marc said, giving Francine a burning glare of his own. "Someone is playing a cruel, murderous game, and he wants to blame Justin for the crimes."

Francine crossed her arms over her chest. "This is no game. When we report Marguerite's death"—Francine cast a doubtful eye on me—"we have to tell the truth. Surely the inspector will come to only one conclusion, that Justin is the murderer."

"But he has no motive," Marc said, "no reason to kill an innocent woman."

"Well ..." Francine looked away. "She did insult him last night."

Marc shook his head. "Saying that he is a murder suspect is hardly an insult. Fear is a natural response."

"True," Francine said, "but since everything points a finger at Justin, he won't be able to escape arrest this time. Maybe it would be better for all of us if he were in jail until the investigation is complete."

Tension shot through my muscles, but I forced myself to relax. "If I am arrested, they will halt the investigation. Why bother working on a case they believe to be solved?"

"What is the alternative?" Marc asked. "You cannot deny that you're the most obvious suspect, though it seems impossible to me."

"I can leave. Go into hiding. Maybe being out of the inspector's view will allow me to do some investigating myself."

Marc clasped my shoulder with a firm grip. "When we report the murder, we'll have to tell the truth, of course, but I will do everything in my power to convince the inspector of your innocence."

"He should turn himself in," Francine said. "Running will add to the evidence against him."

I laughed under my breath. "Better to be an intact suspect than a headless prisoner."

"Agreed," Marc said. "And your running will give us time to find the real murderer."

Francine kept her arms tightly crossed. "Assuming for the moment that Justin is innocent, that means this murderer could still be lurking nearby. We're all vulnerable."

Scowling, Marc scanned the area as if looking for someone to attack. "The murderer is lily-livered. Hanging a woman, burning a doctor in a dark library, and stabbing a sleeper are cowardly acts. I have no fear of him."

"Maybe you don't, but I do. I would feel much safer if I had a gun."

"I'll get a revolver for you," Marc said. "I assume you remember how to shoot."

"Without a doubt."

"And I will search the house thoroughly. Whoever killed Marguerite probably left long ago, but I'll make sure you're safe."

"One problem with our plan." I pushed a hand into my pockets and withdrew the carriage fare. "This is all the money I have for food. It won't last long."

"Then come here in the dead of night," Marc said. "We'll set something out for you." He looked at Francine. "Right?"

She gave a resigned nod. "Of course. Far be it from me to turn anyone away."

"Agreed." Marc touched my arm. "Where will you go? Obviously we won't tell anyone."

The urge to glance at Francine made my eyes hurt, but I kept them trained on Marc. "I shouldn't tell you. That way you won't have to lie for my sake."

"You're right, of course." Marc shook my hand. "Thank you, my friend."

"If I may offer a suggestion ..." Francine pulled me close and whispered, though Marc could hear her with ease. "Go to the catacombs." As she spoke, she slid something into my pocket out of Marc's view. "Even if the inspector looks for you there, you could easily evade him."

I gazed into her imploring eyes. She wanted me to search for the ring, which meant she hadn't told Marc about it yet. "I will certainly do my best to avoid the inspector."

"You should go now." She set a hand on my back and pushed me toward the rear door. "You can return for your personals later."

"Why the rush?" I asked while resisting her push.

"The inspector said he might visit again this morning. Remember? The report from Scotland Yard?"

I gave in to her push but stopped just outside the door and turned back. "If he has the report, please learn as much as you can and pass the information along to me."

"How will we get it to you?" Marc asked.

"Francine knows where the entrance to the catacombs is. I'll stay nearby for a little while."

"Go," she said. "I'll come to the school this evening. Right before dark. Look for me then."

"What about your mother's funeral? Won't you be busy with arrangements?"

"Marc will help. Don't worry."

I gave them both parting nods and hurried toward the school once again. Along the way, I checked my pocket and found the brooches inside. Francine had entrusted me with a valuable treasure. Maybe she wasn't suspicious of me after all.

As I continued at a slower pace, I tried to gather the scattered fragments of this mystery and piece them together. Since I, of course, did not kill Marguerite, the only potential suspects were Marc, Francine, and the newly resurrected Jacqueline, or, perhaps, a stalking stranger who had not yet been revealed. If a murderer were still about, it seemed odd that Marc and Francine would be so calm. They reacted strongly to Marguerite's death, but only for a few moments. Afterward, they carried on as if they had experienced only a minor incident—spilled coffee or a broken teacup.

Yet, even that was explainable. They were still grief stricken over their mother. Another death merely added to their numbness.

The thought of a lingering stalker gave me pause. I halted and turned. The house still lay in view about two hundred yards away. A figure wearing a hooded cloak and carrying a satchel walked from the side yard, stopped at the street, and looked at me, his eyes shaded by the hood.

I resumed a quick stride and glanced back. The stranger walked in the same direction and at the same pace, obviously following me.

As I accelerated, he did as well. Soon we were out of sight of the house and nearing the graveyard where Siobhan's body lay. Dread pounced on me like a ravenous beast. Was I the murderer's next target?

Chapter Thirteen

Just as I flexed my muscles to run, Marc's words came to mind. *The murderer is lily-livered. I have no fear of him.*

Emboldened, I stopped and turned toward the stranger. When he noticed, he slowed his pace but continued toward me. Although the beast gnawed at my confidence, I hardened my frame and set my feet. I had to belie my fear and give this stalker reason to fear me instead.

As he drew close, he lowered the hood, revealing the familiar face of Inspector Fortier.

I relaxed my muscles but kept my mind on guard. Surely he would ask questions I couldn't answer. Maybe striking first would work to my advantage.

"Inspector, why were you sneaking about the Noëls' home, and why are you following me now?"

At first his thinned lips communicated annoyance, but they bent into an agreeable smile. "I hoped to ask for your help in my investigation."

"Of course. How may I help?"

"By answering some questions. And perhaps in another way." He looked toward the house, though it was now far out of sight. "I arrived about an hour ago. The comings and goings have been most interesting."

"If you mean Marc and Francine, they left the house for a little while to have a private conversation."

"Private might not be the best word. Perhaps macabre." He nodded toward the graveyard. "They went in there."

"Really?" I feigned surprise.

Still carrying the satchel, he gestured with his free hand. "Come. Let me show you."

I followed him into the graveyard through the iron gateway, left partially open by a previous visitor. We walked straight to the mausoleum and stopped at its closed door. "They went inside," he said. "They opened a girl's crypt. Since they whispered, I don't know who she is or why they visited her."

I ran a hand along the stone door. "How did they get in?"

"Mademoiselle Noël had a tiny key." He ran a finger across the keyhole. "It was small, but it worked."

"How interesting."

"Do you know anything at all about this girl or why they came?"

I hesitated, which was enough for him to conclude that I did know something. I had to provide a tidbit, something to satisfy him without giving away too much. "She's a family member. A sister, I think. My guess is that brooch Francine searched for held the key. Her mother's death incited her and her brother to visit their departed sister's tomb."

The inspector nodded. "That explains a great deal. And it gives me something to go on. Thank you."

"Anytime I can help, let me know."

"Maybe you *can* help more." He set the satchel down, opened it, and withdrew an empty glass vial, crouching as he showed it to me. "I found this in Dr. Cousineau's pocket."

"Oh? Was it empty when you found it?"

"Yes, except for traces of arsenic."

"Arsenic? Are you sure?"

"Quite sure." He returned the vial to the satchel and straightened. "Madame Noël was poisoned. She was dead before she was hanged."

"Dr. Cousineau killed her?"

"That seems to be the obvious answer, but he likely had an accomplice. And maybe you can help me ascertain who."

"If I can, but how?"

The inspector again looked toward Marc and Francine's house. "You have spent time at the Noëls' home. Have you noticed if they keep a supply of rat poison?"

"What? Do you think—"

"Just answer the question, please." His face was expressionless, no hint of suspicion toward anyone.

"I haven't seen any. I'm sure thousands of homes have a ready supply."

"Yes, but their occupants didn't stand to inherit wealth from Madame Noël's death."

"I suppose that's true." No doubt the inspector was targeting Marc or Francine, but which one? Maybe both?

"One more question that might seem odd." The inspector furrowed his brow and stared as if daring me to speak a lie. "Do you know if the Noëls ever owned a dog?"

"A dog?" Francine's story about the attempted poisoning flashed to mind. Since the inspector asked about a dog, he probably already knew about its demise. "They had one. It died not long ago."

"Old age? Sickness? An accident?"

"It was young, so most likely an accident."

"Thank you." Crouching again, he reached into the satchel and withdrew a portfolio. "On a separate topic," he said while rising, "this dossier arrived on the late train. It contains more information about you and your family than I expected."

"From Scotland Yard?"

"Yes." He drew a single sheet from the portfolio and read it aloud. "Your father, Cameron Trotter, murdered his wife, Cassidy Trotter, when you were seven years old. You ran outside to—"

"No." I shook my head. "No, that's not true. He didn't kill my mother. She's still—"

"Still alive?" He pulled out several more sheets and flipped through them. "I read about your protestations. You said that your mother was with you, and it was another woman he killed. Yet your mother's corpse was identified by your neighbor."

I looked at the pages, but the small letters made reading them from a distance impossible. "I remember, but my neighbor barely knew us. She misidentified the victim."

"Did you see the victim?"

"Not her face. I ran as soon as my mother told me to. I just saw that it was a woman."

The inspector set the final page on top and scanned it. "According to this report, a teacher accompanied you to France. Is that correct?"

I nodded. "A French teacher. Everyone thought it best that I have an interpreter, at least for a few weeks."

"Even though your adoptive parents were bilingual?"

"They both worked for a living. They didn't have time to teach me as quickly as I needed to learn."

"That makes perfect sense." He restored the papers to the portfolio, then the portfolio to the satchel, with slow, deliberate moves, as if letting his questions settle. When he finished, he picked up the satchel and looked at me. "Thank you, Monsieur Trotter. That's all for now."

"You're welcome, but I don't think I helped you much."

"On the contrary. I am now more certain than ever of the murderer's identity. Combining your answers with the testimony of various neighbors, I have pieced together enough evidence to draw a reasonable conclusion. Now I have to prove it."

"Who is the murderer?

He smiled. "Now, Monsieur Trotter, what kind of inspector would I be if I revealed that information before the proper time?"

"But if you were certain that I did it, you would arrest me again."

"I will neither confirm nor deny your assumption." He set a hand on my shoulder. His touch felt oddly comforting. "But I will say this. The murder of Madame Noël made you look guilty. Dr. Cousineau's death may well have been merely an accident, or perhaps you killed him to conceal your earlier crimes. In any case, if another murder happens and you have no alibi, it will be impossible to avoid arresting you, especially since the papers will unleash a firestorm of fearmongering." He looked straight at me. "Go into hiding. Escape from the world's watchful stare. Allow me to investigate without interference."

We looked at each other. The sincerity in his eyes was undeniable. Maybe it would be best to trust him with information about the latest murder, even though it might put me in danger. My honesty could pay dividends in the long run. "Inspector, you need to go back to the Noëls' house. Ask them what happened last night."

His brow lifted. "Why can't you tell me?"

"Because ..." I slid a hand into my pocket and averted my eyes from his piercing gaze. "Just go. Trust me. You need to know what happened."

"Very well. Since you won't divulge the information." He glanced toward the house. "Where were you going at such an early hour?"

"To search for clues, exactly as you were." I looked around the graveyard as its details clarified in the brightening morn. In the daylight, with more tombstones and mausolea visible, it seemed ghostlier than ever. "Something strange is going on, Inspector. Perhaps sinister. Even unearthly."

"Unearthly?"

I had said too much. He wasn't ready for stories about resurrected martyrs and their students. "Unearthly in the sense that it has to do with the departed." I touched the mausoleum's door again. "I think this girl is Madame Noël's firstborn, and somehow she was involved in the girl's death. If I go into hiding now, I won't be able to look into it any further."

"Then trust me to investigate. I will get to the bottom of this."

"I'm sure you will." I turned and walked toward the gate. "Until next time, Inspector."

"Where will you go?"

I kept my focus on the gate well ahead. "If I told you, my hiding place wouldn't be secure, now would it?"

"I suppose not. I will wait here until you're out of sight." His voice faded. "But I might need to contact you about my findings."

I called, nearly shouting. "Then tell Marc and Francine. I will speak to them from time to time."

"I can do that."

I hurried on, now at a fast trot, taking a winding path through the city to ensure that no one could follow. As had happened during my other lonely journeys, Justice came to mind. When we were young, we often frolicked happily along forest paths, through pristine meadows, and beside busy city streets, not caring about hidden dangers, never worried about the future. We just lived. We loved. We needed nothing else but each other.

Tears welled. I suppressed a sob. How I wished I could go back to those bright, innocent days. But it was too late. Much too late. Somehow I had to make her happy in spite of the darkness.

I returned to the brook. A temporary bridge had been constructed to span the water, nothing more than three logs tied in parallel, a challenge to cross since they were not fastened securely. Every step caused the logs to separate slightly, but I managed to get to the other side without a spill.

When I arrived at the school, I climbed into the shaft and shut the trapdoor. Enclosed in the dark tube, a sense of security wrapped me in a comforting coil as if I had reentered my mother's womb—safe from harm and probing eyes.

Below, a weak light appeared. I accelerated my descent, calling, "Joan? Michael? Who's down there?"

No one answered, only a slight breezy sound—the passage of air in the subterranean corridor.

When I set my feet on the bone-littered floor, careful to make as little noise as possible, I looked around. The light came from the schoolroom. As I walked toward it, I called again, "Joan? Michael?"

I peered around the corner. Joan lay on the floor, motionless. Her lantern burned nearby, its flame low and weak.

Breathless, I rushed in, sat next to her, and pulled her into my lap. I checked for a heartbeat but found nothing. She was dead.

Yet, wasn't she a ghost, dead for centuries?

I spoke sharply into her ear. "Joan. Can you hear me?"

Her eyes fluttered open. A smile broke through on her gaunt face. "Justin?"

"Yes." I swallowed to quell a spasm. "Joan, what happened?"

"Pierre … he stole my life lantern."

I nodded toward the one on the floor. "That's not it?"

"No. Pierre suffered one of his fits of rage. He said he was going to end my new existence in this world, so he took my lantern and ran away. In this maze of passages, it was impossible to find him. It was all I could do to return here and find Michael. He and Jean are looking for Pierre now."

"I should help."

When I shifted her to the floor and set her upright with her back against the wall, she grasped my arm, her eyes pleading. "Stay with me. I beg you."

"But I need to find the—"

"No. You'll get lost." She pulled me closer. "Justin, when I died, I was surrounded by villains who wanted me to suffer, also by strangers who did nothing to stop the injustice. When I leave this world again, I want to be held by a friend. Don't let me perish alone … again."

"Of course not. Never." I sat next to her and wrapped her in both arms. "Michael told me you have a connection with your lantern. Do you feel it?"

"I do, but I think Pierre kept moving, so I could not follow the sensation. I had not the strength."

"So if you had the strength, you could keep trying to find him?"

"Yes, but I don't—"

"Then let's go." I pushed the lantern's handle into her hand and scooped her into my arms. "Guide my steps."

Chapter Fourteen

As Joan held the lamp and whispered directions, I hurried through low, narrow corridors, some littered with bones, some covered with ankle-deep water, and others clear and dry. The lantern provided enough light to see only two or three steps in front, making the forks and turns appear without warning.

Although Joan weighed no more than a hundred pounds, after a mile or so, her weight became quite a burden. I whispered to her, "I know you're able to disappear or become semitransparent. What would happen if you did that now? Could I still carry you? Could you travel with me?"

"No, Justin. I would become immaterial and pass through your grasp, and I am too weak to travel on my own." She sighed. "Stop. You should rest."

"This passage is wet. Let's find a place where I can put you down." I turned into a wider, dry corridor and set Joan next to a wall. The lantern's glow revealed the wall's construction—stacked skulls from floor to ceiling. "Do you still feel your life lantern?"

"Yes. It is close. We should start looking again when you've rested." Joan stared at our surroundings with sad eyes. "Hundreds of people lie entombed in this chamber. Maybe thousands."

"And millions more in other chambers." The diary's entry returned to mind. Could this be the wall of skulls it mentioned? A stone glittered from the nose hole in a skull near the floor, likely placed there by a devoted visitor. I plucked it out and looked it over—a white oblong quartz stone, worthless to thieves but perhaps valuable to the deceased or his visiting loved one.

After setting the stone back in place, I reached into my pocket and touched the brooches. Maybe soon they would light the way to solving a mystery.

"Joan, I have to check something. I won't go far." I took the lantern and walked along the wall, holding the light close to the skulls. Their hollow eyes seemed to stare with black orbs, and their dark mouths called out in silent mourning, as if crying, *Why have we been abandoned here?* They once lay in places of honor and respectful memory. Now they were nothing more than an odd curiosity for occasional visitors, a wall of macabre humor to draw gasps from thrill-seeking adventurers.

I paused and tried to recall the exact message in Francine's book. Didn't the last sentence say something about finding the ring *near* the wall of skulls?

"Just another minute, Joan." I walked across the corridor to the opposite wall, this one made of a conglomeration of bones and fewer skulls.

"Justin?" She extended a hand, gasping. "Justin, I need you."

I rushed to her side and let her lean on my shoulder. "What is it?"

"My last moment is nigh. I feel the end coming. Pierre Cauchon has killed me again."

"No. No. I don't believe it. I won't." My thoughts scrambled, but one question bullied to the forefront. Might the ring really provide protection? If I could find it, maybe I could stop her second death.

"Joan," I whispered, "did you have a ring during your battles?"

She nodded weakly. "Two. One given to me by my parents at my first communion, and one given to me later by my brother. They were too big for my fingers, so I wore one on each thumb."

"Did the rings protect you during your battles?"

"Of course not, Justin. God's holy angels protected me."

"Then why did your persecutors take your rings?"

"To accuse me of witchcraft. Pierre ... Bishop Cauchon ... was filled with superstition. He believed the rings protected me by dark arts."

"And maybe he believed the rings might protect you from the fire. He wanted you to burn."

She blinked. "What prompted you to ask about my ring? How would you know about it?"

"Joan, your fame reaches from one end of the world to the other. You are the most revered heroine in history, save for Mother Mary herself. Stories about you have passed down from generation to generation. To France, you are the darling of the ages, which is the reason Francine tried to imitate you at the masquerade party. She adores you."

She stared at me. "I had no idea."

"Is it possible, Joan, that God endowed the ring with protective power? Is it possible that the holy angels made sure that you wore it every day?"

She lifted her thumb and looked at it. "It is possible. I suffered a wound once that many thought must be fatal, but I recovered. Perhaps the ring allows injury but prevents death."

"Then hold on." I eased away from her and cast the lantern's light on the wall of bones. As my eyes adjusted, a distinct cross took shape—femora, tibiae, and fibulae in the vertical piece, ending with a pair of feet, and humeri, radii, and ulnae in the horizontal piece, ending with a hand on each side. A single skull had been wedged where the head of the crucifixion victim would be.

I examined each hand closely. Neither wore the coveted ring.

I withdrew the brooches and joined them into a dual scarab. As before, they emitted a green glow. A girl wailed from far away. I set the scarab close to my ear, heightening the call. I extended the scarab toward Joan. "Do you hear that?"

She shook her head.

I walked to her and held it close to her ear. "Now?"

"No. Nothing at all."

How could she not hear it? When Francine entered my bedroom and set the scarab over my face, was she somehow testing me to see if I could hear the cry? Did passing the test assure her that I would be able to find the ring? If so, how could I use this ability?

I retraced my steps to the cross. My line of sight met that of the skull, as if the intended victim were my exact height. This skull's mouth seemed more eerie than the others, locked in a forever scream of torment.

I set my ear close to the mouth. The same wail came forth—distant, forlorn. I set the scarab inside and balanced it on the mandible. The green glow spread upward and flowed from the skull's eyes. The wail strengthened, louder and louder, reaching a painful volume.

Joan covered her ears. "I hear it now."

A cracking noise issued from the skull. The forehead split vertically at the center. Blood poured from the fissure and flowed into the mouth. As it covered the scarab, the glow turned red and shot out through the eyes like red fire.

More cracking noises followed, this time from the cross's hands and feet positions. The bones split at every endpoint. Again blood flowed from the wounds and drained across the bones below them.

I shifted the lantern from wound to wound, searching for any sign of the ring. The left hand sizzled, and the fingers burned away, revealing another hand behind the first. A ring encircled one of its fingers.

I set the lantern down and, with a respectful touch, slid the ring from the finger. The moment it was free, the wailing ceased. I retrieved the scarab from the mouth, wiped the blood against my trousers, and slid it into my pocket.

The wall rumbled. Grit and pebbles rained from the ceiling inches above my head. The chamber might collapse at any moment.

"Justin?" Joan pointed farther down the corridor. "I see a light. It's coming this way."

A weak, wavering light drifted toward us. As it drew closer, the outline of a boy carrying a lantern clarified.

"It's Pierre," I whispered.

Pierre halted barely out of reach. "Your time on earth has elapsed, Joan." His deep voice sounded more like a man's than a boy's. "Now you will die at my hand a second time."

I took a hard step toward him, but he backed away just as quickly. "You cannot catch me. I am faster, and I know these tunnels far better than you do."

"What do you want?"

"To watch Joan die." He looked at the lantern. "The fuel should run out in a few minutes."

"Pierre," Joan said, "you will die as well. Then you will be judged. Condemned."

"Judged? Yes. Condemned? I think not. You have been using your witchcraft to make me think I am a child and that you are my schoolmaster. The truth is that this was a test to see if I could overcome your spell and vanquish you again. Now that I have finally thrown off your dark magic, I can send you to hellfire once and for all."

His words raised a question that seemed impertinent in this crisis, but I hoped it would lead to a good end. "Pierre, did you push the bookshelf over to stop us from saving Dr. Cousineau?"

He scowled. "Yes, and I also set him on fire. As I told you before, he deserved it."

"But you also said it was an accident. I thought you hated lies, or maybe you meant other people's lies."

"I don't answer to you," he said with a sneer. "Only to God."

"Does God approve of killing an innocent man? How can you possibly think murder will lead you to anything but condemnation?"

"He wasn't innocent. He helped someone hang a woman. I saw him do it."

I kept a firm stare on him. In his state of rage, his memories had grown clear. I could probably get more information if I had time, but I had to persuade him to turn off Joan's lantern. "You're right, Pierre, he was guilty of a horrible crime. But now you need to—"

"And Joan is also guilty. I have to put an end to her. We will go together to see whom the judge condemns. I am tired of waiting."

He tipped the lantern. I lunged and swiped at it, but he twisted out of the way, making me rush past him. The moment I pivoted to try again, he threw the lantern on the floor. When it broke, fuel spilled. Flames erupted. More rocks fell. As the ceiling gave way, I put the ring on my little finger, ran past Pierre, and threw myself over Joan. Rocks pounded my back. Bones jabbed me from every direction. Yet, nothing penetrated my skin. The blows hurt, though not as much as I had feared.

As I arched my back to rise, the weight of the debris pushed me down. I searched for Joan beneath me, but she was no longer there.

"I am weak, Justin," Joan called from above, "but I will try to move the stones."

Grunts followed as well as the sound of rocks tumbling away. Bracing my arms and legs, I again pushed upward with my back. After a few moments, Joan had lightened the load enough to allow me to break through.

I stood with Joan in the same room but with a new, higher ceiling. The fire from Joan's shattered life lantern crackled under a pile of debris, providing a weak glow. The lantern we had used to come to this place lay next to the wall, dark but protected by a pile of broken bones.

Searching frantically for Joan's life lantern, I grabbed stones and slung them away, grunting and shaking with each heave. Finally, I uncovered glass shards on the cave floor amidst the waning flames. Pierre, semitransparent, rose through the remaining stones and stood upright. He blinked at me as if stupefied.

I picked up our search lantern and relit it in the light of the spill's dwindling flame, which now sputtered and crackled. A spark leaped to Pierre and settled on his chest. The spark ignited into a fire that spread in a ring. He batted at it with his hands but to no avail.

Within seconds, the flames engulfed him in a raging inferno. Pierre screamed and clawed at his melting face. The fire roared in an eerie cadence, as if speaking dark, foreboding words.

Joan cried out, "No! Dear God in Heaven, I beg of you, give us more time!"

The fire evaporated. Pierre liquefied into a sizzling, bubbling pool from which putrid smoke rose in a violent twirl.

Joan's legs buckled. She dropped to her knees next to the oily pool and pounded the floor with her fists. "Oh, Pierre, what have you done? Such folly! You have wasted your soul!"

Her head began fading to transparency as did her legs. She was leaving this world. I pulled the ring off, rushed to her, and grasped her wrist. As I fought against her continued flailing, I pried open her fist and pushed the ring over her thumb. Then I drew back, breathless as I waited to see what would happen.

Her hands on the floor, she let her head hang over the rising smoke, as she whispered through sobbing spasms. "I'm sorry, Pierre. I failed you. I am so, so sorry."

After a few moments of silence, she straightened, her body restored, still on her knees as she stared at Pierre's residue, sniffling and whispering something too quiet to hear.

I stepped close again and dared to speak. "Joan? You're still here. Should you have departed by now?"

Her face dripping with perspiration, she gazed at me, gaunt and trembling. "I thought so. I have been asking for understanding, but I hear no answer."

"Maybe the ring saved you."

Her tremors easing, she touched the ring. "My mother's gift. Endowed by God with protective power."

"Then the legends are true."

"Perhaps so. I have no other explanation."

I extended a hand. "Would you like to get up?"

She grasped my wrist and rode my pull to her feet. Giving me a demure smile, she whispered, "Thank you."

I looked at the spot where Pierre once stood, now a blackened smudge. "Such a tragedy. I am deeply sorry, Joan."

"Thank you for saying so." She sighed. "It is truly a great loss."

"I wish I could have spoken the right words at the end, but I failed."

"Reaching Pierre was not your responsibility. Besides, his latest act proved that he was beyond reach. Words of wisdom were like a whip to him. He was so obdurate, no amount of persuasion could have set him on the right path."

"Was the fire his judgment?"

She bowed her head. "I fear it was only the beginning."

"What of Jean? Is he as stubborn as Pierre?"

"Probably more so, but Michael has a way with Jean that penetrates his resolve. I am hopeful for a better result."

"Then I'll hope with you." I nodded toward the way we came. "Shall we return to your schoolroom? Maybe Michael and Jean are already there."

She smiled again, though sadness weighed down her eyes. "This time, I will walk."

We climbed over multiple piles of rocks and bones and, with the lantern lighting the way, retraced our steps. After several minutes, the lantern sizzled and snapped before finally dying, leaving us in total darkness.

Joan slid her fingers along my arm until they found my hand. "Do you trust me?" she asked.

"Without a doubt. I would trust you with my life."

"Then follow my lead. Walk without hesitation."

She pulled my hand. I followed her stride for stride. For now, we were walking on a dry, bare floor, which made it easy to trust her. Would I be able to do so across the bones?

As we walked, Joan spoke in a calm tone that eased my tensions. "Justin, have you yet discerned who Michael and Jean are?"

"Michael told me he's from Spain and that Jean was a pastor who burned Michael at the stake, or arranged for the burning, I suppose. I don't know the details."

"Those statements are correct. Jean was, indeed, a pastor." Joan let out a long sigh. "Do you find it odd that clergymen, people who are called to teach as Christ did, are sometimes the last to turn the other cheek, the first to torment a neighbor whom they are supposed to love as themselves, and the most eager to bear false witness that condemns their enemies to the flames?"

"Odd is a mild word. Damning is more accurate."

"Yet I hesitate to use it. I am no one's judge."

"True. Forgive me."

"Granted." Our feet sloshed in shallow water, but Joan's firm hand kept my confidence high. "Justin, I knew priests who were humble servants, beautiful examples of Christ's love and beneficence. But I have also known priests who demonstrated none of those qualities."

"As have I."

"My question is, what are the people to do? When the shepherd is more crooked than his crook, should they be obedient lambs? Where are they to go for counsel and spiritual succor?"

"I have often wondered that." I shrugged, though she couldn't see the gesture. "I just stopped attending services."

"I don't blame you for that decision, but it is one I could never make. In any case, I give you this warning. If you attend services faithfully, a crooked shepherd will use that against you. Such faithful attendance means that you should have known better than to do whatever sins he accuses you of committing. If you no longer attend services, a crooked shepherd will use that against you as well. You are clearly a heathen from whom no good thing can come. You are obviously guilty of whatever crime he conjures. You will be condemned by his hand no matter what you do."

"I suppose the lambs had better stay in a straight line or else they will be the next sacrifice."

"For the crooked shepherd, yes. The good shepherd, however, will search high and low for a wayward lamb, facing lion and wolf to rescue him and bring him back into the fold. Such is the difference between darkness and light."

We came upon a floor of bones, slowing our progress. As we navigated the uneven terrain, Joan stopped talking, but she maintained a steady pace.

Soon, a flame flickered ahead. Joan whispered, "It's Michael's life candle. He is burning it to light our way."

As she accelerated, I kept up, still clutching her hand. Although I no longer needed a guide, holding the hand of Joan of Arc was a treasure. Why release it if I didn't have to? "Why would he use the candle instead of a lantern? The flame has to be weaker."

"Because he knows I am drawn to it. The feeling has guided my way through the maze of tunnels."

"Isn't that dangerous for him, spending his life fuel?"

"Yes, but Michael is a good shepherd. He would spend anything to find a lost lamb."

When we neared the flickering light, the chamber clarified. The candle stood propped in a pile of bones directly under the ladder leading to the surface. Michael and Jean were nowhere in sight.

Chapter Fifteen

Joan released my hand and ran ahead, calling, "Michael? Jean?" She stopped at the ladder and looked up. "There you are."

"Indeed." Michael climbed down from the ladder and stood gingerly on the bones. He then extended my carpetbag toward me. "Someone left this near the access door."

I took the bag. "It's mine. Thank you."

"You're welcome." He looked up and called, "Come, Jean. They are here. And close the door above you."

I set the bag down and opened it. Something wrapped in a cloth lay on top, warm to the touch. If Francine had provided a hot meal, she must have left the bag only a short time earlier.

When Jean reached the bottom, Michael picked up the candle and blew it out. Another light shone from the school chamber. We walked there and sat in a circle around a lantern, Michael to my left, Jean across from me, and Joan to my right, facing the doorway to the corridor. After a moment of silence, Joan looked at Michael and said, "Pierre has gone to judgment."

"I am sorry to hear that. This is the worst news possible."

Jean covered his face with his hands. A whimper broke through, then gentle sobs.

As Michael rubbed Jean's back, his brow dipped low. "Joan, how is it that you are still here? Shouldn't you have gone to your reward?"

"Reward?" Joan lowered her head. "I failed. What reward do I deserve?"

"The reward due to a loving, forgiving saint. You volunteered to try to turn the heart of your own murderer from darkness to light."

"I do not deny that love and the desire to forgive drove me to volunteer, but all good qualities are gifts. I simply chose to receive them. That deserves no reward."

"Even so, the question remains unanswered. My understanding is that we teachers are to perish from this earth when our duties are finished."

I raised a finger. "I have a theory about her ring."

"Justin." Joan touched my arm. "If I may, I would like to explain. I know much more about it."

"By all means."

Joan rubbed her ring as she provided a summary of our search in the tunnels, the discovery of the ring, and the ceiling collapse. She also gave more history behind the gift of her two rings, including how her captors took one immediately and the second during the trial.

When she finished, I touched her ring. "May I have a closer look?"

"Certainly."

I brought her hand near my eyes and turned the ring slowly on her thumb. Made of dull metal, perhaps vermeil, it was etched with three crosses as well as the letters JHS-MAR. "What does the inscription mean?"

"The letters stand for Jesus and Mary."

"Justin?" Francine walked in, wearing riding trousers. When she saw me, she halted and flashed a nervous smile. "I … I noticed that your bag was taken, so I thought I'd look for you."

"I'm glad you came." I could hardly contain my excitement. Soon Francine would speak face to face with her longtime heroine. "It's about time you saw my hideout, don't you think?"

She scanned the room. "This is certainly a good place to hide. It takes a long time to climb down, but your light was visible from up there, so I kept going." She wrinkled her nose. "But how can you stand being in this … this exposed graveyard? I must have stepped on a hundred bones to get here from the ladder. Real bones. Dead people scattered everywhere. It's a nightmare."

"You get used to it." I couldn't contain my excitement a moment longer. "Look, Francine." I displayed Joan's hand. "I found the ring near the wall of skulls, just as the diary said."

She blinked at the inadequate light. "You did?"

"And I still have your brooch." I rose, withdrew the scarab, and gave it to her. "It helped me find the ring."

"That's wonderful." She slid the scarab into her pocket and took a step closer.

I raised a halting hand. "Introductions first." I nodded toward Michael and Jean in turn. "The man is Michael, and the boy is Jean. I then gestured toward Joan. "And this is none other than Joan of Arc."

"Joan of Arc?" Francine stiffened. "*The* Joan of Arc?"

I laughed. "Yes, isn't it amazing? And now Joan has her ring. Of course, it wouldn't be right for you to claim it since it belonged to her first."

"Of course." Francine took a step back, her body trembling. "Well ... maybe I should go."

"Don't be frightened. You're among friends."

"Friends? Really?" She swallowed. "They ... they do look friendly, Justin, but this place is—"

"Haunting. Yes, I know. As you said, it's a good place to hide."

"I ... I have to go."

"But you haven't said a word to Joan. After all the years reading about her, surely you wondered about her thoughts and feelings while planning and executing the great battles, while talking to angels, while suffering under trial for crimes she didn't commit. Don't you have questions for her?"

Her lips quivered. "I do ... but ... but ..." She turned and hurried away to the sound of bones crunching under her steps.

"Excuse me a moment," I said to the others as I followed. When I reached the ladder, she had already ascended a dozen rungs. "Francine. Wait."

"No. I will not spend another second in that awful place." Grunting, she continued her ascent. As I climbed, I said nothing, choosing instead to watch her feet and to be ready to catch her, should she slip. Although loose slats caused a temporary pause now and then, she regained her balance each time and hurried on.

When she reached the open trapdoor, she climbed out and disappeared from view. I scrambled to the surface and squinted in the light of the midday sun. Soon I found her running toward the brook.

I sprinted in her direction but was not able to catch her before she jumped onto the makeshift bridge. Balancing with arms extended to her sides, she began an unsteady journey across.

When I arrived, I dared not join her on the bridge lest I be the cause of a spill. "Francine, please come back. We need to talk."

"No." She broke into a run. A tie line snapped, and the logs separated. She toppled to the side and fell into the brook, still swollen by the recent storm.

When she surfaced, flailing and splashing, I leaped in and wrapped her in my arms. "It's not over your head. Just put your feet down. You'll see."

She complied and stood next to me in chest-deep water, shivering. I guided her to the city-side shore and sloshed with her up to the bank. "The sun's warm. Let's sit and have a talk." I found a patch of grass in a sunny spot and sat with her face-to-face, our legs crossed in front.

She wrung out her hair and let the water drip to her side. "I apologize for my outburst. I was just surprised. Terrified, really."

"No apology is necessary." I laughed. "When I saw Joan for the first time, I was also frightened."

"The *first* time?"

"Yes, I have seen her multiple times now."

Francine spread her hair over her shoulders. "When was the first time?"

I nodded toward the schoolhouse ruins. "During the party. Joan was in the library. I thought she was you, since you look so much alike."

Francine's brow lifted. "So that's why you said we were together up there when we weren't."

"Right. And Michael and Jean were there as well."

"The man and the boy?"

"Yes." I leaned forward and spoke in low tones. "Francine, you and I have seen Joan of Arc with our own eyes, but I don't think anyone will believe it. We need to keep this secret between us."

She leaned forward as well and copied my near whisper. "Of course. I would never reveal this to anyone."

I drew back. "Good. That's good."

She did the same. "Where is the ring?"

I looked across the brook at the school. "Joan is still wearing it. It has protective powers, just as you thought. If she takes it off, she'll lose her grip on this world and fly to heaven."

"Ah. I see." Francine nodded. "We wouldn't want that to happen."

"At least not until she's ready to go. And I hope she confirms my alibi with Marc. She's the one who taught me how to stitch his wound."

"She did? Well, she is a helpful one, isn't she?"

"Yes, I assume she had a lot of practice on the battlefield."

"That's to be expected." Francine leaned closer again and whispered, "Why is Joan here?"

I kept my voice normal. It seemed odd to whisper with no one else around, though I had been the first to lower my voice. "That's a long story that's even more unbelievable than her presence."

"Really?" Francine braced her hands on the grass at her sides, angling her body to catch more sunlight. "I have time. It would be better to arrive home dry and not have to explain why I took a spill in the brook."

"If you say so." I took in a deep breath and began the story, starting from Madame Noël's slap and providing every detail I could recall. Throughout the tale, I kept my gaze locked on Francine. Her eyes never shifted from mine, though her mouth dropped open from time to time, and she gasped at the most shocking events, including when Siobhan collected the little-girl version of Jacqueline Noël.

146

When I finished with a tired sigh, she leaned close once again and slid her hand into mine. "Justin, you suffered unbelievable turmoil. I wish I could help you."

I shook my head. "I don't see how. If you tell Marc or the inspector my story, they'll think I'm insane. I wouldn't have told you if you hadn't seen our ghostly visitors yourself."

"I understand." She touched my bare finger. "The ring would help them believe."

"But Joan needs it or she'll—"

"I know. I know. But wouldn't she want to leave now that her mission here is complete? Who would want to stay here if she can go to heaven?"

"You're right, but she seems content for now."

"Maybe that won't last. Just be ready to collect the ring when she tires of this war-torn, sin-sick world." Francine wrapped both of my hands in hers. "Think of it, Justin. The ring will help confirm your alibi, at least that you were with Joan in the library. You won't be a suspect, and we can find the real killer. Not only that, we'll have a powerful ring that can protect us from harm."

"Us? When Joan leaves, won't it be yours?"

She straightened. "Well ... yes ... of course ... but ..." She looked up as if searching for the right words, then gazed at me again, our hands still clasped. "Justin, I know I was rude to you earlier. I was wrong to suspect you of murder."

"I understand. The evidence pointed straight at me."

"But now I know better, so I would like to renew our relationship, that is, if you still have feelings for me."

Heat rose into my cheeks. "Of course I do. I was worried that your feelings for me were gone."

"Gone? Hardly. You're a man of high character, dashing, courteous. Any woman would be flattered by your attention."

I fidgeted. "Are you flattered?"

"More than flattered." She edged closer, her voice again low. "Justin, the reason I said the ring would protect *us* is that I hoped to someday be your wife."

"My wife? Francine, are you proposing to me? Isn't that ... well ..."

"Unusual? Scandalous?" She laughed. "Since when have I cared about that?"

"Well ... then I accept. Marrying you would be a dream come true. I have loved you from afar for ever so long."

She slid her hands away and presented her ring finger. "Then shall we seal our engagement with Joan's ring? When she is pleased to leave the earth, bring it to me, and we'll tell the world about our plans. I think she'll decide soon."

"You're probably right." I lifted her hand and kissed her knuckles. "Until then, Francine."

She leaned even closer and kissed me on the lips. When she drew back, she whispered, "Until then."

Chapter Sixteen

Francine rose and walked toward the city center. Her damp trousers clung to her legs and hips, outlining a sleek form. She seemed to accentuate her assets with a swagger, evidence of her words in plain sight. Surely a woman of her standing who wore trousers in public cared nothing about scandal.

I forced my eyes to look away. My heart thudded, and my breaths grew shallow and rapid. Although she had kissed me once before, this touch meant so much more. It was a promise, a covenant. All I had to do was prove my innocence with Joan's ring, thereby ending the law's pursuit, which would allow me to join Francine forever. After all, who would want to be engaged to a murder suspect?

Soon, Francine disappeared in the distance. I jumped up and waded across the brook, soaking my clothes again. Yet that didn't matter. I needed to ask Joan about her future plans, but I had to do so without a hint of persuasion. This was her life, her ring, her eternity.

Within a few minutes, I arrived again in the catacombs school room. Joan still sat where she was before with a lantern near her feet. Michael and Jean had left.

Joan smiled, though her eyes gave away lingering sadness. "Have you been swimming?"

I suppressed a shiver. "I had to cross the brook. The bridge is out." I sat next to her, close enough for our knees to touch. "What will you do now, Joan? Your mission here is complete."

"I have been thinking about that." She twirled the ring around her thumb. "Since you are in danger of arrest and execution, I should do something to help you."

"I could present the ring as evidence that you were really in the library," I said. "The inspector in the case is an intelligent man. He'll understand its uniqueness."

Joan laughed. "Nonsense, Justin. Did the cold water addle your brain?"

"What do you mean?"

"A mere ring will prove nothing. You found it in a wall of bones, a lucky discovery your persecutors will say. Trust me. I know the wiles of those who seek the blood of the innocent."

"Then how can you help?"

"I will bear witness of the truth myself." She rose to her feet and extended a hand down to me. "Come. Escort me to your inspector. I will have a word with him."

"But ..." I took her hand and let her help me rise. "But how can you prove that you're who you say you are?"

"With the ring, exactly as we discussed. And since I'm a witness to your presence in the library, what does it matter who I am? A witness is a witness."

"Yes, that's true, but—"

"You are quite fond of your buts." She spread her arms. "I am ready to help you. Tell me what to do."

I gazed at her open stance. Wearing her traditional battle armor, she looked little like the woman who recently pranced away in a swaggering gait. Yet, Joan's insistence matched Francine's perfectly. I couldn't say no to such an offer. "Let's go to Francine's house. We'll discuss the situation with her and Marc before speaking to Inspector Fortier."

Joan nodded. "Excellent. I wasn't able to talk to Francine earlier. I tried to find an appropriate place to interject a word, but I never saw an opening."

"I apologize for that. She and I dominated the conversation. What did you want to say?"

"I wanted to ask her a question about her costume at the masquerade party. I saw her in the library that evening, but she was praying, so I had no opportunity then."

"You were close enough to hear that she was praying?"

Joan nodded. "She said, 'Mary, Mother of God, drive the demons away from me now, and purge my own demons as I pursue the path set before me.' "

"I had no idea she was so tormented."

"Indeed, which is why I left quietly."

"What did you want to ask about her costume?"

"I was stunned by how similar her battledress was to my own. Yet, I noticed one difference that intrigued me. The rivets in her armor were metal, while mine are wooden. Hers seemed far sturdier, so I hoped to learn more about them."

"Interesting, but if you had spoken to her, you might have frightened her."

"Yes, I understand that now. I'm glad I let her be."

"Well, maybe you'll have another chance to meet her." I picked up the lantern but decided to leave my bag and the food behind, though hunger burned in my belly. Hauling it up would be a toilsome chore. "Let's go."

After climbing the ladder, Joan and I walked to the river's edge. I paused, not anxious to again suffer another round of wet shivers.

Joan set a foot in the water, then drew it back. "The chill won't hurt me, but you will catch your death if you keep wading across."

"I'm afraid I don't have much choice."

"Of course you do. We can fashion a temporary bridge until a more permanent one can be constructed."

"Do you have the skill to do that? I certainly don't."

"My men and I built countless bridges during our campaigns. We merely need to find suitable materials." She looked at the school building and nodded. "Yes, I think we can do this."

We collected some of the school's rubble, such as roof pieces and scorched timber, and began working. Joan not only issued orders like a seasoned general, she also added considerable muscle to the tasks, matching my strength as we carried and placed heavy objects. How the ghost of a young female could do that remains a mystery to this day.

When we finished and crossed the bridge, we walked side by side into the city. As I looked at her, her face smeared with dirt, sweat glistening on her forehead, and grime marring her battledress, reality hit hard. Her appearance would raise questions, too many questions. And my clothes were not yet dry, which would add to the mystery. I would have to invent a tale.

Soon, we reached the outskirts of the city's center. As expected, many people stopped and stared. Even a fiacre driver reined in his horses and stopped.

I hurried past, but the driver called out, "Monsieur? Aren't you the gentleman who saved the inspector?"

I stopped and turned. The carriage driver who had transported me earlier stared from his perch. I gave him a genial nod. "Yes, my good man. It is I."

He gestured toward his passenger seat. "Do you need a ride? No charge for you."

"Certainly. I would like that."

When we climbed aboard, I told him our destination. As the horse trotted along, he called without looking back at us. "I gave you a ride not only because you're a hero. Everyone was staring at you. I thought you'd like to avoid that."

I laughed. "Thank you, but you might recall that I'm an actor. I'm accustomed to being stared at."

"I remember, but the clothing is—"

"Props for a play. A battle scene."

"A sea battle?"

I laughed again. "I got wet crossing the brook near the burned school building. The bridge is out. Even the temporary bridge failed."

"Well, I suppose I shouldn't be surprised at anything an actor decides to do, but I wouldn't parade in the streets looking like that."

"Which makes your gesture that much more appreciated."

While the driver switched the subject to cooking and began a long discourse about his achievements as a chef, Joan stayed quiet, taking in the sights and sounds of the busy Sunday afternoon

152

in Paris. Although she had likely seen some of the sights before, being burdened with Pierre as they hurried from place to place probably made enjoying her outings impossible.

When we arrived at the Noëls' house, I thanked the driver and walked to the front door, followed closely by Joan. She called with a hiss. "Justin. Your trousers."

I looked back. Strings of weeds hung from my waistband across my buttocks. No wonder the driver asked about a sea battle. Maybe most of the people were staring at me instead of Joan.

I pulled the weeds off and slung them to the side. "Thank you for telling me."

"I only wish I had seen it earlier."

"No harm done." I knocked on the door. When Francine answered, I offered a head bow. "I brought Joan. May we come in?"

"Of course." Francine looked past me and bowed her head. "Welcome, Joan. I am honored by your visit."

"Thank you," Joan said. "The honor is mine."

Francine waited for us to enter and closed the door. Now wearing a lovely pink house dress, she looked at us and smiled. "You're still wet. I'll get some of Marc's clothes for you. He's out for a while."

As she turned, I said, "Do you have something for Joan to wear? Her battle clothes are filthy. I'm sure you're the same size."

Francine pivoted back, her cheeks reddening. "Oh ... yes ... I can do that." She turned again and walked down the hallway.

I guided Joan into the sitting room. The family tree still lay on the table in the same condition as before. I pointed out the relevant names to Joan and explained what I knew, finishing with, "I can't believe that young Madame Noël could commit such a horrific murder. Marguerite never did anything to her."

"I believe it," Joan said. "When Pierre and I first began our time together, he was filled with rage. I had to prevent an act of violence several times each day. It took a week or more for him to settle."

A moment later, Francine returned with an armful of clothes. She handed me a pair of trousers and a shirt, then unfolded a pretty green dress and let it hang from her fingers. "I hope this is suitable."

Joan smiled. "It's lovely. Thank you."

Francine fidgeted. "Well ... then ... um ... you know where the wash basin is." Seemingly unsure of what to say next, Francine laid the dress over the table. "Marc is at a neighbor's house. I'm sure he'll want to talk to you. I'll get him." She hurried to the front door and exited.

Joan looked at me with a confused aspect. "Is it customary in these times to leave an unmarried couple alone to change clothes?"

"No. Francine's flustered. Having Joan of Arc as a guest is distracting her. I told you how famous you are."

"Yes, I haven't learned to accept that yet."

"Do you like the dress she left for you?"

"It is lovely." Joan ran a finger along the green material. "But if you want me to convince others that I am the general of the French army, the Maid of Orléans, then I should keep my battle clothes on."

"You're right, but you don't have to look like you're returning from battle. You should wash."

She smiled. "I would like that."

I showed her the washroom and gave her privacy while I returned the green dress to Francine's room and laid it on her bed. Then I paced the floor, thinking about how I could explain all that I had seen. Yet, the barest of summaries seemed insane, even to myself.

When Joan finished, I took my turn and put on the fresh trousers and shirt. They were too big, of course, but not uncomfortably so. I returned with Joan to the sitting room, put my dirty clothes under a chair, and sat there while Joan chose the chair to my right. To my surprise, Francine had not yet returned with Marc. A neighbor's house couldn't be that far away. What might be keeping them so long?

The delay gave me an occasion to converse with Joan. She talked about her life as a child, how angels visited her, and the events surrounding her call to save France. As she spoke, I kept my gaze fixed on her lovely face—youthful and perfect in spite of the many years that had passed since her era. And with a freshly washed face and brushed hair, she looked quite beautiful.

Soon, Marc entered the front door, followed by Inspector Fortier and the bishop who had given the anti-reformers homily. Francine came in last and closed the door. She whispered to the bishop and gestured toward Joan. He nodded in a disagreeable manner.

A lump grew in my throat. No wonder she had taken so long. They had gathered others who were interested in meeting Joan, but for what reason?

The inspector wore the cloak I had seen him in earlier, though now with the hood down, while the bishop wore a white cassock with a black sash that hung around his neck. Both men trained their stares on me as they approached.

Joan whispered, "This is not a friendly council. It is an inquisition, and you are the target. I have seen prosecutorial eyes too many times to think otherwise."

I gave her a calming hand signal and stayed quiet. Joan was right. The authority of the law and the Church had come to rain fire on me. It would be best to say as little as possible.

Francine found chairs for everyone and made a circle, her to my left, then Marc to her left, then the inspector across from me, and then the bishop to Joan's right. The bishop continued staring at me, his expression unreadable.

The inspector cleared his throat. "If I may begin, Monsieur Trotter …"

"Yes." I steeled my body to keep from trembling. "Please do."

"Francine summoned the bishop and me because you made a rather incredible claim."

"What claim, Inspector?"

"Well, let's put it this way. You believe the real Joan of Arc is sitting next to you."

LET THE GHOSTS SPEAK

I offered a disarming smile. "I know it's hard to believe, Inspector, considering her apparent age, but she has proven to my satisfaction that she is, indeed, the true Joan of Arc."

The bishop touched Joan's chair arm. "What proof did she give you?"

His sharp stare blazed right past Joan, telling me that she was correct. This inquisition was aimed at me alone. They wouldn't bother to ask her any questions. "She knows everything there is to know about her history. She is even wearing the ring her parents gave her for her first communion." I gave Joan a nod. "Show them."

She lifted her hand, making the ring easy to see. After a moment, she lowered her hand to her lap and whispered, "I don't think they're convinced."

"We'll know soon." I smiled at the bishop. "If you have any further questions about the ring, I'm sure she'll be willing to answer them."

The bishop stared once more, his jaw tense.

After several seconds of awkward silence, the inspector spoke again. "Monsieur Trotter, when we last talked, you insisted that I return here to learn something important. I assume you meant the tragic murder of Marguerite Arnaud. My investigation concluded that the Noëls' fire poker was the weapon that slashed and killed her."

"I assumed the same," I said.

"Did you, in fact, have that poker in your possession when the Noëls returned home from their morning walk?"

I nodded. "I did, but—"

"And was the end of the poker cleansed of all blood and ash?"

"Yes, but let me explain—"

Marc raised a finger. "He presented the poker to me voluntarily, stating that it might be the murder weapon. I'm certain he didn't commit the crime. No murderer in his right mind would—"

"Isn't that the only question remaining?" the inspector asked. "Whether he is a cold, calculating murderer or instead an insane one?"

"What?" I clutched my chair's armrests. "I am not a murderer, nor am I insane."

The bishop's cheeks flamed. "Let me settle the question once and for all." He turned to me and pointed a finger. "What is engraved on the ring?"

"Why don't you ask Joan? She is far more articulate than I."

The bishop vaulted from his seat and stormed toward the door. "I refuse to continue this charade. We are mollifying a madman. Arrest him and be done with it."

Joan whispered, "I am hurting your cause, Justin." She slid the ring off and laid it in my palm. Her voice faded along with her presence. "Thank you for everything. I will pray for you." Seconds later, she was gone.

My throat tightened, and my arms wilted. Joan had flown to heaven. Yet, I had to stay strong.

I gestured toward her chair. "You see. She vanished. Now do you believe me?"

"Oh, Justin." Francine covered her face with her hands and wept. "Why are you doing this to yourself?"

The bishop stalked back and pointed at Francine as he shot a hot glare at me. "Do you see what your madness has wrought? You have broken this woman's heart many times over. In spite of the shaky alibi Marc provided out of loyalty, it is clear to me that you killed Francine's mother and her doctor. Then you turned your murderous rampage on her housekeeper, and now you're playing the fool, pretending that Joan of Arc is here."

"*Was* here," I said.

"Impertinent fool." He slapped my face. The blow nearly tipped my chair over, but I recovered and straightened. The sting of the slap burned my cheek.

I gave him a defiant glare. "The other cheek awaits you."

He reared back, but, after glancing at Francine, he lowered his hand and muttered, "You will get what's coming to you."

"You asked what's engraved on the ring." I opened my hand, revealing the ring sitting on my palm. "See for yourself."

He plucked the ring and drew it close to his doubtful eyes. As he examined it, the tension in his brow eased, and his mouth slowly dropped open.

"Well?" the inspector prompted.

"This is …" He cleared his throat and turned to the inspector. "This is, without a doubt, the ring that belonged to Joan of Arc. It bears the engravings that she described during her trial." He stared at me again, this time with genuine curiosity instead of anger. "Where did you get it?"

"I followed a trail of clues." I looked at Francine. She gazed at the ring with tear-filled eyes, leaning forward as if yearning to touch it. "She gave me the first clue."

While everyone looked on with rapt attention, I related the events regarding Madame Noël's brooch, its partner in the mausoleum crypt, the Gaelic note in the diary, and the discovery of the ring near the wall of skulls. Although I included Joan's role, I omitted any reference to other ghosts. They already believed me insane. Why add to their evidence?

As I spoke, I glanced at Marc and Francine. He gave her curious looks, obviously learning some of the facts for the first time. Whether or not he was offended by her lack of forthrightness, I couldn't tell.

I concluded with, "Francine saw the ring when she visited me in the catacombs. Joan was wearing it then."

The bishop showed Francine the ring. "Is that true? Had you seen this ring before now?"

She fixed her gaze on the bishop. If I could ever read an expression, this was the time. She begged for an indulgence to lie, but she could not bring herself to speak anything but the truth to a bishop of the Church.

She exhaled as she replied. "I did see it in the catacombs."

"On the finger of Joan?" the bishop asked.

She shook her head. "In Justin's hand. We were alone there."

Mother, you once told me that those who love with pure passion and those who hate with hot fury have one aspect in common. What is plain to everyone else is hidden from their eyes. Even at my tender age, I understood what you meant. And now, after I had experienced the depths of both love and hate, the meaning of your wise words struck more profoundly than ever. My love for Francine and for Joan had blinded me to the truth. Francine never saw Joan, nor had anyone else—not the people in the room, not the fiacre driver, not the people in the streets who stared at the weeds hanging from my trousers rather than at Joan. I had sat like a fool next to an empty chair, at least in everyone else's eyes. It was no wonder they thought me insane.

"I was looking for him," Francine continued, "because I was supplying him with food. I saw that the food was gone, so I ..." She looked away. "I descended into the catacombs to make sure it was he who took it."

The bishop's eyes widened. "That hideout of murderers and thieves? What possessed you to do something so dangerous?"

"Mercy possessed me, Bishop. Once I verified that Justin had taken the food, I left immediately."

"As any good Christian woman should." The bishop set the ring in Francine's hand. "Even by this madman's account, the ring belongs to you." He then turned to the inspector. "Although he is clearly insane, an asylum would be a waste of time and money. My judgment is that he should be executed. He is a deranged murderer."

The inspector spoke in a calm, soothing tone. "He is deranged, to be sure, but I still doubt his guilt."

The bishop roared, "What? How can you have doubts? He had the poker. He was the only person in the house when Marguerite was murdered, and he hallucinates visions conjured by demons. The evidence is overwhelming."

The inspector waved a hand. "I am aware of the facts of the case, and I assume there is sufficient evidence to convict Monsieur Trotter of perhaps one murder, but that doesn't make him guilty of any. Too many questions beg for answers."

"We'll see about that." The bishop stalked across the room and left the house, slamming the door. We jumped at the sound, then stared at each other as if trying to read minds.

After a quiet moment, Francine brushed tears from her cheeks. "Inspector, what questions remain unanswered?"

"It would be premature to reveal that at this time." The inspector rose and bowed. "Watch Monsieur Trotter closely. Perhaps even hide him. Insane or not, he is not the murderer. It would be unjust for him to suffer the guillotine or the bishop's wrath."

Marc thanked the inspector and escorted him to the door. While they chatted there for a moment, Francine looked at me, her gaze intent, piercing. "Do you know which questions beg for answers?"

"All I know is he received a report about me from Scotland Yard, but I didn't read it. Maybe something in the report raised questions."

"I see." She glanced at the clothes under my chair. "What did you do with the dress I lent you?"

"I laid it on your bed. Joan thought it better to stay in her battledress, because ..." I shook my head. "What's the use explaining? You don't believe she was here. You think I'm mad."

"Shouldn't I?" She looked at the door until Marc and the inspector walked outside. She then laid a hand on my arm. "Justin, give me a reason to believe you. I don't want to think you mad."

"Where did I get a needle and thread to stitch Marc's wound? How did I learn to stitch or to cauterize his wound? Or the inspector's wound. How could I possibly find the ring in a dark, endless maze of bones?" I slid my hand into hers. "I'll tell you how. Joan guided me step by step. It would have been impossible without her."

"Justin, you could have learned those surgical skills elsewhere. And finding the ring as you described might have happened, but it also might be the result of mere chance. How can I be sure you're telling the truth? Do you have any proof that is undeniable?"

I searched my memory. What proof could I supply? Had Joan said anything that no one else could have known? Then the answer came. I whispered again. "Joan told me the words you prayed while you thought you were alone in the library. You said, 'Mary,

160

Mother of God, drive the demons away from me now, and purge my own demons as I pursue the path set before me."

Francine gasped. "That prayer was a bare whisper. No one but Mary herself could have heard me."

"Except for someone standing next to you."

"That's true, Justin, but it could have been you standing close, and I was unaware."

"Except for another fact Joan told me. She said your costume was accurate except for the rivets in the armor. Yours are metal. Hers were wooden."

"I knew that. I hoped for perfect authenticity, but the metal rivets are more ..." Francine's mouth dropped open. "You really *did* see Joan, didn't you?"

"As clearly as I am seeing you now."

She lifted the ring, pinched in her fingers. "And this really is a protective ring."

"Without a doubt. It protected me from a ceiling collapse in the catacombs, and it kept Joan from leaving this world."

Francine looked up, as if contemplating. "Then it's all true. Every word of it."

"Every word of what?"

She withdrew the diary from a dress pocket and flipped through the pages, scanning them with frantic eyes. After a moment, she stopped and looked at me. "Remember what Marc said about Grandmother Claire's diamond pendant?"

"Yes. Of course."

Francine touched a page. "I found more about it here. She says it's a priceless treasure created to honor Joan of Arc after her death. The pendant was given to the family and came into her possession, but she was greedy and paranoid, and believed others in her family were trying to steal it. Such were her delusions. She, therefore, hid it in the catacombs and set a deadly trap for anyone who might try to steal it."

"A trap? How strange."

"Yes, but that's all she wrote about it." Francine closed the diary. "I thought the idea was absurd, perhaps rambling madness, but now I'm not so sure."

"Are there any clues that might give away the location?"

"None at all. It would be such a shame for a priceless treasure to rot in that horrid place. If I sold it, think of all the good I could do with the money. Feed the hungry. Clothe the naked. Everything Joan would have wanted."

I nodded. "I can't argue with that motivation."

"Then help me find it. Think, Justin. Think."

"Well, if Claire set a deadly trap, then she would have to be able to avoid the trap herself."

"Perhaps, but then might others find the way to avoid it as well?"

I imagined a woman creeping through the catacombs and coming upon a dragon guarding the pendant. No one could pass such a beast without getting burned alive. Unless …

"Claire could wear the ring. It would protect her from the trap."

"Of course." Francine seemed to effervesce. "She hid the ring so no one else could find the pendant. Since she knew where it was, she could retrieve it and be under its protection."

"And since no one wants to linger in the catacombs, the pendant is probably close to the ring. The collapsing ceiling might have been the deadly trap. Maybe it exposed the pendant's hiding place."

"And at the time you didn't know to look for it, but now you can." Francine pushed the ring into my palm and closed my fingers around it. "Put it on and flee to the catacombs."

"Today? Now?"

She nodded. "The bishop's fury always leads to action. You must leave at once."

"What might he do?"

"Any number of things. Perhaps incite a mob. Send them to my house to demand your head."

"I can't allow you to suffer that." I rose from my chair. "When should I come out of hiding?"

"I will give you a signal." She stood and tapped her chin as she spoke. "I will pretend that I am helping the bishop by telling him that you would never return to the catacombs because that's the obvious place to search, that you told me you would take refuge in the countryside, that you are an experienced huntsman who can survive for months in the wild."

"Which is far from the truth," I said.

"No matter. He will believe me. Then you *will* hide in the catacombs and search for the pendant. I will bring food to the school each night along with a note that will include any relevant news. I have a friend who knows Gaelic, and I will ask him to write my message. That way, no one else will be able to understand it."

"That should work."

"Let's hope so." She reopened my hand, revealing the ring. "Justin Trotter, someday your torment will be over. When that blessed day comes, return to my arms, put this ring on my finger, and marry me." She kissed me, her lips soft and supple on mine. When she drew back she whispered, "I will look forward to our union."

My mouth dried out, but I managed a coherent reply as I put the ring on my little finger. "Whether I find the pendant or not?"

"Of course. But I'm certain you will find it." She touched her bodice well below her neckline, her hand lingering over her mother's brooch, its former greenish glow no longer evident in the light of day. "Then you will set it right here."

I swallowed, though I tried to conceal the motion as well as my uncertainty. "I will do my best. Of that you can be sure."

Chapter Seventeen

When Marc returned, Francine told him about my escape plan, though she said nothing about my hope to find the pendant. After giving me one of his carpetbags filled with provisions and also furnishing me with an oversized cloak, she shooed me through the scullery and out the back door with a warning to make sure no one was following.

I walked toward the old school yet again. Wind and cold rain forced me to turn my collar up and keep my head low, a benefit for a fugitive who hoped to scurry unnoticed into the shadows.

As I had hoped, no one followed. When I crossed the bridge Joan and I had made, I looked back and carefully scanned the road. Rain swept across the scene, painting a veil over the city backdrop. A steeple loomed less than a mile away, the standard bearer for the cathedral, the largest of the churches in my persecutor's diocese, the same church I attended with Francine not long ago. Then it represented a mere annoyance. Now it stood as an enemy. I had to stay clear of its stalking shadow.

I salvaged the tie lines from the broken log bridge and fashioned a long rope. After fastening one end to the open trapdoor, I tied the other to the bag and lowered it to the bottom. Then, I descended into the catacombs. No light shone from below, telling me that Michael and Jean were probably not there.

Once I set my feet on the bones, I lit a match and ignited the lantern, then pulled the rope to close the door. When it shut, my lantern seemed brighter than ever, prompting me to turn it down to save fuel.

After untying the lantern, I carried it into the schoolroom, retrieved a blanket from the carpetbag, and laid it neatly on the floor. Then I doused the lantern and reclined on my makeshift bed, such that it was.

As I lay in total darkness, a gentle prodding nudged my thoughts. What about Justice? She would expect me to come for her, as I promised. But that was now impossible. Somehow I had to get a message to her.

Once I had pledged to do so, the prodding quieted along with every other sound, save for my heartbeat and breathing. I drifted toward sleep thinking about the daunting task ahead. Claire's deadly trap might be much more dangerous than a fragile ceiling. A dragon was out of the question, of course, but who could tell what other ideas she might have invented?

In any case, it would probably be good to rest and regain my strength. The search for the pendant might require a lot of stamina. I had to be ready.

I slept, but for how long I did not know. When I awakened, a new light appeared in the corridor. Michael walked in with his black candle in hand. A small flame burned on the wick, and a sad expression weighed down his features. "Justin," he said with a melancholy tone, "your presence tells me that not all is well."

I rose to a sitting position and relit my lantern. "And you being alone while burning your life candle tells me that things might be worse for you."

"True." He sat next to me and blew out his candle. "Jean has left again. This time I don't think he will return. My candle can find no trace of him."

Michael's sad eyes spoke of deep sorrow, even agony. "How does Jean escape so often, so easily?" I asked. "You seem to allow him a lot of freedom."

"Jean has always been free to come and go as he pleases. When I search for him, it is to remind him of his responsibilities to learn his love lessons, but I never take him by force."

"But why wouldn't you force him? His eternity is at stake."

Michael chuckled. "How do you force someone to love? Do you put him in a cage? Do you tie him down? You might drag him to his chair and force him to listen, but love cannot be bought with a leash and bell collar."

"I understand, but haven't you told him he will go to condemnation? That is, if you believe in that sort of thing."

"Ah. You have raised the crux of the issue yourself, the tension between what he has been told and what he believes."

"And what does he believe?"

"That all things are predestined. His fate is determined. He can do nothing to change what has been ordained."

"Even so, why follow a path that leads to destruction if you hope to avoid it?"

"One of the many points I have made to him."

"Do *you* believe everything is predestined?"

Michael laughed again, this time with a hint of derision. "Of course not. Such an idea is pure folly. If God put us on the earth merely to watch us act out a script, and he then punishes us with eternal fire simply because we played a villain's role that he wrote for us, a role that we *had* to play, mind you, then he would be quite the cruel monster, don't you think?"

"Indeed. The cruelest."

Michael rolled the candle over and over, now not much longer than a stub. "God is love, not cruelty. Jean gives lip service to God's love, but his words and actions indicate that he flinches when God lifts a hand."

"Which is why he thought you would beat him for the loss of his primer, if it wasn't all just a prank."

"That is a good example." Michael heaved a sigh. "Failing to convince Jean of God's love has been my greatest disappointment."

"How much time do you think you have left?"

"A week or two at the most. Why do you ask?"

"I thought he might accompany me for a while. I hope to visit my sister. Her love is beyond compare. Seeing is believing, especially when it is shown from a new point of view."

"You don't mind a little boy tagging after you?"

"Not at all. Besides, no one can see him, correct?"

Michael pointed at me. "You can see him. And the horse saw him, the one that spilled the carriage."

"That's true. Then tell me, who can see you and Jean, and who cannot?"

"I don't know for certain. Perhaps those who possess an innocent or hopeful outlook on life. Or maybe those who have seen something so traumatic that it ripped away all blinders, making them able to see the spiritual world."

"Like seeing my father with blood on his hands after he hanged a woman?"

Michael stared at me for a moment, pity and compassion in his eyes. "That is likely the reason. The tragic sight burned scales away from your eyes."

"At least there was one benefit."

"And a drawback," Michael added.

"A drawback?"

"From what I have seen, a gift of vision often comes with blindness. The gifted one is able to see what others cannot, yet at the same time he cannot see what is apparent to everyone else."

I nodded. "My mother used to say something like that."

"She must have been a wise woman."

"*Is* a wise woman. She's still alive ... somewhere."

Michael's eyes probed deeply, as if his own gift of vision pierced a veil. As he looked at me, only his gentle respiration added to the sound of my own. "Justin, have people told you that your mother is dead?"

"Yes. How did you know?"

"It was apparent in your tone." He breathed another deep sigh. "I am a physician, Justin, and it seems that my diagnosis is correct."

"What diagnosis?"

"Blindness. You cannot see what everyone else sees."

"Are you saying my mother is dead?" Unbidden anger infused my voice. "I know she's not. After my father was arrested, I talked to her. She comforted me for days."

"For days? What happened after that?"

"She said she had to leave, but she would come back someday."

"And you're still waiting."

"What choice do I have? It's not as if I sat around doing nothing. I went on with my life."

Michael shook his head. "Oh, Justin, Justin, Justin, you are so perceptive, but your blindness will be your downfall."

"But I'm not blind to the truth about my mother. I tell you I was with her. How can you deny a personal eyewitness?"

"I will speak no more on that topic. Whether or not you are right, the result is relatively harmless. My concern is that you are blind to more current facts that could bring you harm."

"Blind to what? Tell me."

"If I told you, you would not believe me. You need to learn to see the truth for yourself."

I spread my hands. "But if I'm blind, how can I do that?"

"As the Scripture teaches, a little child shall lead them."

"Lead me where?"

"Is a funeral still in the offing?"

"I think so, but I've lost track of time. It's tomorrow, I think, or maybe later this morning."

"Then my advice is for you to attend the service. I will persuade Jean to accompany you. He has vast insight into many things and the courage to speak with brutal honesty." A flame reappeared on Michael's life candle. "Maybe Jean will help you open your eyes."

"All right. Thank you." The need to find the pendant returned to mind, but it could wait while the funeral could not. Still, attending the service carried a great risk. "I'm somewhat of a fugitive, at least from church persecutors. The bishop is likely to go over the inspector's head in his efforts to take *my* head. If I go to the funeral, someone will recognize me."

"If it is well known that you are a fugitive in hiding, no one will look for you. After all, what murderer would attend his victim's funeral? A simple disguise will keep you safe. Perhaps a fake mustache or beard."

"I suppose I could come up with something."

"To be safer, you could avoid the church service and attend only the committal rite at graveside. That should be enlightening

Bryan Davis

enough. I am assuming, of course, that normal Catholic ritual will be followed."

"With Francine, normal isn't often the best assumption, but I'll follow your advice and go straight to the cemetery." In the light of the candle, I retrieved my pocket watch and looked at the time—almost five o'clock in the morning. If it was still working properly after all the brook crossings, I had slept most of the night. "Michael, you should douse your candle. My lantern has plenty of fuel."

"Thank you, but I am using the candle to call for Jean."

"Why would he come now when he wouldn't before?"

"We have a connection. He knows that I call with an interesting opportunity instead of a scolding rebuke."

Wax dripped to the floor, further decreasing the candle's remaining life. "I hope he hurries."

While we waited, I ate some of the food Francine had provided. Then I found a knife and small mirror among the supplies and began cutting my hair. It was already fairly short, barely covering my ears and not quite reaching my collar, but I was able to cut enough to alter my appearance and collect hair to fashion a wispy mustache. The only missing item was some sort of glue to apply the hair to my face.

Another drop of black wax fell to the floor. I touched the drop, stickier than expected, and the color matched my hair. Maybe it would do. I would just have to stay away from close inspection as well as heat. I also opted to take the knife along to scrape the disguise off if needed, and since I now often traveled alone and at night, the blade could serve as a means of protection, even if only to frighten a potential attacker away.

After about fifteen minutes, Jean arrived, and Michael blew out the candle. "Jean," Michael said, "how would you like to accompany Justin for a while?"

He smiled. "On the surface? Out in the open?"

"Yes. Justin wants to attend a funeral, and he needs you to pretend to be his …" Michael looked us both over. "His nephew,

169

I suppose, or perhaps his younger brother. Justin doesn't look old enough to have a son your age."

"I assume you think some people will be able to see him," I said.

"Yes, which might make interactions difficult, since some people will see him, and others will not."

"That could be confusing." I took Jean's hand. "You will be my brother. I never had one, so I think I'll enjoy this bit of theater."

Jean looked up at me. "You'll need a new name."

"You're right." I looked in the mirror and studied my face. Although the facial hair masked my identity fairly well, I was still obviously born an Englishman. "I will be Charles."

Jean and I climbed to the surface. With dawn still waiting to break the darkness, we were able to creep out of the school area and cross the bridge undetected. By the time we reached a main thoroughfare, the first rays of Monday morning arrived. We walked hand in hand toward the cemetery, nodding and smiling at the market owners and other businessmen as they swept entryways, washed windows, or set wares out to be scrutinized.

When we arrived at the cemetery's entry gate, we found it open again. We stayed outside, waiting for other mourners to join us. Might they arrive individually or come en masse from the church? Since I had arrived in Paris, I had witnessed a number of religious processions, usually in celebration of Corpus Christi or to install a newly arriving bishop. Whether or not Madame Noël's funeral would give rise to processional pomp remained to be seen.

I checked my pocket watch—8:25. Francine said the burial would be at nine after the mass. We would just have to wait. As the sun rose, the topcoat Francine had given me grew warm, but I kept it on. Although she might recognize it, no one else likely would, and the size made me look larger than I really was.

Soon, people dressed in black began to arrive, some on foot and some disembarking from carriages. They gathered in groups here and there outside the cemetery, all talking quietly. A few carried notebooks—reporters, most likely. The papers couldn't let an event like this go by without telling the world every detail, along with adding the usual dose of hyperbole.

At exactly nine, a hearse stopped in front of the gate, its horse and driver draped in black. Several men unloaded a coffin and carried it into the cemetery. Marc and Francine walked behind the coffin with hands folded in front. Dressed in black and her face covered by a dark yet sheer veil, Francine kept her gaze forward, as did Marc.

I exhaled. They didn't see me. And no one else seemed to pay any attention to the mustachioed stranger and his young companion.

When the pallbearers had proceeded about thirty yards into the cemetery, the other mourners followed. Jean and I blended into the crowd and maintained their pace.

Keeping my head low, I glanced around. To my left and a few steps ahead, Inspector Fortier walked with elegant precision, his hat off and his hair lifting in a freshening breeze, but I recognized no one else. And no priest seemed to be in the procession. Whoever was officiating either had not yet arrived or was not wearing his vestments.

Soon, the pallbearers stopped at an open gravesite with no tombstone. While two men dressed in work clothes helped them set the coffin next to the grave, Francine held a handkerchief over her face and wept. Marc draped an arm over her shoulders and whispered into her ear—words of comfort, no doubt.

Moments later, Marc broke away from Francine, lifted his head high, and scanned the crowd. "Has anyone seen the bishop?"

Several heads shook while others turned this way and that as if searching for a telltale cassock.

While we waited, I looked at Jean. "What do you think of this so far?"

He wrinkled his nose. "Strange. I hope my mourners didn't do this. Why make such a fuss over a body that will be food for worms?"

I contemplated his words. Indeed, as Michael had indicated, Jean did have a lot of wisdom, and his manner of speaking belied his apparent age. If he decided to converse with people who could see him, they might wonder at his intellect and maturity.

A man approached me, perhaps thirty-five years old and dressed in a splendid black suit. He held the hand of a pretty young girl. Adorned with black curls that brushed her shoulders, she appeared to be about eleven or twelve years old. "Are you a friend of the family's?" the man asked.

"An acquaintance."

"An Englishman?"

"Until seven years old. I have fully adopted Paris." I extended a hand. "Charles Bennett."

"I also hail from England." He shook my hand. "Cameron Trotter."

I pulled free and stepped back. That was my father's name. I studied his face. Indeed, he looked exactly like my father. Then I shifted my gaze to his shoes. Since my father owned a shoe company, he always wore the finest shoes, and the Oxfords this man wore were exquisite. Moments earlier, I had given him a mere glance and failed to notice the resemblance. Now it seemed obvious. Yet, my father would be considerably older now, fifty at least.

He tilted his head. "Is something wrong? You're staring."

"No. No." I blinked and forced a smile. "It's just that you remind me of someone."

"Ah. I have heard that before. I suppose I have a common face."

"And is this young lady your daughter?" I asked.

"Yes. This is Justice."

"Justice?" A light-headed feeling washed through. A second look revealed that this girl resembled my sister, though my Justice was already blind by this age. How odd that, in such a short span of time, I would meet two girls of different ages who looked so much like her.

The girl smiled at me. "What does the writing on your ring mean? It says JHSMAR."

"Oh, that?" I took the ring off and showed the inscription to her. "The letters stand for Jesus and Mary."

She studied the ring for a moment before looking at me again. Her gaze seemed to search my mind for something. I know not what.

I slid the ring back on. "How could you see the letters from where you stood?"

She shrugged. "It was easy."

"Justice often sees more than she should," Cameron said. "I am trying to teach her to turn a blind eye when the occasion calls for it."

A mental vision of my Justice appeared. Her pitiful early attempts at learning to weave baskets had often sent me from the room weeping, though her efforts had improved of late. "How can blindness ever be desirable?" I asked.

"Blindness to race. Blindness to nationality. Blindness to circumstances. These are all precious gifts. Unfortunately, Justice has much to learn in these areas. She sees everything."

"Interesting."

Jean pulled away from me and took Justice's hand. "I'm Jean. Would you like to play?"

"Yes." She looked up at Cameron. "May we?"

"Very well." He nodded toward a patch of grass. "Play over there, and stay out of trouble."

Jean's departure provided the opportunity I needed to question Cameron further. Could he and Justice be a ghost pairing? If so, how could that be since Justice was still alive?

Then dread overwhelmed my senses. *Was* my sister still alive? Had something happened to her?

A firm hand gripped my elbow. "Monsieur, may I have a private word with you?"

I turned toward the man—Inspector Fortier. Cameron excused himself and walked toward Jean and Justice.

The inspector studied my face. "Well, that is a fine disguise. I thought you might come, so I have been watching for you."

"You are thorough, I must say."

"I try to be."

"I thought when you couldn't find me at the church service you wouldn't look for me here."

"There was no church service. We gathered there, but after Francine looked out over the mourners, she announced that the mass and all rites would be conducted at graveside."

"By what authority could she do that?"

The inspector offered a wry smile. "Money, most likely. Whatever the reason, I heard that her announcement caused quite an uproar, and the bishop is still furious. It might take some time, or a few more coins in his cassock, for him to regain his composure."

I studied the inspector's face for a hint of anger. Apparently his relationship with the Church was less than genial, but his expression revealed nothing. Perhaps an event in his past damaged his faith. "Pardon my ignorance," I said, "but conducting mass at graveside seems highly irregular, even for Francine's whims."

"It is unusual, but I suspect it's not a whim. She made the decision after studying the crowd at length. I am still considering possible reasons. It's all part of my investigation."

"I see." I lowered my voice. "Have you made any progress?"

"Yes, but my discoveries have to remain a secret for now." He nodded toward the grassy area. "Who is the boy? I saw him with you earlier."

I wanted to blurt out, "You can see him?" but I kept my composure. Yet, I had to invent a new role for Jean since the inspector likely knew by now that I had no brothers. "His name is Jean. I just met him. Considering the clothes he's wearing, I assume he might be the son of one of the diggers."

"A friendly boy, then, considering that he was holding your hand."

"Yes, quite affectionate."

"Is that so?" The inspector gave me a sideways glance and lowered his voice. "Justin, may I speak frankly?"

I replied in like manner. "Please do."

174

"I am one of your few allies in this investigation. It is of paramount importance that you tell me the truth at all times."

"Do you mean about Jean?"

"About Jean or anything else. And let me give you more advice. Trust no one, not even Marc or Francine."

"Do you still suspect that they were involved in the murders?"

"I am leaving all options open. Just guard your words with everyone."

"I agree, but *everyone* includes you."

"Touché, Justin. Yet keep in mind that I cannot fully investigate the murders unless I am aware of all potential suspects." He backed away. "If you decide to talk, leave the trapdoor open. I will find you."

A rise in murmurs turned my attention to the gravesite. The bishop now stood in front of the grave with a crucifix in hand. While people gathered around, Jean rejoined me. Justice returned to Cameron and held his hand as they took places in the midst of the crowd.

"I like Justice," Jean said. "I hope she can be my friend."

Before I could reply, the bishop began speaking. "Welcome. I apologize for being late. We will begin without further delay." He cleared his throat and started a Latin recitation.

I looked at Marc and Francine. Although he stared straight at the bishop, she glanced around as if searching for someone. Then she trained her gaze on me. Since I couldn't avert my eyes without creating more suspicion, I gave her a genial smile.

For a moment, she studied me. Then, after nodding in a knowing fashion, she returned her attention to the bishop. She recognized me. Perhaps now I would learn whether or not she was really an ally. Since the bishop wanted my head on a platter, she could easily expose me.

After a few more moments of Latin monologue, the bishop began giving bread to a line of mourners. Not being Catholic, I stayed away as did Cameron, but for some reason, Justice stood at the line's tail end.

When everyone had partaken, the bishop drank from a goblet, put away the implements, and began speaking again, though his speech became slurred. His face reddened, and his eyes bulged. Then he clutched his throat and collapsed.

Bedlam ensued. A mob of people, including the inspector, rushed toward the bishop. Others called for a doctor. Reporters barked questions and furiously wrote notes.

When a doctor pushed through, he examined the bishop, then spoke to the inspector. Whispers of "Dead" and "Poisoned" filtered from the knot of people and spread throughout the crowd. Fear spread like a wild contagion. How many others would be affected by the tainted elements?

Francine pushed her way through the frenzy and sidled up to me. "You'd better leave. Quietly. You're a stranger here and therefore a likely suspect."

"How could I be a suspect? I didn't go anywhere near the cup."

"You have a good point." Francine's eyes narrowed as she scanned the crowd. "No one else is showing symptoms. Maybe only the wine was poisoned."

"True. I suppose anyone in line could have put something in the goblet."

"That's not likely. Those in line after the culprit would have noticed." Francine looked at me. "Who was last in line? Did you notice?"

I searched for Justice, but she was nowhere in sight. "A young girl, but I don't see her now."

"No, it has to be someone else. A young person wouldn't poison someone." Francine gripped my arm. "Oh, Justin, this is so frightening. Who would murder the bishop?"

"I suppose since he wants me beheaded that makes me the most likely suspect once again, but I assure you that I didn't—"

"Of course you didn't, but you should leave. Now."

"Surely someone will notice my departure."

"Does it matter? No one else knows Justin Trotter is here. Now is your only chance. Go while everyone is distracted."

I grasped Jean's hand and backed away. As Francine guessed, no one paid any attention to me—that is, no one except Justice, now visible in the crowd. Still holding Cameron's hand, she stared straight at us, unblinking.

I pivoted and walked away with Jean, not too fast, not too slow. I still felt Justice's stare as if needles pricked my back, and I expected someone to shout after me at any moment. But no shout ever came.

When we reached a point well out of sight of the funeral crowd, I accelerated to a brisk march. "Do you have any idea who poisoned the bishop?" I asked Jean.

"I have a guess."

"Justice? She was at the end of the line."

"I saw her there, but she didn't do it."

When we reached the cemetery's gate, I looked back once more. Again, no one followed. We exited and continued at a brisk pace toward the schoolhouse. "How do you know?"

"Francine was in front of her. I think she did it."

"Francine? Why would she poison the goblet?"

Jean shrugged. "It's just a guess. I didn't see her do it. But I did see that the bishop didn't give Justice any bread."

"Oh? That's interesting." The idea that Cameron and Justice might both be ghosts came to mind, which could mean that the bishop never saw her. Her invisibility would have made it easier for her to slip poison into the wine. "Back to Francine. You believe her to be a witch. Are you sure you carry no prejudice against her?"

"Maybe. But you seem to think she can do no wrong."

Now out of sight of the funeral goers, I halted and looked at him. "Of course she can do wrong. Everyone has that potential. I simply don't think she can murder someone."

His expression darkened. "You don't know witches like I do. A witch can murder and make you think she's an angel. Beware of her arts."

I suppressed a laugh. "Jean, Francine is no witch. She gives her time and energy to a number of charities. She is well-known throughout Paris as a friend of the poor."

"As I was in Geneva." Jean's voice deepened. "And you know what I did." He glared at me with flaming eyes, raising a shudder.

Although I didn't understand the Geneva reference, I knew he had participated in Michael's death. And now he seemed to be reverting to his adult mind. Was he about to have an episode of rage? I had to calm him down.

"All right. I'll watch for evidence that Francine is guilty of murder."

He half closed an eye. "Will you?"

I stared at him. I had made my statement rashly, without regard for whether or not I really meant it. Now that Jean was challenging its veracity, I couldn't help but hesitate.

He whispered, "I have to go back to Michael."

"Why so soon?"

"I can't do what Michael asked. I'm sorry." He ran ahead and shrank in the distance.

Chapter Eighteen

After looking back again and finding no one in sight, I followed Jean at a jog. When I arrived at the school's remains, I opened the trapdoor and, guessing that I might need the rope for my next journey, untied it from the door's handle and carried it with me as I descended once again into the catacombs. I found my lantern in the schoolroom and lit it. With the exception of my bag of supplies, the chamber was empty—no sign of Michael or Jean, though new drips of black wax had accumulated in a spot near a corner. Based on the size of the candle when I last saw it, they didn't have much time left.

I looked at the ring on my little finger. It was time to search for the pendant, but could I trace my way through the maze without Joan's help? If so, I also had to make sure I could find my way back.

After cutting as much rope as I thought I could carry, I gathered it into a coil and hoisted it over my shoulder. I then slid the knife behind my waistband, held the lantern in front, and walked across the littered bones, stopping every few steps to set one of the longer bones on top so that it aligned with my path.

The process slowed my pace, but I was in no hurry. I had plenty of fuel in the lamp, and no one in the land of the living wanted to see me, except those who hoped to see my head in a basket or a treasure in my hand.

Mother, during this tedious expedition, a million thoughts fought for attention. You came to mind at nearly every turn, most likely because I once again fumbled through a dark corridor. For the first time in years, some of your long-forgotten words returned to memory. As we ascended the stairs on that nightmarish climb to the attic, you whispered, "Be brave, my son. You will not always have me with you when you travel through dark passages. Courage is strengthened when you learn to walk alone."

You were a prophetess. I have walked without you through many dark passages, and venturing alone in a hall of death proved that my courage had indeed strengthened. Thank you, Mother, for preparing me for this journey.

After nearly half an hour, I found the room with the collapsed ceiling and lifted the lantern high. As I pivoted in place, the light shifted, illuminating a higher ceiling and the walls around what used to be an upper chamber, once hidden from view and now exposed by the collapse.

A large metal hook protruded from the ceiling about twenty feet above my head. Perhaps the upper chamber held the key to finding the pendant, but the walls were sheer, impossible to climb. The only way to ascend was to attach the rope to the hook and pull myself up there.

I fashioned a loop at the end of the rope and cast it several times before catching it on the hook. After testing the rope to ensure the hook could support my weight, I used the knife to cut a piece of rope and tied the lantern and knife to my waist in spite of the potential danger.

I set my feet against a wall and, pulling hand over hand, climbed toward the top. Since I had no practice with an effort like this, the going was slow and painful, but I managed to ascend to a point about a yard below the ceiling. There I rested, one hand clutching a knot in the rope and the other holding the lantern as I shone its light around.

The glow passed across a dark, rectangular hole in the opposite wall, perhaps a doorway at my level. If I had chosen to climb against that wall, I might already be there. Now I had to choose between descending and climbing again or swinging across, another feat I had never tried before. Yet, since my hands and legs ached, I probably couldn't climb again without a long rest.

After securing the lantern once more and taking a deep breath, I pushed off the wall and swung toward the doorway. As I drew close, the lantern shifted. The flame burned my thigh. With a yelp, I batted at the lantern and lost my grip. I flew the rest of the way and plunged into the opening, then crashed onto a solid floor and rolled until my momentum eased. Although my shoulder throbbed, no bones seemed to be broken, and I was safely inside a new corridor.

I climbed to my feet, detached the lantern—its glass shield cracked from the tumble—and shone the light at the doorway. My end of the rope had fallen back to the floor where I had started, impossible to reach. Returning would require a precipitous descent, or a miracle, though it already seemed a miracle that I survived the climb, the lantern's flame, and the perilous flight across the void. Perhaps Joan's ring had protected me at every turn. Yet, its power couldn't provide me with a rope. I would have to face that obstacle after exploring this new chamber.

The thought raised a new puzzle in my mind. How could Claire have created this elaborate series of obstacles? Did she have help? If so, who was her helper, and what became of him or her? The helper would have known about this hiding place. As paranoid as Claire was, why would she share her secret with someone else?

After taking a short rest, I ventured into the new passage, again carrying the lantern. The ceiling stayed about a foot above my head as the passage curved to the left until the doorway behind me angled out of sight.

When the path straightened, a new glimmer appeared in the center of my field of vision, as if hovering in midair. I walked toward it, always glancing from side to side to look for more obstacles. Yet, none appeared.

When I drew within several steps of the glimmer, I halted. At eye level, a diamond pendant dangled from a gold chain. The chain looped around another hook embedded in the ceiling.

All I had to do was walk to the pendant and release it from the hook. The task was easy, frighteningly easy. Yet, maybe since I had already come through a series of obstacles, there were none remaining.

I shook my head. No. The dangling prize was designed to tantalize, to lure, to cause a man to forget caution and rush forward. Something had to be amiss.

Taking slow, careful steps, I tested my weight on the floor with each small advance. It felt sturdy and gave no sign of impending collapse, but I still couldn't trust it.

I lowered myself to my hands and knees to distribute my weight and continued at a crawl, pushing the lantern as I progressed. When I reached a point directly under the pendant, I looked at the chain where it looped over the hook. I couldn't reach it from my all-fours position, though the task would be easy if I were to stand.

Using the lantern's light, I studied the floor. Every inch appeared to be solid, not a crack or crevice in sight.

What should my next step be? I couldn't wait here for eternity or retreat without the prize.

I looked at the ring. Even if Claire had set a final trap, the ring would protect me. It had already proven its power.

Moving slowly, I rose to a standing position, lifted the chain from the hook, and draped it over my neck. Nothing happened. All was well.

I blew a relieved sigh. Now to find my way back. The moment I picked up the lantern, the floor collapsed. I threw my arms out and grabbed the edge of the expanding hole. The lantern tumbled to the bottom and lay on its side, revealing sharp stakes below. More dirt crumbled beneath my fingers, and I plunged toward the protruding spears.

Chapter Nineteen

When I crashed, the wooden stakes snapped, though one pierced my shirt and jabbed a rib. I sat up, pulled the stake from my side, and tossed it away. Unhindered by the shallow stab, I righted the lantern and looked around. This new chamber was no more than a box, perhaps ten feet in every dimension.

Above, the floor of the corridor was out of reach, and again the walls were sheer—stone without protrusions that could support hand or foot. I couldn't climb out. The ring had indeed protected me once more, but, as before, it couldn't provide a rope.

I sat and thought about every possible use of the stakes, the lantern, and the pendant, but no device could possibly get me to the top. I was stuck, maybe forever. Claire's scheme had worked, though without the fatal consequence she had envisioned.

Still, unless I could conceive of a way to escape, I would eventually succumb to dehydration, an alternative cause of death that Claire might have had in mind. During these dark moments, her malice seemed to permeate my dismal prison, threatening my sanity to the point that I cried for help, knowing that my voice reached only earless skulls in the vast maze of bones.

A moment after my third shout echoed back to me, the end of a rope fell into my lap, and a voice from above followed. "You seem to be in quite a predicament."

I looked up. Inspector Fortier stood at the edge of the collapsed floor, the rope in hand. "I am, Inspector. Thank you." I retied the lantern, and, with the inspector's help, climbed into the upper passage. Once I stood securely, I dusted off my clothes. "Did you follow my trail of bones?"

"And your voice. Following the bones was easy, though the climb to this level was far more challenging, and since I had to cut away a section of the rope to rescue you, returning might be difficult." He picked up his own lantern. "Shall we go? We'll talk on the way back."

The remaining rope proved to be long enough, making our drop to the lower chamber relatively easy, as was retracing our steps toward the school chamber.

"Do you intend to arrest me?" I asked.

"Why would I do that?"

"The bishop's murder. I guessed that I would be a suspect."

"No, Monsieur Trotter. I watched you at the funeral from the moment you arrived. Among other reasons for coming here, I wanted to ask what you saw."

"I don't think you would believe me."

"Give me a chance."

While I explained my most recent journey, stopping at times to locate the proper bone and make the correct turn, the inspector listened intently, offering only a question or comment to clarify. I omitted the ring's protective power, leaving him to assume that the sharp stakes had broken due to age, and flying through the upper opening without injury was the result of luck.

I then provided my account of the funeral, though I bypassed the truths that he certainly wouldn't believe, such as seeing a man who appeared to be the ghost of my father as well as my being accompanied by a formerly dead persecutor.

When I mentioned Justice, the conversation took an intriguing turn.

"How interesting that her name matches your sister's," he said, now walking abreast of me in a wider corridor. "It is not a common name."

"That crossed my mind as well, which leads me to a request."

"Name it. I'll do what I can."

"Could you check on my sister for me? I haven't seen her since all of this began."

He glanced down for a moment as if trying to decide whether or not to answer. When he looked again at me, he set a hand on my elbow. "I saw her after the funeral."

I halted. "You did? Where? Why?"

"Because of the bishop's murder, I had to hurry to my office to make a report. She was there waiting for me. She had expected you to come to her residence. When you failed to arrive, she went to your flat and couldn't find you there. The commissaire suggested that she might learn your whereabouts from me, and he led her to my office."

"Was she well?"

"Well enough. Worried, as you might expect. I did notice a welt on her cheek. I assumed she bumped into something, so I didn't ask about it. Why embarrass a blind girl?"

I fumed inside. The welt likely came from Madame Dupont's hand. "Where is she now?"

"Come, and I'll tell you more." He marched ahead.

I strode quickly to match his fast pace. When we arrived at the schoolroom and set our lanterns down, the inspector looked me over. "You appear to be exhausted. Your ordeal and stress have taken their toll."

"Yes, yes, but it's nothing. Tell me about Justice."

"She's here." The inspector pointed upward. "Waiting at the surface on the other side of the brook."

"What? You left her there alone?"

"Of course not. My wife is with her. I couldn't travel with Justice without another woman along."

"I have to see her."

When I took a step toward the ladder, the inspector grabbed my arm. "What do you plan to do with her?"

"Do with her? What do you mean?"

"Along the way she talked about how you and she were going to find a place to stay together. I didn't have the heart to tell her that you're in hiding. She doesn't even know you're in the catacombs. I told her to wait patiently while I looked for you. She is quite a trusting soul."

"Yes. Trusting. Innocent. Naïve. She needs someone to watch over her."

"How will you do that? You have no income, no safe place to stay."

"I know, but she can't return to where she was. The woman who looks after her is abusive. That welt is likely the result of a savage slap."

The inspector's brow lifted. "I can look into charging this woman, if you wish."

"Even if you do, Justice would still have to leave. I promised I would take her in. I can't abandon her now."

"But where will you go?" He spread his hands. "Here? In the catacombs? Ridiculous. Even if so, how will you survive? What will you eat? Do you think Francine will bring enough food every day to—"

"You knew about that?"

"I am a detective. Of course I knew. I have kept my eye on Francine's movements for quite some time."

"Then you know of her willingness to serve others. Maybe she would take Justice in."

"Certainly she would if asked," the inspector said. "But would it be appropriate to put such a burden on her at a time like this? With the tragic death of her mother, the emotional exhaustion from the funeral, and the legal annoyances in the settling of the estate, she will have enough burdens already, not to mention the fact that a murder has taken place at her house, and the murderer is still at large."

"You raise good points, Inspector, but do you have a solution?"

He cleared his throat and straightened his sleeves in a nervous sort of way. "Well, I was thinking she might live with us. My wife was a nurse until our daughter came along, so she is more than capable of caring for your sister."

I looked into the inspector's compassionate eyes. No doubt he would do all he could to ensure Justice's good fortunes, but there was more to consider. "How old is your daughter?"

He hesitated a moment before answering. "One year last week."

"Then your wife is already busy. A one-year-old is quite a handful."

"This is true, but we are more than willing to help, and you have no viable alternatives."

"I can't argue with that." I patted his back. "Thank you for the kind offer. We'll ask Justice about it."

With both lanterns in tow, we climbed to the top. When I surfaced, two carriages stood in view on the far side of the brook. One carried Justice and a woman I didn't recognize, and the other carried Francine and an elderly male driver.

I walked toward them, the inspector following. As I drew closer, the unfamiliar woman spoke to Justice while looking at me. Justice climbed down from the carriage and spread her arms, calling, "Justin?"

I ran across the makeshift bridge and into her embrace. As we held each other, I kissed her cheek. "I'm here, Justice. I'm here."

"I'm so glad." She kissed me in return and drew back, her blank eyes wandering. The welt on her cheek, red and swollen, seemed to burn a hole in my heart. "Where have you been?" she asked. "You smell … musty, I think. And I smell lantern oil."

Mother, it would be impossible to describe the delight I felt in seeing Justice. Although it had been such a short time, with all that had happened, and with the danger I was facing, I wondered if I would ever see her again. The thought of lying to keep her blissfully ignorant didn't cross my mind until the moment I wrote this account. I am thankful that telling the truth was a more natural response.

"I was in the catacombs, and I needed a lantern there." I guided Justice's hand to my lantern. As she ran her fingers along its handle, I glanced at Francine. She sat quietly in the bench seat behind her driver, presumably Denis, her carriage alongside Justice's. "Some people think I committed murder," I continued, "so I have to hide from those who would have my head in a basket."

Instead of an expression of shock, she offered a sad sort of smile. "I know, Justin."

"You do?"

She nodded. "About the suspicions. The commissaire told me you were probably hiding. But no one mentioned the catacombs. I heard water running, and I smelled charred remains, so I guessed where we are. Francine confirmed my guess."

I glanced at Francine again before looking again at Justice. "Do you believe I'm innocent?"

"Of course. You are gentle and kind. You wouldn't harm anyone."

"Thank you for believing in me."

"Always." She turned to the carriage she had been riding. "Madame Fortier, would you hand the basket to me?"

Madame Fortier, a light-haired woman in her mid-thirties, held a sleeping child in her lap. She passed a woven fruit basket to Justice. The inspector joined his wife and climbed into the driver's seat. Sad doubt weighed down the couple's expressions as he put on his hat and took the reins.

Justice held the basket by its handle and showed it to me. "You see, Justin? It's perfect." She ran a hand along the bottom. "Not a single flaw. Surely it will sell at the market."

I looked the basket over. Indeed, she had woven it with great care and precision. Yet, one of the flat reeds was discolored, an obvious flaw to anyone with sight. The price of the basket would have to be discounted, perhaps severely.

Again, I could not lie, but love doesn't always demand the whole truth. "Your weaving skills are excellent, Justice. I am so proud of you."

Her face lit up like the sun. "Thank you. Now I can contribute to our household income. That is, as soon as your name has been cleared."

"I'm sure you can, but until that time comes, I need you to go—"

"No, Justin." Her eyes grew wide and wet. "I cannot go back to that woman." She touched the welt on her cheek. "This is the one you can see. I have three more you cannot see, including a burn." Justice broke into sobs. "She has gone mad, I tell you. Mad."

I pulled her close and let her weep against my chest. As I shushed her, I whispered, "You're not going back there, my dearest. Never again." I looked at the inspector. He brushed a tear away and averted his eyes.

When Justice drew back, she sniffed, her own tears beginning to spill. "Where will I go?"

I dabbed at her tears with a clean portion of my sleeve. "The good inspector and his wife have offered to take you in. She is a former nurse so she is well qualified to care for you."

At this point, Francine climbed down from her carriage and drew closer.

Justice whispered, "They have a little girl, Justin, and they are grieving the recent death of an older daughter. How could I add to their burdens?"

I whispered in return. "An older daughter died? When? Why?"

"I don't know what caused her death, but she was ten years old and passed away in Inspector Fortier's arms only six months ago. He wept as he told the story. I didn't want to ask him for more details."

"Ten years old?" A lump swelled in my throat. "I had no idea."

Justice ran a hand along my arm. "Of course you didn't, but now you know why I don't want to go there. No matter how loving they are, I will be a burden."

I brushed away a tear of my own, grief spiking my voice. "But I have no other options. I can't let you—"

"You have other options," Francine said as she walked closer. "I will take her."

Justice turned toward her. "You will?"

"The very reason I came." Francine curled her arm through Justice's and looked at me. "Gossip is swirling in the city. I heard about Justice's search for you, and I guessed that she would need a roof over her head. I am more than happy to provide it."

"Francine," I said, "of course I thought of you right away, but I assumed with all the burdens you're carrying that you—"

"My burdens? Justin, yours are far heavier. I am delighted to lift at least this one for you."

"Considering what happened to Marguerite, do you have any concerns about safety?"

"We have doubled our locks, including on the guest bedroom. She will be safe."

I tried to invent a new challenge, but nothing came to mind. Francine's insistence was holding sway. "I'm glad to hear about the locks."

"Then it's settled." Francine took Justice's basket and guided her toward me. "Say good-bye to your brother, and we will be on our way."

Justice kissed me on the cheek. "Come and see me soon."

"I will." I kissed hers in return. "Very soon."

Francine leaned close to me, her words soft. "Did you find it?"

I nodded.

Her voice lowered further. "Midnight tonight. Everyone should be asleep by then."

"I'll be there."

While Francine led Justice toward her carriage, I stepped closer to Inspector Fortier as he sat in his seat. "Are you content with this solution?"

"Content, though I do have reservations." He touched the brim of his hat. "I will contact you when I have news about the case." He gave the reins a snap, and the horse trotted away with its load.

When Francine's carriage followed with Justice on board, I watched their progress until both carriages drove out of sight. Then, I walked in their path. I couldn't hide in the catacombs until I was certain that Justice would be safe from any lurking menace. I needed to check on the security precautions myself.

Mother, watching Justice leave was the hardest thing I had ever done in my life. She was so vulnerable, so easily victimized. She reminded me of the chick you once showed me, freshly hatched from an egg, wet and struggling to stand. It chirped, calling for its mother, though it had no idea where she was or what she looked like. Such is innocent blindness. A chick, or a young woman, has to trust in the goodness of someone else, believe that the wing she nestles under is one of protection.

Of Francine's wings of protection, I had no doubts of my own. Yet Jean's accusations of witchcraft still haunted my thoughts. I had to brush them away. It was superstitious nonsense. Besides, Francine would surely treat Justice kindly and keep her safe, not only for the obvious altruistic reasons but also—if someone were so unkind to suggest it—for self-serving ones. Caring for the blind sister of the man who was accused of murdering her mother would greatly enhance her reputation among the socialites, especially in her church. That thought provided comfort as I continued the long walk to the Noëls' house.

Chapter Twenty

When I arrived at the Noëls' house, I crept around to the back alley and surveyed the rear door and windows. Everything seemed secure. I walked to the other end of the alley and found the inspector standing near the corner of the front street. I backed out of sight and peered around the last house in the row. Why would he station himself there? Maybe he wasn't convinced that extra locks would be enough to keep the occupants safe. And if he wasn't convinced, then I shouldn't be either.

The inspector walked toward the alley. I ducked behind a low brick wall and watched him over the top edge. He drew a revolver from his coat and scanned the area. After a few moments, he put the gun away and returned to his former station.

Now out of his line of sight, I hurried back to the rear of the Noëls' house and hid behind a waist-high planter box. Misty rain spread through the air. Cold wind added a chill. Inspector Fortier would probably leave soon, which meant that I had to remain as Justice's lone guard. Rain, cold, and hunger mattered nothing. I had to protect Justice.

The sky darkened to evening's shade. Thunder rolled far away. Black clouds loomed on the horizon, promising a downpour. Able now to move unseen, I stepped away from my hiding place and into the alley. At the alley's end, opposite of my entry direction, three figures drew closer, shrouded in darkness.

A swinging lantern in the hand of the smallest figure illuminated Jean's face. He ran ahead, calling, "Justin, we found you."

When he arrived, he pointed at the two others as they drew closer at a slower pace. One man hobbled while the other supported him. Soon, they came into the light. Michael, carrying a carpetbag on one side, supported Cameron Trotter by the arm on the other.

I rushed to them and grasped Cameron. We helped him sit with his back to the house opposite the Noëls' home. Jean gave the lantern to me, whispering, "This is ours, but you can use it till we leave."

After setting the carpetbag down, Michael knelt next to Cameron and gestured for me to come closer. "This man says he knows you. He is one of us and has lost his ward, a girl named Justice. He searched for hours until his candle melted to a mere wafer. The candle's light led him to this area, but he was unable to find her. When I discovered him, he had already collapsed. I helped him rise, and he maintained enough sensibility to move his legs, but he hasn't been able to tell me who he is."

"He's the ghost version of my father." I crouched and set the lantern close to Cameron. He appeared wan and wasted, as if devoured by malnutrition. "Father, were you looking for me?"

His eyes fluttered open. "Justin?"

I leaned close. "Yes. I'm here."

He slid his hand into mine. "You must find Justice. She is not yet blind."

"Do you mean my sister? She is already blind."

"No, no. Not your sister. Until Justice is blind, she is dangerous. You must pursue her. Stop her before it's too late."

"Too late? Do you mean before your time here is over?"

"My time is over, Justin. Hers will go on. She was never human. She cannot die, but her purposes can be thwarted. She must be fully blind so she can never do to others what she did to me."

"How? Why?"

"Don't you remember?" He caressed my cheek. "You saw me, Justin, but you ran before I could explain."

"The night you killed that woman?"

"But I didn't kill her, I …" His eyes widened, and he looked skyward. For a moment, he smiled. Then his head lolled to the side. Seconds later, he faded and disappeared.

The tingle of his touch lingered, growing hot on my cheek. I climbed to my feet, staggered to the wall on quaking legs, and leaned against it. "Michael, what does all this mean?"

"I don't know." He rose and joined me. "But it seems that you need to find Justice, whoever she is."

"I've seen her. The first time was on a city street, then soon after at the masquerade party. She appeared to be Jean's age. I saw her once again at the funeral. She was older, maybe eleven or twelve."

"How odd," Michael said. "Jean doesn't age, nor did Pierre."

"Maybe Justice is even older now, so I have to search for a female of any age, but where and how? And what did he mean by her needing to be blind?"

"Again, I don't know."

"I can help," Jean said, looking at Michael. "Justin and I can search for her together."

Michael frowned. "You have yet to pass the test. We have time for only one more trial."

"The test?" I asked.

"It is the reason we were in the area. Jean hoped you would witness his final trial."

Jean took my hand. "I'm going with Justin. To blazes with the trial."

"Your lack of temperance might send you to blazes." Michael's stern expression faded as he let out a long sigh. "Perhaps we have time, depending on how long the search takes."

"She must be close," Jean said. "Justin's father was coming this way."

I pulled my coat close and shivered. The misty rain stopped, but thunder in the distance promised more bad weather. "Now that darkness has fallen, I don't see any hope of finding her."

"Then what should we do?" Jean asked.

"I'm not sure. If only—"

A stroke of lightning interrupted. The flash illuminated the Noëls' house and a face in the window. Justice stared at us, though not my sister. Although they looked alike, somehow I knew. Then

194

darkness veiled her. Another stroke crashed somewhere nearby. This time, she was gone.

I whispered, "She's inside." Large raindrops pelted my head. A deluge would follow soon. "I need to get in there. She might cause trouble."

"I believe you're right." Michael gestured toward the carpetbag he had brought. "I collected your belongings and put them in there. I assumed you weren't returning to the catacombs."

I nodded. "Thank you."

Michael took Jean's hand. "Now that you have found her, we'll be going."

"No." Jean pulled away. "I want to stay. I want to help."

Michael stooped and looked at him eye to eye. "Jean, your eternity is at stake. We have time for one trial. One. You know what such a trial entails. Think carefully about your decision. I will honor it."

Jean looked at me, then at the Noëls' house. After a few seconds, he lowered his head. "I will go with you."

"Good." Michael straightened and picked up the lantern. "There is no time to lose."

"What about the storm?" I asked.

"It won't affect us." He faded to near transparency. In the dim flash from a distant lightning strike, raindrops passed through his body. "Godspeed to you, Justin. I greatly appreciate our talks. I hope we meet again someday." They walked away and blended into the darkness.

Their departure drained me, as if I had lost two dear friends. Although dead, they seemed more alive to me than nearly anyone who had crossed my path here in Paris. For their help and encouragement, I am grateful to this day.

Now alone and with only occasional thunder interrupting the silence, my father's words echoed. *She was never human. She cannot die ... she must be fully blind. ... I didn't kill her.*

Since he was the teacher and Justice was the student, he couldn't have been a murderer. After all these years, the truth finally came out, spoken by the ghost of my father. He was innocent of the crime. Yet, who was this girl named Justice whom he was assigned to teach, and why did he want her to be blind?

A clap of thunder jolted me from my trance. I hurried to the Noëls' door and found it locked. Since it was still a few hours before midnight, Francine was not yet expecting me.

Rain poured in sheets. Wind banged a shutter at the closest window. I knocked on the door and called for Francine, but the howling storm drowned out my voice, and the shutter matched the sounds of my pounding fist. My attempts were futile.

I found a crate in the alley, set it under the window, and stood on top. Now able to reach high enough, I held the banging shutter against the wall, opened the sash, and climbed in.

Once inside, I looked out. The carpetbag still sat in the alley. Trying to retrieve it now would result in my getting soaked. It wasn't worth the trouble. I closed the window and sat on the floor. The shutter reprised its pounding, and rain pelted the window pane. Now somewhat wet, I looked around to gain my bearings, aided by an occasional flash of lightning. I sat in the dining room next to the table. The low-hanging cloth blocked my view of the house's sitting room, which lay beyond the dining room's doorway.

Footsteps approached. Flickering candlelight appeared. I peeked around the table's corner. Francine halted at the doorway, carrying a candelabrum and looking at the window. When the shutter banged once more, she strode toward it.

Not wanting to startle her or explain my presence, I slid between two chairs and hid under the table, concealed by the cloth, though I peered out from under it.

She opened the window, reached out into the pouring rain, and pulled the shutter into place, then fastened it to the one on the other side and closed the sash. Now wet, she dripped water to the floor at the base of the window, thereby concealing the puddles I had caused. She let out a sigh and a frustrated murmur, then left the room, though the light remained.

I slid out a bit and looked around. The candelabrum sat on the table. Francine would probably be back soon to clean up the mess.

After a few moments, a tapping sound came from the sitting room, barely audible over the storm's din. I hid myself again and waited. Soon, shoes appeared below an ankle-length skirt, then knees lowered to the floor. Fingers touched the floor here and there as if searching for the extent of the water's spread. Yet, the candles provided plenty of light to see the boundaries.

I raised the cloth a few inches. Justice—my sister—mopped the puddles with a towel, her expression determined as she swept the towel throughout the area. Her cane lay on the floor nearby.

I opened my mouth to whisper, but Francine's voice interrupted from the doorway. "When you finish, I'll show you how to arrange the laundry, then you may go to bed."

Careful to make no noise, I lowered the cloth and held my breath.

"Thank you." Justice felt the floor, now dry. She picked up her cane and walked out, the cane's taps fading.

Footsteps approached again. The candlelight flickered and slowly diminished as the sounds retreated. Francine was gone.

I stayed in place, wanting to make sure everyone had walked well away. Why was she putting Justice to work, a blind girl who had just arrived? Yet, it was Francine's manner to request effort from those she helped, so it shouldn't have come as a surprise.

Mother, you often told me what the good book says—those who will not work should not eat. I agree in principle. But a blind girl? Perhaps Francine planned to use easy tasks as a way to teach Justice the customs and layout of this house, to help her function independently. Since Justice was industrious and would want to work for her keep, they likely agreed upon the arrangement. Maybe Justice even suggested it. Who was I to judge?

Deep within the house, a clock chimed nine times. In three hours I would meet with Francine. In three hours I would give her the pendant and slide the ring onto her finger. In three hours I would be engaged to marry the woman I had loved from afar for so long.

Yet, I still had to find the other Justice, the missing ghost who refused to pass into eternity. Searching in stealth was probably the best plan.

Hoping to dry well enough to walk around the house, I waited until the clock struck eleven. Now that the household had likely retired for the night, I slid out from under the table, shed the coat I had borrowed from Marc, and draped it over a chair seat, out of sight. Since I hadn't been in the rain for more than a minute, it had dried quite well.

Again guided by occasional lightning flashes, I crept out of the dining room and into the sitting area. A small table had been set up there, but I was unable to see any details. Walking now from memory, I made my way to the scullery, where I found a small candle and matches. After lighting the candle, I returned to the sitting room.

A flowery tablecloth covered the small table. At the center, a bottle of wine stood next to a tall candle set in an ornate holder. A crystal goblet sat at each place, both already filled, as if poised for a celebration. Francine was ready for me.

I felt the ring on my finger. I was ready for her.

Since I stood at the end of the hall, I had a view of the bedroom entries. Every door was closed, including Marguerite's former room, where Justice likely slept. Whether or not her door was locked, I couldn't tell.

The memory of Marguerite's bloody corpse raised a new shudder. Could the ghostly Justice be the murderer? No matter what the danger, it was up to me to find her.

Still holding the small candle, I walked toward my sister's room. As I passed Francine's, I stopped. Dim light leaked through the gap under the door, and low whispers emanated from inside.

I leaned close and listened.

"Marc, I need you to go."

"In this storm? Can't it wait till morning?"

"If the fever gets worse, she could be dead by morning. I would go, but I'm in my nightgown."

I stiffened. *She*? Was Francine talking about Justice?

Marc sighed. "Very well. But since I have to walk, I'll be gone more than an hour."

"I think she'll be all right for that long."

I opened Justice's door, ducked inside, and pulled it nearly closed, thankful that she had left it unlocked. I peeked through the gap. Carrying a lantern, Marc exited Francine's room and shut her door with an authoritative click. He then exhaled loudly and turned toward her room. "Please forgive my frustration. I'm tired."

The door opened a crack. "I know, Marc," Francine said. "All is forgiven. I will see you soon."

I closed Justice's door and tiptoed to her bedside. Wearing a plain white nightgown, she lay on her back with her hands folded over her chest, peaceful and quiet. I set a palm on her forehead— warm, but not hot. Maybe her fever was breaking.

I pulled my hand back and whispered, "Justice?"

She let out a slight gasp. "Justin, is that you?"

"Yes. I am here."

She felt for my hand and grasped it. "Why did you come?"

"To check on you. To make sure you're all right."

"I am well. Tired, but well."

"Do you have a fever?"

"No. Why do you ask?"

I looked toward the door. Maybe Francine was talking about someone else, a neighbor perhaps. "I thought you felt a little warm."

"Well ... I have been ... um ... walking around the house a lot to learn where the rooms are." She pulled my hand to her cheek. "How are you?"

"I got a bit wet from the storm, but I'm dry now. Tired. Worried about you. Other than that, I'm fine." I lifted her hand and tried to rub warmth into her cold skin. "How are you and Francine getting along?"

A few seconds passed before Justice replied. "I am ... adjusting."

"Adjusting? What do you mean?"

"Well ... Francine is ... I'm not sure how to say it."

199

"Making you do housework?"

"Not making, Justin. I volunteered. I need to be useful. I was trying to say that Francine is somewhat aloof. I need to adjust to her personality."

"Much better than living with Madame Dupont, I assume." She tightened our clasp. "Oh, yes, Justin. Francine would never strike me. I am certain of that."

"Good to hear." I patted her hand. "Go back to sleep now."

A new flash added to the candlelight, illuminating her tear-filled eyes. "Thank you for coming. Please visit again soon."

"I will." I kissed her forehead and walked to the door. After verifying that no one was in the hall, I exited and closed the door behind me. Again walking on tiptoes, I crept to the small table and sat in the chair farther from the bedrooms. Since the napkin at this place was plain and the other was trimmed with lace, this setting was likely mine.

I withdrew my pocket watch and read the time—half past eleven. After putting it back, I blew out the candle and sat in silence. Francine was probably changing from her nightgown to something more presentable. Yet why would she have put the nightgown on in the first place since she was planning to meet with me? Perhaps she took a nap so she would be well rested.

In any case, in mere minutes, Francine would probably come out from her bedroom and unlock the back door in anticipation of my arrival. It would be best for me to retrieve my coat and wait outside in spite of the driving rain.

When I set my feet to rise from my chair, another lightning flash lit the room. Justice stood motionless at the side of the table, a hand on each goblet.

I suppressed a gasp and whispered, "What are you doing here?"

Wearing a black traveling dress and jacket, she struck a match and tried to light the table's candle, but she missed her aim, and the flame passed by the wick. When she tried and failed again, I grasped her wrist and guided her next effort successfully. The candle's glow bathed her gaunt face in a yellowish tint. Although she was now the same apparent age as my sister and her eyesight had severely worsened, she had to be my father's ghostly ward.

She blew out the match and looked straight at me with glazed-over eyes. "I am here to protect you and your sister."

My throat tightened. "From whom?"

She leaned close and replied in a whispered hiss. "The murderer."

The seriousness in her voice further shook me. My voice spiked louder than I intended. "Who is the murderer?"

"It is your own blindness that prevents you from seeing the obvious."

Francine's bedroom door opened. She appeared in the hallway with a lantern in front. "Hello? Who's out there?"

Justice turned and hurried toward the dining room, extending her hands to guide her way.

I called, "It's me, Francine. Justin."

She walked into the sitting area and lowered a revolver. Now wearing a sky-blue dress trimmed with lace and her mother's brooch pinned on a lapel, she breathed a sigh of relief. "You frightened me. Marc went out for medicine, and I knew he couldn't have come home so quickly."

"I arrived early. I knocked, but no one answered. The storm was bad, so I came in through a window."

"Ah." She set the gun on the table and looked me over. "Where is the coat you borrowed from Marc?"

"In the dining room. I laid it over a chair to dry."

"Good. I'll start a fire."

When she stepped toward the fireplace, I grasped her arm. "No. Stay. We should talk."

Her expression turned curious. "If you wish." She sat in her chair and set the lantern on the floor. She then propped her elbows on the table with her chin resting in her hands, her smile coy. In the low lighting, her brooch emitted a dim green aura. "What do you want to talk about, Justin Trotter?"

Jitters ran along my body. Maybe some wine would calm my nerves. "Shall we start with a drink?"

"Um ... let's wait. You look like you're excited to tell me something."

I smiled. She was playing the role of the naïve maiden, unaware of what her suitor had in mind. I could play along with a flair. "Mademoiselle," I said, adding drama to my tone, "I have a gift for you, taken from the jaws of a dragon."

I pulled the chain over my head and let the pendant dangle in front of the candle. As the pendant swayed, the diamond reflected the light. Dazzling colors danced across the tablecloth's flowers like bejeweled bees. "How lovely it would look shimmering against your fair bosom."

She fanned her face with a hand and replied with a girlish voice. "Oh, Justin, you're so romantic."

I leaned across the table and slid the chain over her head. When it came to rest around her milky white neck, I set the pendant in front of her chest and drew back. "A beautiful pendant for a beautiful woman."

"Thank you. You are so kind." She touched the diamond. "And you solved Grandmother Claire's final mystery. You truly are a man of many talents."

When I reseated myself, I pulled the ring off my finger. "And now ..." My hands shook terribly as I swallowed hard. "I would like to ask you a question."

"Justin." Francine laid a hand over mine. "You're so nervous. Maybe we *should* have a drink now."

"Yes, I think that would help."

She lifted her goblet and whispered, "To our future."

I set the ring on the table and lifted my goblet. "Yes, to our future."

I took one sip and set the goblet down, while Francine drank the entire contents of hers. She nodded toward my wine. "Is it not to your liking?"

"It's excellent. I try to savor a good wine."

"Justin, the sooner you relax, the sooner you can ask your question." She set her hand on mine. "Please. Drink the rest. We have much to talk about."

Her touch sent a shiver along my arm. Why the insistence on drinking the wine? It wouldn't act that quickly to calm my nerves. The brooch's glow brightened and sent a soothing sensation into my mind, as if wooing me to drop my defenses. As I reached for the goblet, Jean's words broke through. *Beware of her arts.* I looked at the ring on the table. Francine had declined my invitation to drink earlier, then became insistent when I took the ring off and removed its protective power. Had she poisoned my wine? Was Jean right after all?

Francine compressed my hand. "Justin? Is something wrong? You're staring."

The dining room shutter banged. I looked that way. Had Justice opened the window? "I'd better see to that."

"Don't worry yourself. It happens during every storm."

"I prefer to avoid the distraction." I slid the ring back on my finger, picked up my goblet, and walked into the dining room, light from the table candle guiding my way. The window was open, and a rainy breeze flowed in. I looked outside. Illuminated by distant lightning, the ghostly Justice, still dressed in black travel clothes, wandered along the alley. Rain and wind assaulted her, whipping her dress and hair as her hands groped for anything that might support her.

I shouted through the wet breeze slapping my face. "Justice!"

A man carrying a lantern ran to her and gathered her into his arms. The lantern cast a glow across his face—Inspector Fortier. He looked at me and nodded. She would be cared for.

"Justin?" Francine called, her voice drawing closer.

I poured my wine out the window, set the goblet on the dining room table, and turned. She walked in, carrying the candle. "Why did you call for Justice?"

"I thought I saw her out there." I secured the shutter and closed the window. "Just my imagination, I suppose."

Francine picked up my goblet. As we walked back, she let out a humming laugh. "Perhaps another ghost?"

"Perhaps."

When we seated ourselves, she set my empty goblet next to hers and the candle back in place, then looked at me expectantly. "How are you feeling now? Still nervous?"

"I'm feeling—"

A bedroom door opened down the hall. "Justin? Did you call me?" A tapping sound followed—a cane against the floor.

I whispered, "Justice is coming."

"She shouldn't be here," Francine said. "I don't want her ..." She blinked. "Something's wrong."

"What?"

She raised a hand to her throat and rasped, "It's burning."

"Something in the wine?" I touched my own throat. "I don't feel anything."

Justice walked in, her cane in hand. "Justin, you're still here."

"*Still* here?" Francine rose from her seat and stared at us in turn. Her face flushed deep red, and her voice roughened. "You two conspired against me."

I pushed my chair back and stood. "Conspired? What are you talking about?"

Francine laid a hand on her stomach. A tight grimace twisted her face. "You poisoned me!"

"Poisoned?"

When I took a step toward her, she picked up the gun and aimed it at me. "Give me the ring."

"Francine, you're probably suffering from some kind of—"

"Give me the ring." She shifted the gun toward Justice. "Now."

"Francine, no!" The shutter banged again, making me flinch, but I dared not look that way.

"Now, Justin," Francine said, her tone hardening, though her body swayed as if ready to topple.

Justice trembled. "Justin? What's happening?"

"Stay calm." I grasped the ring around my finger. "I'll give it to you if you'll put the gun down."

A shot rang out. Blood spattered from Francine's arm. She dropped her gun and collapsed, motionless.

Inspector Fortier ran in from the dining room with a smoking gun in hand. He put it away under his coat and knelt at Francine's side. "I struck her wrist," he said, dripping rainwater as he lifted her bleeding arm. "It's not much more than a scratch. Why would she pass out?"

"She claimed that I poisoned her." I pulled my sister into my arms and held her close. "Then she threatened Justice."

The inspector's eyes darted from Justice to the dining room and back again. "How did she get inside and change clothes so quickly? I left her in my carriage and ran here."

I kept my mouth closed. Explaining would make me look more insane than ever, as would putting the ring on Francine's finger to try to save her life. Of course, basic decency demanded that I do so without concern for appearances, but the confusion of the moment petrified me. Protecting Justice from harm overwhelmed every other thought.

"And," he continued, "why would anyone threaten a helpless, blind—"

The front door opened. Marc walked in, soaking wet. "I have the fever medicine," he said as he closed the door. "A carriage driver gave me a ride home, so it didn't take long." He looked at us. When his gaze fell on Francine and the inspector, he rushed to her side. "Francine? What happened?"

"We have reason to believe that she has been poisoned," the inspector said. "She also suffered a minor bullet wound to her wrist."

Marc lifted Francine and carried her to the sofa. The moment he laid her down, he ran to the door. "I'll catch the carriage."

When the door slammed, I picked up the lantern Francine had brought and guided Justice closer to the sofa. Under the glow, Francine lay on her back, heaving shallow, labored breaths.

Inspector Fortier lifted Francine's goblet and sniffed it. "No telltale odor." He swirled the dram of wine that remained. "I will subject this to a Marsh test."

"Marsh test?" I asked.

"To detect arsenic."

"Is she showing symptoms of arsenic poisoning?"

Francine rolled to her side and vomited on the floor. Red liquid spewed, but whether it was wine or blood, I could not tell. When she finished, she shifted to her back again and moaned.

"Without a doubt," the inspector said. "We can hope, however, her vomiting episode expelled much of the poison."

Marc banged the door open. Breathless and dripping, he ran to the sofa and lifted Francine again. "I caught the carriage. We're going to a doctor."

"Take her," the inspector said. "But wait for me. I'll be there by the time you get her settled in the carriage."

Marc hurried out with Francine, leaving the door open.

The inspector slid the goblet into an inner coat pocket. He looked at me and whispered, "If Francine denounces you, you will have no hope. I have opinions on what really happened here, but I won't act on them until I have facts. Do what you must to ensure your safety." He glanced briefly at Justice. "If your sister is here alone when I return, I will take her to my home." He shut the door with a hard thud.

Chapter Twenty-One

I pulled Justice close with one hand, the other still holding the lantern. She trembled in my grasp. "Who could have poisoned her?" she asked.

An image of her namesake came to mind. Could the ghostly Justice have delivered the poison? Yet, she had said that she was there to protect me and my sister, not to kill Francine. Nothing made sense.

The odor of vomit rose from the floor. I turned with Justice and guided her toward her bedroom. "My dearest, you heard what Francine said. She thinks you and I poisoned her."

"I did hear, but it seemed so absurd. We wouldn't hurt anyone."

"People will believe *you* wouldn't hurt anyone, but I'm afraid my reputation is not as pristine."

"What are you going to do? Hide again?"

Her question felt like a slap, though she surely didn't mean it that way. I had hidden too many times. I felt like a coward. "I'm staying with you until the inspector returns to take you to his house. He is a good man. You'll be fine there."

When we arrived at her room, I led her to the bed. She sat on it and looked up at me with imploring eyes, a habit she gained before she went blind. "What will you do then?"

I set the lantern on the floor. "I have no place to go. Certainly I can't stay here."

"The catacombs again?"

"Most likely, until I can arrange a new identity. But no matter what happens, I'll make sure you have a comfortable place to live."

"I don't see how I can be comfortable knowing you're in that place. I want to be with you. You're my brother. We should be together."

"Even in the catacombs?"

"Justin, I'm blind. I won't be able to see how awful it is."

"We would have no food, no water. I would have to scavenge at night."

"But we could—"

I set a finger on her lips. "No more arguing. You don't want me to go to prison, do you?"

"Of course not."

"The only way I can stay free is by being able to move quickly. I might have to run from my pursuers, and you would slow me down."

She sighed. "That's true."

"Then it's settled. We'll wait here until the inspector comes. I assume he'll return by dawn." I grasped her shoulders. "I love you, Justice. You are a treasure above all treasures."

"I love you, too, Justin."

When she released my hand, her fingers ran along mine. "What's this? A ring?"

I lifted my hand and looked at the ring. "It's an artifact I found in the catacombs, a ring that was once owned by Joan of Arc. Legends say it protected her from death, and based on what I've been through, I think it might be true."

"Then you believe in its power."

"I do." I took the ring off and stared at the engraving. Maybe the names were more than a simple reminder of heavenly helpers. Maybe they represented an appeal for protection. I slid it onto her finger. "I want you to have it."

She twisted it back and forth. "But if you're on the run, you'll need it more than I do."

"I can take care of myself. If you wear it, I'll feel like Joan's angels are watching over you."

She held the ring hand close to her chest. "In that case, thank you."

"You're welcome." I picked up the lantern. "Change out of your nightgown and pack your things. You'll want to be ready when the inspector arrives."

"I will." She hugged herself and shivered. "It's getting cold in here."

"It is, indeed. The storm must have brought a surge of cold air."

She ran a hand along my sleeve. "No coat?"

"I borrowed one from Marc. I'll get it." I carried the lantern out to the sitting room and set it on the small table, where it would cast light around most of the house, including down the hall toward the bedrooms. I returned to the dining room and picked up the coat. A strong, frigid breeze poured in from the open window, explaining the chill in the house. Outside, the rain had ceased, leaving behind an early taste of winter.

I secured the shutter, closed the window, and put the coat on before returning to Justice's room. I waited by the door until she signaled that she had changed clothes.

When I entered, she was wearing the ragged gray dress she had on when she visited my flat. I touched a loose thread on one of the sleeves. "Justice, have you noticed this seam near your elbow?"

"Yes, but whenever I sewed for Madame Dupont, she wouldn't let me use her supplies for my own clothes."

"I'm sure Francine has plenty to spare. I'll get a needle and a spool of thread." I entered Francine's bedroom, found her sewing table in the corner, and picked up a needle and a spool of thread that appeared to be gray, though the dim light made the color uncertain.

When I returned to Justice's room, I gave her the supplies and helped her pack her clothes and personal items in a travel bag. When we finished, she put her coat on, and we walked together to the sitting room.

Justice sniffed the air. "I heard Francine vomit. I should clean up the mess."

"I'll do it."

Justice grasped my arm, her expression hopeful. "Together?"

I smiled. "Together."

Using a basin of water, a cleanser, and scrubbing cloths, we cleaned away the vomit, all the while reminiscing about days gone by. For some reason, concern about Francine melted away. Justice and I had each other. We were content.

When we finished, we sat on the sofa and waited for someone to return with news. Most likely the inspector would arrive first. He probably recorded Francine's belief that Justice and I poisoned her, and he would have to report it, but as long as he believed we were innocent, we had nothing to fear, at least for a while.

Still, a question gnawed at the back of my mind. If we were innocent, then whom would the inspector blame for the poisoning? No one else could have done it.

As we waited, we leaned our heads together, talking and laughing at times, dozing at others. Joy filled my heart. I had reunited with my best friend, a jewel of a woman I never should have left behind. I should have had more faith that we could have survived on our own. Her determination would have made the difference.

The front door opened, shaking us from slumber. A cold wind ushered Francine into the room, her face pale and pain streaked. Her blue, lace-trimmed dress bore wrinkles and vomit stains. When she saw us, she halted and blinked, as if unable to see clearly. "Justin? Justice?"

"Yes." I rose from the sofa, pulling Justice to her feet. "Where are Marc and Inspector Fortier?"

"Outside, preparing the inspector's carriage for travel." Her face hardened. "Why are you still here?"

"Where else would we be?"

"Murderers usually try to flee from prosecution."

"Murderers? We didn't—"

"Justin, don't try to deceive me again." Clutching her stomach, she hobbled to the table and picked up her revolver.

I stepped in front of Justice. "Francine, no. Don't."

She aimed the gun at me and called, "Justin, don't shoot. I'll do anything you say. Just don't shoot."

"What?" I glanced from Francine to Justice, then back to Francine. She was setting up an alibi for murdering me. I pushed

Justice down and leaped toward Francine. She fired the gun. The bullet hit me in the shoulder, knocking me back a step.

Justice screamed, "Marc? Inspector? Where are you?"

As I stood in place, pain shredded my thoughts. I couldn't move. Francine walked closer and cried out, "Justin, you shot yourself. Oh, dear God, you shot yourself. Give me the gun. Don't shoot yourself again."

Now just out of reach, she looked at my hand, perhaps to check for the ring, then aimed the gun at my forehead and whispered, "First you. Then your sister, if she's not convinced you committed suicide."

I lunged, grabbed her wrist, and wrestled her to the floor. As we fought, Francine screamed, "Marc! Help! Justin is trying to kill me!" She wrenched her arm free and pulled the trigger. The gun fired. The bullet sped past my head and nearly hit Justice.

"Justice!" I shouted. "Get down." Just as Francine squeezed the trigger again, I turned the barrel toward her. A new blast erupted. Blood splashed from her chest. She stopped struggling and looked at me, bitterness in her eyes as she gurgled through a mouthful of blood. "I will see you in hell."

She closed her eyes and stopped breathing.

Justice, now lying on the floor, called, "Justin? Are you there? What's happening?"

"I'm here. I'm all right." The pendant lay in a pool of blood on Francine's chest. I took the gun from her hand and struggled to my feet, gasping. "Francine is dead. She tried … to kill me. She said … I shot myself to … hide her actions from you."

Justice rose and grasped my arm. "You sound hurt."

"I am hurt. She shot me … in the shoulder. I don't know … how badly I'm wounded."

She pushed her shoulder under my arm. "Lean on me."

Still holding the gun, I shifted my weight to her. "Thank you."

She ran a hand along my back. "You have a hole here, too. The bullet went through."

At that moment, Marc walked in. When he saw Francine, he rushed to her, crouched, and checked her heart. "She's dead."

"She tried to—"

He leaped up and snatched the gun from me. "You killed her!" I raised my hands. The pain from the wound stabbed mercilessly and throttled my senses. "Marc. She ... I ..."

"Justice," Marc said, "move out of the way. I don't want you to get hurt."

The inspector stormed into the room, his own gun drawn. "Monsieur Noël, put your weapon down."

"Not until I avenge my sister's death." When he set his finger on the trigger, I pushed Justice away and ran toward the door. Marc fired. A bullet grazed my ear and thumped into the wall. I dashed outside and into darkness.

As I made my way along the street, the inspector shouted from the house. "Monsieur Trotter. You need medical attention."

Indeed, my shirt clung to my chest and back, and blood soaked the front of my shirt. If the bleeding didn't slow soon, I would die.

I pressed a hand against the shoulder wound and slowed to a walk. My heart thumped. Every beat echoed in my wound as a painful jab, as if someone were ramming the fire poker into my shoulder. Although the pain sent searing heat though my body, a sense of peace eased the torture. The inspector would be sure to take care of Justice. She would be safe no matter what happened to me.

As a bitter wind blew from the north, I bundled the coat closer. It seemed that every force of nature pushed me toward the catacombs. What choice did I have? I had to stay out of sight until Marc's anger subsided. Soon, Justice would explain that I shot Francine in self defense. Then all would be well.

I followed my usual route to the old schoolhouse, familiar enough that I no longer had to think about which turns to make. Every step ached. Every gust of wind tore at my wound as if reaching into it with icy fingers. But I had to go on.

Trying to take my mind off the pain, I studied my surroundings. A city clock showed twenty past six, perhaps an hour before dawn. At a coffee house on one street, soft music played while customers chatted and laughed, oblivious to the cares of the world.

On the next street, a painted woman called to me from a sheltered doorway and lifted her skirt in a provocative manner. Why would she be out at this early morning hour? Perhaps a slow night for business.

I turned my head and walked on without replying. The prostitute's words replayed in my mind, a call to warmth in her embrace. I neither loved nor loathed such women. I pitied them. And their sad state spiked my anxiety.

Every time I saw a streetwalker or a brothel worker, I wondered if Justice would have to resort to that profession if I were unable to find suitable keep for her. Since she was young, pretty, and vulnerable, the vultures of the trade would swoop down on her, likely not caring that she was blind, or perhaps relishing her handicap, knowing they could take advantage of her. The rodents they called customers would probably look upon her as an interesting novelty.

The thoughts made me ill. I shook them away and hurried on, still pressing a hand against my wound. Since I had made it this far, maybe I had a chance to survive. All I had to do was stop the bleeding, but could I cauterize and stitch two wounds without help? Surely not the one on my back.

By the time I arrived at the brook, the setting moon peeked through a break in the clouds. The bridge Joan and I had constructed was still intact, and the brook flowed safely below, though swollen by the storm. Drainage from the hills would probably make it rise even more, which might tear the bridge apart. All the better. I would be more secluded, safe from Marc or whoever might want to find me.

When I set my feet on the floor of the catacombs, I felt my way to the schoolroom and found my supplies, including the lantern and matches. I blinked at the darkness. This is what my poor sister saw all day, every day—no sun, no moon, no starlight. She never enjoyed smiles, flowers, rolling meadows, or sunrises. Of course she had seen them years ago, which allowed her to view these delights in her mind's eye, but was it worse to lose the precious gift of sight or never have it at all?

Of all the human conditions, perhaps blindness was the worst—not only physical blindness, but mental, emotional, and spiritual blindness as well.

That thought resurrected the ghostly Justice's words. *It is your own blindness that prevents you from seeing the obvious.*

Then Michael's warning came to mind. *You cannot see what everyone else sees. Your blindness will be your downfall.*

Finally, Jean's sad words returned. *I can't do what Michael asked. I'm sorry.*

Three different ghosts had referred either directly or indirectly to my blindness, though none of them explained. Yet, one truth I did know—sitting in the darkness and wallowing in self pity would never help me see the truth.

I shed the coat and rummaged through my bag. I found the matches, lit the lantern, and set it on the table. A folded page of parchment lay on the floor along with a pen, as if a writer had left in haste. I picked it up. It was sealed with black wax. On the outside, it read, "To Justin Trotter."

I broke the seal and opened it. Written in French with a near-perfect script, the note said:

Justin,

I administered Jean's final test. Since you and he grew close, I thought it only fair to let you know the result.

The test was simple in design, yet difficult for me to administer and for Jean to endure. I created an image from the past, much like the one you witnessed of the brawlers in the drinking establishment. In this scenario, I was on trial for heresy, and Jean was my interrogator.

As you have also witnessed, Jean reverted to his former self and became enraged at me, slinging verbal arrows and invectives unfit for any mouth, much less for one as youthful as Jean's.

At a pause in his diatribe, I said, "You have written in your own works that no church has the authority to bind the consciences of men and that those who kill heretics are savage butchers. And now you seek to have me killed, a man who has done you no wrong, a man who simply disagrees with your doctrines." I then looked Jean in the eyes and said, "Are you still blind to your hypocrisy even after all I have taught you? Are you still blind to the innocence of someone you hate, just as your friend Justin is to the guilt of someone he loves?"

Jean stared at me for an extended time, then he ...

Justin, I have reconsidered. I will not tell you what happened to Jean, because you must set your mind on your future, not his. It is enough to say that we have both finished our time here, and I was granted an extra hour to write this message.

I pray that you will open your eyes to the truth. Remove the scales from your eyes. It is the only way you can survive and take care of your beloved sister.

Your friend,
Michael Servetus

My hand trembled. The letter slipped away and floated to the floor. The moment it struck the stone, it withered until it crumbled into dust.

Tears flooded my eyes. For Michael, for Jean, for Pierre, for Joan, and most of all for my father. I had no chance to speak to him about anything important, that I loved him, that I missed him, that I wished he were here to tell me what to do. They had all left this world for a second time, never to return.

The tears burned. It seemed that flames ignited and sizzled across my eyes. Like a ghost, Francine appeared in front of me, holding the brooch as she entered the mausoleum, as she took the other brooch from the dead girl, as she asked me to find the ring and the pendant, and, finally, as she waited for me to take off the ring before suggesting that we drink wine.

In the images, she poisoned her mother and worked with Dr. Cousineau to hang her body. She brutally stabbed Marguerite with the poker, meticulously washed the end, and put it back in place at the hearth. She pointed a gun at me and then at Justice, ready to shoot us in order to get the ring and avoid dying from the poison.

215

How did Francine realize so quickly that she had been poisoned? Was it a mere guess? No. She knew what lurked in one of those wine goblets. The ghostly Justice had not poisoned her. She merely switched the goblets to protect me, and by so doing, she protected my sister.

A mask fell from Francine's face, revealing a monster, a devious witch. This was my blindness. All along, Francine had been the killer, and I was too sightless to realize it. She conspired with Dr. Cousineau to kill her mother to get the inheritance and the clues to finding a treasure. But why kill a poor, innocent woman like Marguerite? To keep me running? To make sure I stayed in the catacombs? Might that have been the motivation for the bishop's murder as well, to keep him from doing harm to me before I could find the pendant she lusted for?

What a fool I had been! A blind fool who sought the love of a brutal killer and in so doing abandoned a woman who loved me with all her heart. And now I had escaped to the catacombs once again, another cowardly run to my shelter where I could hide encased in dead men's bones.

I shook my head hard. No. I couldn't stay here. I had to go back to Justice. She needed me. Wounded or not, I could make it back to her.

I grabbed the lantern, tied its line to my waist, and struggled back up the ladder. Pain and exhaustion slowed my progress. Muscles cramped. Blood streamed down my chest and back. But I had to keep going. I had to find Justice.

When I arrived at the top, I staggered toward the brook, morning's first rays providing light. Cold wind knifed through my clothes. In my hurry, I had left Marc's coat behind in the catacombs. No matter. With thoughts of Justice driving me forward, I could brave the chill, if only I could get there without bleeding to death.

At the opposite side of the brook, two women stood near the bridge—Justice and the prostitute I had seen earlier. The prostitute whispered into Justice's ear, then turned and walked toward the city.

Justice set a foot on the bridge. Water rushed over the sagging center, threatening to tear the platform away. No one but a blind person would dare try to cross.

I grabbed the lantern's handle and ran as fast I could, shouting, "Justice! Stop!"

The sound of rushing water swallowed my cry. The moment she set her full weight on the bridge, it gave way. She toppled into the brook and disappeared.

Chapter Twenty-Two

I dashed to the water's edge and dove in. In the underwater dimness, I searched with wide-open eyes and flailing arms. After several seconds, my fingers brushed flesh. I latched onto a wrist and held on as I splashed toward shore.

Several seconds later, I pulled Justice onto the school side of the brook. I knelt, sat her upright, and slapped her on the back as she coughed up streams of water. Blood oozed from a cut on her scalp and another on her lip, perhaps from striking rocks or part of the bridge. Both wounds had already swelled more than I would have guessed possible in such a short time.

When she finished coughing and began breathing with wheezing gasps, I sat and gathered her into my arms. "Oh, Justice, why did you come? You could have drowned."

She whispered fractured phrases through the wheezing. "I had to ... find you ... help you ... stop bleeding. ... I brought the ... needle and thread."

Barely able to speak, I whispered, "Marc and the inspector just let you leave?"

Her voice settled to a low, sniffling lament. "They were busy with Francine's body. While they tended to her, I sneaked out the back door and walked in the school's direction. I asked others for help, and a kind woman showed me the way." She touched the cut on her lip. "I bumped into some things, but it doesn't hurt much."

I rose and helped her stand. The frigid wind cut through our wet clothes and made us both shiver. The threadbare dress she wore clung to her body like a second skin. She could die in a matter of minutes. "We have to get you warm, or you'll catch your death."

I felt for the lantern, but it was gone. The current must have stripped the line from my body. With the bridge torn away, we couldn't cross the brook unless we walked at least three miles to the next bridge. We would freeze by then. And I couldn't build a fire, since everything that could burn was too wet.

My own wounds stabbed me again. The cold water had temporarily numbed them, but now the pain returned with a sharper edge. "We'll have to go to the catacombs. It's warmer there." I helped Justice walk to the trapdoor. I stepped onto the ladder first and coaxed her down with constant instructions and affirmations, mimicking how Jean had guided my steps on the sometimes unreliable rungs. Although new pain spiked with every grasp of a rung, I forced a calm voice, not wanting to worry Justice any further. The process was already exceedingly difficult. No need to add to her distress. Since we were both saturated and shivering, our feet often slipped, but, taking plenty of time and care, we eventually reached the bottom safely.

Still shaking violently, we walked into the schoolroom and sat against a wall. Although it was warmer here, with no fire and our clothing soaked, we would soon become chilled to the bone.

"Take off your shirt," Justice said, her voice rasping as if still choking on water. "I want to feel your bullet holes."

With her help, I did so. Every move sent new peals of pain across my body. Her fingers ran along my shoulder until they touched the bullet's entry point. "You're still bleeding badly. I should sew the wounds closed."

"Do you know how to do that?"

"The inspector ..." She coughed and wheezed. "The inspector told me you sewed his wound. If you teach me, I can do it."

"In the dark? With both of us shivering?"

"Darkness means nothing to me. And one skill I have learned while living with Madame Dupont is how to keep my hands steady in spite of bad circumstances." She coughed several times, as if still struggling to eject water trapped in her lungs. "Let's start ..." Her voice was little more than a grating whisper. "Now."

As I talked her through the procedure, her fingers grew colder and colder on my skin. Shivers and coughs interrupted, and the stitching slowed.

"Justice, you should take off your wet clothing and put on a coat I left here. It's completely dark, so I am as blind as you are."

"All right. Thank you."

While Justice disrobed, I found the coat and spread it open. When she was ready, I helped her slide her arms through the sleeves and wrap it around her body.

"Does that feel better?" I asked.

"Much better, thank you. But what about you? You'll freeze."

"I'll be all right." My teeth chattered as I spoke. I probably didn't sound convincing. "Let's finish the stitches."

Now that Justice was warmer, the procedure went faster, and she settled into the effort without further guidance. While she stitched the back wound, I grew faint and dizzy, and stronger shivers shook my body.

"Justin, I have one more stitch to do. Try to stay still."

"I can't." My body quaked, and the dizziness worsened. "I think I'm going to faint."

"You lost too much blood, and you're freezing to death. We should wrap up together in the coat."

"My trousers will get you wet."

"Take them off."

The thought of such close, intimate contact with Justice incited nausea. "I can't. I mean, we can't. We shouldn't."

"Justin, the alternative is death. I didn't risk my life only to let you die simply because of propriety. Besides, I'm your sister. We trust each other. Take off your trousers and join me. We'll both get warm that way."

Her voice was smooth and gentle. She wanted to save my life. Of course we would maintain innocence. I would rather die than violate her trust.

After taking off my trousers, I sat at her side and slid my arm through one sleeve while she kept her arm in the other. Fortunately Marc's coat, since he was a bear of a man, was big enough to enclose us both.

As we sat against the wall, our skin warmed, and our shivers ebbed. I imagined myself as a little boy in a washtub with Justice, leaning close, splashing each other, naked and unashamed. She had always been my friend, my closest confidante, the only person I could trust with every word, every thought. To think that I had left her with Francine, a woman who turned out to be a cruel murderer, brought new pangs of guilt to pound at my already fractured conscience.

"Justice," I whispered into her ear, "I'm sorry for leaving you with Madame Dupont. I was wrong."

"No need for apologies, Justin." She yawned. "We were up all night. We should sleep."

"You're right." I also yawned, as if in echo. "Thank you for never losing faith in me."

"You'll never have to worry about my faith in you." She leaned her head against mine. "What we're doing now should make that clear."

"That's true." I relaxed and closed my eyes. Now the darkness felt good, like a blanket of warmth and joy. "I love you, Justice."

"I love you, too, Justin." She clasped my hands in hers. "And I always will."

Soon, she settled into sleep, her respiration wheezing again. I followed her into slumber moments later. Whether or not I dreamed, I don't know. I remember only that I was warm and with my dearest friend in the world.

A light shone in my face. I blinked my eyes open and squinted. Inspector Fortier stood in the schoolroom holding a lantern in a tight fist. He stared at us, his mouth open.

I gasped. What must he be thinking? "Inspector ... I ... we ... we were cold ... freezing. We did this to survive."

Saying nothing, he shifted his arm, casting the light across our clothes.

I whispered to Justice, "Wake up. The inspector's here."

She stayed silent, motionless. The yellow light flickered across her pale cheeks and gray lips.

"Justice?" My voice spiked unbidden. "Justice, wake up!"

The inspector walked close, crouched, and set a hand over her mouth, then pressed his fingers against her neck. "She's dead."

"Dead?"

He rose and glared at me. His jaw quivered as he spoke in a calm tone. "Get up. Cover her and get dressed." He set the lantern down and walked out of the room.

My mind numb, I pulled my arm from the sleeve and closed the front of the coat over Justice. Her body, still limber and lukewarm, slumped. I caught her wrist and let her down gently to the floor.

The sight jolted me out of a senseless trance. I shook uncontrollably and wailed, "Justice! My dear sister! You're dead!" I paced from wall to wall and pulled my hair. "Oh, God, help me! Justice is dead! She's dead!"

"Get dressed," the inspector barked from the corridor.

I bit my lip and halted my lament, though my body continued shaking. I dressed quickly, especially considering my trembling hands and wounded shoulder. All the while, I couldn't take my eyes off my poor sister. Somehow the cold water had infected her lungs and killed her as she slept. And I, like an ignorant fool, slumbered during the attack.

After I clumsily tied my shoes and straightened, I called out a shaky, "I'm dressed."

Inspector Fortier stalked in, strode straight at me, and punched me across the jaw. I backpedaled until I slammed into a wall.

"I believed you!" he roared, his fists tight at his side. "I let you roam freely while you plotted to poison Francine." He pointed at Justice's body. "Then you killed the only person who knew about your crime. You drowned her. Then you ..." He waved his finger from side to side. "Then you had your way with her. Incest with a blind girl. Rape of a corpse. You are worse than a dog. You are a monster."

He drew a revolver and aimed it at me, his hand shaking. "Justin Trotter, you are under arrest for poisoning Francine Noël and drowning Justice Trotter. I hope to God that your head will fall into a basket to the cheers of a crowd."

I raised my hands as far as my aching shoulder would allow. "Inspector, I assure you—"

"Save your lies for the trial." He waved the gun. "Go. I'll be right behind you."

I shuffled to the ladder and began climbing. My wounds ached, and my arms and legs trembled. Grief ravaged my soul. But I couldn't let his false accusations go unchallenged. As I spoke, my words spilled out in a tide of agony. "Inspector, examine her body. You'll see. I didn't do what you think. She fell into the brook. I rescued her. The bridge was out, so to keep from freezing we had to go below. We were wet and cold, so we warmed ourselves in the only way we knew how. It was innocent. Brother and sister trying to survive. She just died in her sleep. I don't know why."

"Keep moving," was his only response.

When we reached the top, morning sun illuminated the horizon, and cold wind assaulted me once more. My clothes, still damp, did nothing to combat the frigid blast.

The inspector waved the gun at a horse and carriage—not his own carriage this time but a Paris police vehicle. "Get in."

I climbed into the rear seat. The inspector put his gun away, clasped one of my wrists in an iron cuff, and fastened a second cuff to a metal bar attached to the carriage. A short, thick chain linked the cuffs. With the twist of a small key, he locked them in place.

He shook the chain and let it drop. "This will keep you from running, but if you even try to escape, I will kill you."

"Inspector, you have to believe—"

"Quiet." He seated himself on the driver's bench, picked up a hat, and put it on. With a shrill whistle, he signaled the horse. It broke into a slow trot along a path that ran parallel to the brook.

"Will you send someone to get Justice?" I asked as I bounced with the carriage. "We can't leave her down there."

"Don't pretend you care. Your acting skills will not avail you."

I looked back toward the school's ruins. My dear sister lay below, cold and lifeless. I couldn't focus my efforts on proving my innocence in the wake of this tragedy. Yet, if I continued speaking about her welfare, the inspector would again dismiss my concerns as self-serving, perhaps hardening him further.

"Very well," I said, "perhaps at least someone could examine her to prove that I'm telling the truth."

The inspector let out a sad sigh. "She will be examined."

As we rode on toward the alternate bridge, I put myself in the inspector's place. He walked in on the most damning scene imaginable. No wonder he hit me. But now he seemed to be softening. Maybe he was reverting to his analytical self. I could attempt appealing to his intellect.

Trying to ignore the cold, I leaned forward. "Inspector, right before the poisoning, you found Justice in the alley. What did she say to you?"

For a long moment, he stayed silent. Then he loosened his grip on the reins. "Justin is in trouble. Francine is trying to kill him."

"And what was she wearing?"

"A black dress."

"Where did she go?"

"I put her in my carriage where she could be out of the rain."

"What did you do?"

"I ran to the Noëls' house. You know the rest."

A strong gust sent icy fingers through my clothes, but I shook off the chill. "When you arrived at the house, Justice was dressed in a nightgown. It was impossible for her to outrun you to the house, change clothes, and appear dry before you arrived."

He twisted toward me and barked, "Stop interrogating me."

"You mentioned the puzzle yourself. I thought now would be a good time to—"

"You thought wrong." He turned forward and stared ahead. "I don't know how she managed it, but obviously she did. Facts are facts."

"Unless there's another explanation."

"What? That you have another sister? A blind girl who looks exactly like Justice? If so, where did she go? She wasn't in the carriage when I returned to it."

I lowered my head. "You wouldn't believe me if I told you."

"No, I wouldn't. This time you can't escape your guilt. You and Justice were the only ones who could have poisoned

Mademoiselle Noël. Then you shot her and fled to your hideout, and your accomplice found a way to join you. Later, I discovered you with Justice's dead body. Naked." A growl spiced his voice. "If I have anything to say about it, you will die for your crimes as soon as possible."

A long pause ensued. The bitter wind continued its unabated assault. The bullet wounds stabbed relentlessly. The loss of my dearest loved one shredded my soul. How could I continue this fruitless debate? The inspector's righteous wrath had closed his ears. And why not? My denials sounded like the ravings of a madman, and explaining further would seal his certainty that I was insane. A verbal defense was out of the question.

"Inspector, will I be allowed to write my explanation of everything that happened?"

"Not only will you be allowed, your explanation will be demanded." He gave the reins a snap, making the horse accelerate. "Not that anyone will believe you."

When we drew near the city center's police headquarters, a small throng of people had gathered close to the entrance. A few carried writing implements of one kind or another. One man turned and pointed at us. "It's Inspector Fortier. He has the murderer in custody."

The crowd streamed from the building and surrounded us, forcing the inspector to halt the carriage.

The inspector snorted. "The circus has begun."

"Is he Justin Trotter?" a young man wearing a beret asked as he pointed a pen at me.

"He is." The inspector stepped to the ground amidst a rise in murmurs and pushed men and women back as if they were annoying dogs. When he drew his gun, the murmurs erupted into shouts.

"Is he dangerous?"

"How many has he killed?"

"I heard about a blind sister. Where is she?"

"Quiet." The inspector unlocked the cuff around the metal bar, attached it to my free wrist, and used the chain to pull me out of the carriage. Like oil rushing from water, the reporters backed away, making a path to the police building.

As he led me between the two groups, the chain in one hand and the gun in the other, I risked a question. "Why here instead of straight to the prison?"

"The public knows about four murders," he said stiffly. "We calm their fears by showing them the culprit in chains."

When he opened the door, he allowed one reporter to enter. Inside, the prefect of police posed for a photo with me, which proved to be a tedious process. A balding man with a mustache that spread into his sideburns, the prefect made a grandiose statement about capturing a notorious villain, an Englishman who thought he could come to this fair nation and conduct a murderous rampage against its citizens, all in an effort to purloin a diamond pendant and a historic artifact.

While the prefect droned on, the inspector whispered, "Give me the ring."

I looked at my hand. The ring was on my finger once again, and I hadn't noticed. I took the ring off and handed it to the inspector. "I gave it to Justice, but she must have slipped it on me before she died."

"She died?" the reporter asked, leaning close. "Isn't Justice your sister?"

I nodded. "Was my sister."

When the prefect finished, the reporter wrote a few notes before looking at the inspector. "Will the bodies be put on display in the morgue's vitrine?"

The inspector sneered. "You would like that, wouldn't you?"

"My readers would, yes."

"The city's vultures will be disappointed this time." The inspector waved a hand. "No more questions. After we finish our work here, we will take him to La Grande Roquette where he will await trial for murder."

An officer escorted the reporter outside where the throng collapsed on him, apparently pecking at him with questions.

For the next several minutes, the inspector sat at a desk and wrote on a number of sheets of paper. Then he stood and gave one to the prefect, who waited nearby.

"A sixth murder," the prefect said as he read the page. "And he violated his own sister."

The inspector nodded. "While she was dead. Or so it seems. We should have a physician examine her."

The prefect stared at me, his cheeks turning red. "Perhaps we should release this information to the other prisoners."

"If I may, sir, I recommend solitary confinement."

The prefect lifted his brow. "Why?"

"He was born in England. It's not a good time for an Englishman to die in our prison without a trial."

The prefect returned the page to the inspector. "You're right. See to it."

"Also, we will need a team of men and women to recover Justice. The women will go with one man into the catacombs to secure the body while those on the surface pull her up."

"I will make the arrangements." The prefect shot another glare at me. "I want every scrap of information about this scoundrel. We will have both the French and English public begging for his head to be put on display."

"I received a dossier about his father from Scotland Yard, but the information was scant. I suspect there is much more to be learned about him."

"What was his father's crime?" the prefect asked.

"Murder."

"Excellent. Go to London. Learn what you can. A demon seed planted in England will incite the public enough to scream for a death sentence. Even the most lenient judge will have to listen. We'll make sure the trial is delayed until you return."

"A thorough investigation might take a few weeks."

The prefect glanced up for a moment before looking again at the inspector. "We'll request January, then. As long as the murderer is locked up, waiting until after Noël to bring justice to the Noëls should be agreeable to all."

"You should use that statement with the reporters. And emphasize *justice*."

"Ah, yes, the sister. I hadn't intended that one. It will look quite good in a quote." The prefect shook the inspector's hand. "Excellent work. Send me a telegram from London to let me know your progress. By the time we're finished, Queen Victoria won't make a peep about it, especially if we take a photo of the deceased sister in the state you found her and send it to her."

The inspector clenched his jaw. "I prefer that we not do that, sir."

"That was a joke, Inspector. A bad one. I apologize for my crassness."

"You have no need to worry. The fault is mine. My anger is getting the best of me." The inspector called for two other officers, and the trio escorted me back to the carriage. One drove while I sat on the back bench between the other and the inspector. The reporters and other onlookers swarmed to a line of carriages and followed.

All three officers stayed quiet, allowing me time to again consider the past few hours. I was a ruined man, already tried and convicted. Only the formalities remained. Also, my only friend in the world was dead, and she and I were being blamed for killing the woman who was the ultimate cause of six deaths, including her own.

Somehow I had to make this right. Whether or not I could clear my name wasn't important, but I needed to tell the world what really happened for the sake of Justice. The poor girl had been stricken blind by smallpox. It would be a tragedy if her good name suffered at the hands of false witnesses. She deserved better. Much better. Maybe someone would believe the truth.

I whispered to the inspector, "I would like to begin my testimony immediately, if I may. I will need paper and pen."

He kept his stare straight ahead. "How much paper?"

"As much as you can spare. I have a lot to write. I expect that it will take the entire time you are gone to England."

He bit his lip as if forbidding the release of a harsh word. After several seconds, he nodded. "I will get what you need."

"What about Justice's burial? Will someone arrange a funeral?"

"A magistrate will see to that, but you should put it out of your mind. You won't be able to attend."

"Then may I ask a favor? Is it possible to have her body returned to England and buried next to my father?"

The inspector stayed quiet for nearly a minute before answering. "I am willing to take her with me to England, but the arrangements would be quite expensive. Who would pay for it?"

"Do you think Marc might?"

The inspector laughed under his breath. "I think not." After another pause, he breathed a sigh. "Perhaps someone can be persuaded. Leave it to me."

"Thank you, Inspector."

When we arrived at the prison, we rolled past the guillotine, elevated on a platform. The top loomed well over our heads. There, if events went as the police hoped, a blade would fall and sever my head from my body.

In a way, I hoped for it as well—a quick end to my misery. All that I ever loved was gone, my father, Francine, and now, even my sister.

And you, Mother, wherever you are. I fear that I shall not see you on this side of heaven.

The prison officials thrust me into a tiny cell, a cube perhaps six feet in all dimensions. The inspector saw to it that I was supplied with a small table, a rickety chair, and a short stack of paper. The jailer promised to try to find pen and ink, but he wasn't sure how long it would take.

Then they locked the door and left me alone.

And I had never been so alone. *Solitary confinement*, the inspector had called it. The thought crushed my soul. Trapped in bitter loneliness, why should I want to live even another day?

Then the answer came, whispered in Justice's own voice. *Vindicate me, Justin. I am innocent.*

Joan's voice rode the air. You must write what you have seen and heard. Only you can provide the antidote to hate and injustice. Michael added, *Your suffering has delivered a gift. Do not forfeit this opportunity to share with the world the truth about freedom of thought and conscience.*

I closed my eyes and called out, "Joan, Michael, Justice, I will try, but how can I remember all the details?"

"I will help you." The voice came from directly in front of me. I opened my eyes. Siobhan stood on the other side of the table, hand in hand with young Jacqueline. Wearing a pretty green dress with a white sash, the bright-eyed girl smiled and said to Siobhan, "Who is this man? I've seen him before."

"Justin Trotter." Siobhan set a pen and inkwell on the table. "You will learn all about him as we help him tell his story."

"How can you help?" I asked. "You don't know what happened."

"No, but I can communicate with Joan, Michael, and Justice. And Jacqueline will begin remembering parts of it when the time comes. It will be good for her training to listen to your tale of love and sacrifice."

I let out a sigh. "You mean a tale of failure."

Siobhan caressed my cheek. "I heard about your tragedies. Perhaps writing about them will provide hope for a better future."

Her touch felt cold but comforting. "How can reliving tragedies give me hope?"

"Not hope for you so much. Hope for others." She drew her hand back. "Your own hope awaits after you finish."

"If you say so." I sat in the chair, filled the pen, and poised it over the paper. "Do you have a suggestion about where I should start?"

"Start by resting, Justin. Sleep. You have witnessed murder and injustice time and again, and the events will likely haunt your dreams. Insanity will knock at your door. Don't let it enter. Each morning when you awaken, purge the haunting images and test yourself to see if your mind is clear. If you can think of Francine without hatred, without vengeance, then you will know that you are sane and are ready to begin writing. Only when love conquers all bitterness and all dread will you be able to let the ghosts speak."

"Will you come every day to help?"

Siobhan nodded. "Every day until you finish. Then I will see if Jacqueline is ready for her test."

I took her advice and slept on the thin straw mat the prison provided. Nightmares assaulted me for three nights, and each morning I awoke with the ghouls still swirling—thoughts of Francine's smile as she beckoned me to drink poisoned wine, Justice's fall into the brook, her pale cheeks moments after she breathed her last, and the inspector's accusing eyes as he drew his fist back to strike me.

As Siobhan predicted, the phantoms of the night shook my spirit. It seemed that sanity fled my grasp, no matter how hard I tried to grip its slippery hands. Each morning I battled the thoughts with such grief and moaning that other prisoners called for me to calm down, even offering heartfelt prayers, though a few hurled curses.

Then, on the fourth morning, I forsook all bitterness and gave up any thought of revenge. Francine was in God's hands. With that I could be content. And this newfound peace brought blessed sanity back into my embrace.

When Siobhan arrived with Jacqueline, I began writing, and you know the rest. It is all here in this manuscript.

Now, dear Mother, I have spent more than a month writing this account, and doing so has helped me greatly. Putting the tale on paper has fully restored my sanity. Not only that, I believe that the account will result in my deliverance from death. You see, as I wrote, I translated each day's work into French for the judge to read, though I left out the personal notes to you. Perhaps now I will have a sympathetic ear in court. The presiding judge will surely see that my account is the only way these events could have taken place. Nothing else makes sense.

Also, I learned from a prison guard that Inspector Fortier did, indeed, accompany Justice's body to England. I don't know who the benefactor was, but I am grateful for his generosity.

I am also happy to report that Jacqueline has progressed quite well. She asked for my forgiveness regarding her behavior toward me at the masquerade party, which I granted without reservation. Siobhan believes her young charge is ready for her final test. I am confident her end will be better than Pierre's. Yet, to this day I have no idea what became of Jean. Siobhan is also unaware of his fate, which is probably for the best. Who am I to inquire of the heavens the eternal state of another man?

I am now writing on my last available page. No matter. I have nothing more to tell you at this time. Inspector Fortier is supposed to return from England today, so my trial will soon be upon us. Yet, I no longer care whether or not I am found guilty. If I live to see many more days, I can begin a new search for you. If I die at the guillotine, I will go to be with Justice and Father.

Mother, I long to see Justice. She was the one light remaining in my life. She trusted me without question and always wanted to be at my side. How I wish I could fulfill that desire now and be with her for eternity.

One more item—a priest has visited me on occasion, a friendly young man, nothing like Francine's hate-filled bishop. Between the priest's words of faith and memories of my martyred friends, I have reason to believe again, and my new faith has given me assurance that death will bring me into Justice's embrace.

She is alive in heaven, as is Father. We all have hope of a reunion.

Here ends my tale. Mother, I hope to see you soon.

Affectionately yours,

Justin

Addendum to the Case Record –
Inspector Paul Fortier

As the lead inspector, I would be remiss if I omitted crucial information that I discovered after I closed the case and submitted it to the judge for examination. Yet, this new information is fraught with great uncertainty and doubt, to say the least, thereby making it unbelievable to any who might read the record. Therefore, when I complete this addendum, I will hide it from contemporary eyes and store it for future viewing. Perhaps those who read it in a later century will do so from a more enlightened perspective. God as my witness, my own era would never understand what I have seen and heard.

I have chosen to employ a style similar to Monsieur Justin Trotter's, that is, from my direct point of view as events unfolded. This way, putting the two accounts together will appear more consistent than otherwise. I will also add annotations from time to time so readers in the future can understand our era's ways, though I can only guess whether or not these will be needed.

I returned from London on a cold December afternoon. I had vowed to come home in time for a joyeux Noël with my family, and I achieved my goal with three days to spare.

Upon my arrival by rail, light rain pelted the city as I walked to La Grande Roquette prison to visit Monsieur Trotter, the case's portfolio tucked under my arm. When I asked for him to be brought to the visitation room, I was informed that he was already there with another guest.

Anxious to learn who that guest might be, I hurried to the room and peeked past the guard. Monsieur Trotter sat at a table across from Monsieur Marc Noël, his one-time friend. A lantern cast a flickering glow across a stack of papers on the table as well as the two men's faces. Both wore morose expressions, though Marc's seemed angry while Justin's was more melancholy, perhaps influenced by wrist irons that dangled to the floor where they attached to leg irons.

"I will be at the trial," Monsieur Noël said in a restrained tone, "but don't expect me to say anything in your defense. I know Francine did some terrible things, but there is no defense for what you did to her. Murder is never justified."

"I shot her in self-defense, Marc. She shot me first."

"Because you poisoned her." Monsieur Noël's voice sharpened. "Don't take me for a fool, Justin. I am an actor, too. I know your tricks, and you are finally unmasked." He set his hands at the sides of his head. "I can't believe I'm discussing this with the man who poisoned my sister, a man who raped his own dead sister. This is madness."

"Then why did you come? Why did you call for me?"

Monsieur Noël took a deep breath and calmed himself. "To appeal to you, Justin. Confess your guilt. Francine is dead. She has paid for her crimes. There is no need to drag her name through the mire in what will surely be a spectacle of a trial if you maintain your innocence."

"Then I would face the guillotine."

"You will face it either way. No jury will acquit a man caught naked in the catacombs with his dead, equally naked sister. If you think otherwise, you are deluded, the victim of your own playacting."

"I am not deluded." Monsieur Trotter touched the stack of papers. "I have written the entire account here. The judge and jury will be persuaded that this is the only possible way everything could have happened."

"The ghost of Joan of Arc?" Monsieur Noël swiped at the stack, sending the pages flying. "No one will believe this excrement. It is a fantasy, your delusion. Even if someone witnessed every word as it played out, he would never utter a syllable of it in public. He would soon be in an asylum."

Bryan Davis

Monsieur Trotter looked at the pages on the floor. "Even if it is a fantasy, it is the only truth I know. How can I speak otherwise?"

"If you speak this rubbish, they'll want to cut your head off twice." Monsieur Noël sighed. "Justin, I have no more to say. Consider my plea. It is true that my mother was a witch of a woman, and my sister was a murderer. Both are dead, and they will face the ultimate judge." He folded his hands in prayerful entreaty. "Let the dead bury the dead. I paid for your sister's burial expenses so your family could have peace. Now let my family have ours. Don't put us through more torment. I have an aunt and three cousins who are in desperate grief. We have suffered enough."

"I didn't realize you paid for the costs." Monsieur Trotter lowered his head. "I will consider your plea."

"If so ..." Monsieur Noël removed Joan of Arc's ring from his little finger and displayed it on his palm. "Since I am an heir, Inspector Fortier gave this to me. As you know, it is a symbol of protection, of honor, of valor. If you confess and thereby avoid destroying my family's name, I will stand at the trial and symbolically extend this toward you, signifying my complete forgiveness and that I will always consider you my friend."

Still looking down, Monsieur Trotter said, "I understand. Again, I will consider your request."

Without another word, Monsieur Noël rose and departed.

Monsieur Trotter crouched and began gathering the scattered pages. The guard helped, and I walked in and added my efforts.

Within a minute or two, we finished and set the pile on the table. "It's a good thing I numbered the pages," Monsieur Trotter said. He gestured toward the visitor's chair. "Shall we talk?"

Once we had seated ourselves, his melancholy expression turned to a more frightened aspect, the look of a condemned prisoner. "Do you bring news from London?"

"I do." I set the portfolio case on the table and folded my hands on it. The last time I saw this man, I wanted to kill him, and he knew it. Now, after learning new information both in London

235

and in Paris, I didn't know what to think. "In fact, I have a great deal of news."

"You found my mother?"

"I did. You see—"

"Excellent." A smile broke his fearful countenance. He slid the stack of paper toward me and spoke with unusual rapidity. "This is my full account. Two copies. One in English for my mother, and one in French for the judge. I trust that you will give them—"

"No. Wait." I held up a hand. "Monsieur Trotter, let me explain."

His smile wilted. "What's wrong? Won't you take the accounts?"

"Of course. Of course." I picked up the pages and slid them into my portfolio case. "But as to the wisdom of delivering the French version to the judge—"

"Inspector." His expression turned serious. "Tell me what you found. Hold nothing back."

"Very well." I folded my hands again. "Justin, I spent three weeks—"

"So, I am Justin now? Not Monsieur Trotter?" His brow lifted. "This change portends bad news, I think."

"Bad news? Yes, but liberating all the same." At that moment, I decided to refer to him as Justin from that time forward. My role as inspector seemed to transform into that of a counselor. "You see, Justin, I retraced every step of the incidents the night your father was arrested, and I followed the case to its end. Correct me if I am wrong in the retelling.

"You heard a loud noise over your head. To investigate, you ascended the stairs to an attic where you found your father with blood-covered hands. A woman hung by a rope from the ceiling with a noose around her neck. Is that correct?"

Justin nodded. "Yes. I told you that once before."

"Forgive me. I am making sure all accounts are consistent."

"I understand. Go on."

"Frightened to no end, you ran downstairs and into the night, shouting for the police."

He nodded again. "My mother told me to run for help."

236

"Justin ..." I leaned closer and looked into his eyes. "She told you no such thing. She was the woman hanging by the rope."

He shook his head hard. "She was sitting on my bed when we heard the noise. Then we walked together up the stairs. The woman hanging in the attic was not my mother."

I settled back in my chair. "Let's say for the moment that your memory is correct. Where, then, did your mother go after she sent you for help?"

"I don't know. You said you found her. Why are you trying to confuse me?"

"I did find her." I withdrew a photograph from my case and set it in front of him. "Since seeing is believing, I had this photograph made. It's your mother's tombstone."

As he stared at it, he bit his lower lip. A tear streamed down his cheek to his chin. "When did she die? I can't read the year."

"Don't you understand?" I took the photograph and slid it back into the case. "She died that night. She was the victim of the hangman's rope."

He shook his head again, his eyes clenched shut. "That can't be true. She was with me. I saw her. Heard her. Felt her touch." After a moment of gentle weeping, he stared at me blankly and quieted.

I took advantage of the silence to continue. "Justin, further investigation led me to learn the following. The police arrested your father for hanging your mother. The investigation and trial were quick, and he was sentenced to be hanged, but the execution was delayed due to an advocate who made several appeals. During this time, you were sent to France, as you know.

"I was able to interview your father's advocate. He claimed that the judge in the trial had invested in a shoe company, and your father's business was a competitor. The judge was glad to remove your father from competition and thereby add to his own fortunes. My investigation revealed that the judge's investment was exactly as the advocate had related, so I dug deeper. The same judge applied the death sentence to two other competitors, though the criminal charges were highly in doubt. This pattern led me to ask for the evidence against your father, but other than the file briefing I already had, everything has been mysteriously lost.

"To make a long story short, your father claimed that your mother committed suicide by hanging herself." I paused to see how Justin would react, but his blank stare continued. "He tried to cut the rope to free her and in so doing sliced his hands, accounting for the blood. The judge refused to believe his story. He declared your mother to be sane, saying that he knew her personally. She would never commit suicide. In fact, he claimed that wounds in her body proved that your father stabbed her even while she dangled. A mortician testified that this was so, but, unfortunately, since the records of her post-mortem examination are missing, I could not verify or disprove that claim.

"Yet, I do have the testimony of your father's advocate, who wasn't at the trial. He was your mother's doctor and claims she was under care for hallucinations. He prescribed a number of treatments, none of which provided relief. In fact, the problem grew worse. The doctor believes that the hallucinations likely drove her to madness.

"So I dug deeper once again, this time literally. I had your mother's body exhumed."

Finally Justin reacted as if jolted by lightning. "You did what?"

"I had your mother's body exhumed and examined for stab wounds. After fifteen years, of course, her body was badly decomposed, but I was able to satisfy myself that she had not been stabbed. The mortician lied, perhaps paid off, but since he is now dead, I was unable to interview him."

While Justin sat quietly absorbing this flood of information, I continued. "One fact is obvious. Since I was able to determine the truth years after the fact, a diligent investigation at the time would have exonerated your father. Therefore, a crooked judge is not the only person to blame. England's entire justice system failed your father. In fact, it is fair to say that the system murdered him."

"Murdered him?" Justin blinked tear-filled eyes. "So my father was a martyr. Persecuted by justice."

"Well ... yes. I suppose you could say that. But now his name will be cleared. He can rest in peace. And it seems appropriate that your mother, even while dead, exonerated him."

Justin's face twisted. "Did you see her body with your own eyes?"

I nodded.

"How can you be sure it was her? Her face couldn't have been recognizable."

"Her doctor was with me. He noted a bone deformity in her foot he knew about. It was a—"

"A bent big toe," Justin said.

"Yes. Apparently it caused a slight limp."

After another quiet pause, Justin whispered, "She was already dead. Her ghost was with me. Sitting on my bed. Walking with me up the stairs. Shouting at me to run for help."

"Justin, the doctor suggested that hallucinations might run in the family, so is it possible that you—"

"No." He added another emphatic shake of the head and raised his voice. "I was not hallucinating. I saw her, just as I am seeing you now."

"But don't you see that it's much more likely that you inherited a—"

"Read my account." He shook a finger at my portfolio case. "It's all there. I have seen other ghosts. Not only my mother. Without them, I couldn't have found the ring. I couldn't have found the pendant. Hallucinations can't give you information you don't already know."

I waved a calming hand. "All right. All right. I'll read your account."

"Good." He took a deep breath and settled himself. "When you finish, let me know what you think."

"I will." I withdrew another sheet of paper from my case. "I have more information. This is the report on your sister's autopsy. The fluid in her lungs was not merely water. If she had drowned and died immediately, the fluid would have been clear, that is, all water. It seems that a small amount of water caused an irritation that led to fluid secretions that built up while she slept. In other words, she drowned in her own fluids. Also, the examination showed that her virginity remained intact. Every part of the report matches your account exactly."

"Then you believe me."

I slid that page back to the case. "I believe that portion. Whether or not a jury will look kindly on your close contact with her is another issue."

"She was freezing. We were both freezing. We had no fire, nowhere to go. It was the only way."

I waved a hand. "I understand that survival instincts can cause us to make difficult choices, but a jury sitting in a warm room might not sympathize with your shivers, especially while well-heeled women wearing corsets and plumage stare at you in disgust."

"Granted, but doesn't the truth of my account in this instance give me more credibility in your eyes?"

"It makes me think you're not a disgusting pervert, if that's what you mean. You still poisoned Mademoiselle Noël. No one else could have done it." I rose, set my hands on the table, and leaned close to him. "I suggest that you take Monsieur Noël's advice. Confess to the poisoning. Perhaps when the autopsy evidence comes to light, the charges of murdering and raping your sister will be dropped, and your sentence will be lighter. I think that plan is your only hope of escaping the guillotine." I picked up the portfolio case. "I will see you at your trial."

I departed and rode a carriage home. After spending time with my wife and daughter until they retired, I stayed up all night reading Justin's French account. The effort was laborious, but it seemed expedient to review the evidence that he asked me to provide to the judge.

Knowing about his hallucinations, I was able to separate fact from fiction and piece ideas together that made sense. Of course, the witchcraft claim was obvious fiction, perhaps a way for Justin to rationalize his so-called blindness and to cast a final stain on Francine's character. The fact column held the ring and pendant, both declared authentic and highly valuable by a reputable expert who also verified that both heirlooms legally belonged to Madame Noël's estate.

The Pierre phantom likely arose from Dr. Cousineau's final words. Had he tried to accuse Francine, his damaged lips unable to form the proper sound? It seemed strange that two men heard Pierre, but no other explanation made sense.

Still, a pair of items refused to take either the fact or fiction category—the ghosts, Jean and Justice. I saw these two with my own eyes at Madame Noël's funeral. On a later day, I gathered an older version of Justice into my arms and carried her through a driving rainstorm. Although the written account was beyond belief, the idea that Justice ran back to the Noëls' faster than I did, changed to a nightgown, and dried her hair before I arrived was every bit as unbelievable, as Justin had claimed. Either the Justice I carried was a ghost, she had an identical sister who was also blind, or she defied all laws of physics. No option made sense.

With such impossibilities in the testimony, what would the judge say when he read it?

I withdrew the English version and looked over the first few pages. As Justin had said, it was identical to the French version save for the addition of personal references to his mother.

Shaking my head, I shoved the pages back into the portfolio case. If I showed either report to the judge, he would be certain of Justin's guilt, call him an insane murderer who conjured phantoms to take the blame. Who in his right mind would ever think that this account could help his cause?

"Then he's not in his right mind," I said out loud. "Unless, of course, it's all true."

I laughed. Even entertaining the idea that the account was true proved that I was tired beyond all reason. I had to get some sleep. After the holiday, I would return to the investigation and be ready to testify at the trial on the third of January.

Case Conclusion

When the day arrived, the public jammed the periphery of the courtroom, mostly rich citizens dressed in cold-weather finery, their eyes and ears intent on hearing every tidbit and mouths relishing the chance to embellish the testimony in risqué gossip. Women dressed in black dominated the public seating area, their attire a sign that they hoped for a death sentence. Ever since the papers began reporting the crimes, the court of public opinion staged their own trials, and the nearly universal pronouncements of "guilty" would surely bleed onto this new stage, the theater we called a courtroom.

You see, readers in the future, during our era in Paris, high-profile trials often became a theater production. Some judges allowed the drama, realizing they could often manipulate the public's reaction to testimony in a manner that might sway the jury toward a conviction. The display was often uncouth, sometimes unjust, but our citizens delighted in the performance.

In keeping with the stage's dramatic effect, the jury sat in a shadowed area, veiled from the rest of the room's occupants, while Justin sat with his appointed counsel facing the jury and the judges' bench above them.

At the bench, three red-robed magistrates settled in place and loomed over the courtroom like scarlet birds of prey. The prosecutor, a longtime friend of mine, sat in a chair at the end of the bench. He was a brilliant man who would skewer Justin alive if he decided not to confess. I hoped for a better outcome. A prolonged trial would do no one any good.

Justin sat with his head high, though his pose was likely part of his acting role. His counsel had probably told him to look as innocent as possible, to be confident in the outcome. Yet, by this time, the magistrate had already interviewed him privately. Justin now knew that I had turned over the official reports, including the autopsy, but not his own account. If he verbally provided a summary to the judge, including the portions about the ghosts, then he was dead already. Soon we would all know.

I ran through the possibilities in my mind. Although Justin did not kill Jacqueline Noël, a fact that would come to light during the trial, demonstrating that someone else must have murdered the Noëls' housemaid would be more difficult. And proving his innocence in Francine Noël's death would likely be impossible. Without a miracle, a guilty verdict was certain.

The presiding judge—the president, as we called him—began the trial with the usual admonition to maintain order and decorum. At a trial like this, his warning would be ignored, and he knew it. Bearing a high brow, white mustache, full cheeks, and infectious smile, he often appeared jovial in spite of the gravity of the trials, and he sometimes employed a biting wit, much to the dismay of those at whom he directed his sharp tongue.

I was the first to testify, determined to undermine the wagging tongues by providing no fuel for their fire. I related the facts of the case in an academic fashion. When called upon to elaborate, I refused to speculate about motives, hearsay, or any other tangents the prosecutor raised. Of course, he gave me no reason to reveal Dr. Cousineau's involvement in Madame Noël's murder, which prompted me to stay quiet about it and bide my time until the defense attorney's turn to question me.

Yet, when the defense attorney raised the issue, just as I opened my mouth to speak, the president bellowed, "Dr. Cousineau is not on trial. You will not mention his name again."

Although the attorney protested with vigor, the president maintained his stance by saying in a mocking fashion, "We will not discuss ghosts in this courtroom, neither those who stay silent in their tombs nor those who rise from the dead and speak to the insane."

Gasps and murmurs rose from those in the public seats. They had no idea what he meant by that highly unusual statement. Yet,

I knew. Justin had surely given his summary to the president. His doom had begun.

The attorney protested once more, but the president waved his hand. "Let's move on. Bring the accused forward to testify." Still holding his head high, Justin stepped up to the dock and faced the judges' bench. The president then pointed at me. "Inspector Fortier, stand in the barreau. I want to question both of you at the same time."

I rose and stood at the center of the central floor space, the barreau, as we called it during our era. Based on the president's dour expression, one that seemed ready to crucify Justin, I expected the worst.

"Inspector," the president said, "did you see Justin Trotter enter the Noëls' house the night Francine Noël was poisoned?"

I nodded. "I did."

"Did he knock on the door? Did she freely invite him in?"

"Whether or not he knocked, I can't be certain. I arrived in the rear alley just as he was climbing through the dining room window."

Whispers rippled across the audience.

"Did you think about questioning him at that time?" the president asked.

"No. It was raining quite heavily, and I assumed he was unable to enter by the door. Since he and Monsieur Marc Noël are close friends, I did not think he was entering with criminal intent."

"At approximately what time did he enter?"

"Nine in the evening."

"And Mademoiselle Noël was poisoned shortly after midnight, correct?"

"Correct."

"Which gave Monsieur Trotter plenty of time to conspire with his sister to poison Mademoiselle Noël."

I glanced at Justin's attorney. He sat in stoic silence, apparently knowing that objecting to these leading questions would be futile. "That would be conjecture," I said. "I have no idea how long it takes to arrange a conspiracy with a blind girl."

"A fair answer." The president turned to Justin. "Monsieur Trotter, did you poison Francine Noël?"

Justin squared his shoulders. "I did not."

"Do you know who did?"

"In a way, she poisoned herself."

Someone in the public gallery laughed, followed by titters from others.

The president glared at them, which stifled the noise. "How did she poison herself?"

Justin kept his gaze on the judges. "Francine poisoned the wine in my goblet. Justice switched the goblets while no one was looking."

New gasps rose, along with murmurs that continued in spite of the president's stares. "If no one was looking, Monsieur Trotter, then how do you know this to be the case? Did Justice confess her crime to you?"

"No. She did not. When I say Justice, I don't mean my sis—"

"Come now, Monsieur Trotter, do you expect us to believe that your sister would not confide in you? You shared everything, did you not? After all, you were found in the catacombs with her, together in a naked embrace, even though she was dead."

A woman swooned and toppled from her seat. While another woman fanned her, several more cried out. Men and women alike crossed themselves.

The president allowed the antics to continue. This reaction was probably exactly what he hoped for.

I looked at the jury. Although shadows veiled their faces, the shaking heads were easy to see. Justin was as good as dead.

I shouted above the din, "Monsieur President, may I speak?"

As he turned toward me, a hush settled across the courtroom. "Until it becomes irrelevant ..." He nodded.

I addressed him directly. "You have done well to point out the inconsistencies in Monsieur Trotter's testimony. By all measures, his account is unbelievable, as you and I know. You have deemed it necessary to expose the obscene elements of the case in order to force him to confess, or at least demonstrate some semblance of contrition for his crimes. A resolve to maintain an unrepentant posture in the face of such damning evidence would reveal him as a beast deserving death."

The president gave me an approving nod, a signal to continue. I turned to Justin and summoned all the passion I could muster. "Justin, I implore you, for the sake of your sister, for the sake of Justice, confess that you were the one who poisoned Francine as an act of vengeful passion. Tell these good people that Justice had nothing to do with it, that she died from drowning and that I found her dead in your arms. Then she will be remembered as a victim instead of an incestuous murderer. The trial will end, and no other unseemly details will come to light that could sully an innocent person's reputation." I took a breath and set a hand over my heart. "Let Justice be honored. Let that poor blind girl, who at this very moment looks down from heaven with perfect eyes, know that her brother loves her more than life itself, that he has purged the ghosts that have haunted him, that he is ready to face the almighty judge who knows every secret and unlocks every mystery."

New murmurs ran across the assembly followed by shushing sounds. Tears flowed down Justin's cheeks as he looked at the president. "Is it true? If I confess, will the trial end?"

The three judges leaned close to each other in conference. Whispers in the crowd restarted and grew until they sounded like leaves rustling in the wind. Justin looked across the buzzing gallery until his scan halted near the back wall. There, Marc Noël rose from his seat, slid Joan's ring off his finger, and extended it toward Justin.

Justin nodded and turned again toward the judges.

When the judges finished their conference, the president said, "We have agreed that if you take full responsibility for Francine Noël's death, we will end the trial and consider every case associated with that series of crimes closed. There will be no need for a jury verdict."

Justin inhaled deeply and squared his shoulders once more. "I take full responsibility for Francine Noël's death, but, if I may, I would like to make a statement before you decide on my punishment."

"If it is short and pertinent," the president said. "I will not tolerate a lengthy rant about your hallucinations."

"I will be brief." Justin cleared his throat and looked out over the crowd. "Justice ... true justice ... is beloved by each one of you, a sister to those who value charity above all. This is why every magistrate needs her presence. She will whisper into his ear, advising him to balance the scales, to consider mercy as he ponders retribution, to expel thoughts of revenge and judge with blindness toward all but the facts set before him.

"We all have ghosts haunting us—deaths, broken relationships, lost opportunities—memories that stab deeply, making us want to bury our ghosts forever. Yet, I advise you to resurrect the memories. They all have something to teach us. Mistakes can be corrected. Wrongs can be made right. Fractured friendships can be restored. Unless we let the ghosts speak, unless we bear the pain and listen to their whispers, our tragedies will remain tragedies for all eternity."

When Justin paused, the president narrowed his eyes. "Are you finished?"

"Yes." Justin folded his hands at his waist. "I am finished."

"So be it." The president raised his voice. "Justin Trotter, as one who values charity, a magistrate who wishes to protect the city from murderous fiends like you, I find you guilty of the murder of Francine Noël. All other charges are dismissed. Barring an appeal, you will be executed by guillotine in one week. May God have mercy on your soul." He rose from his chair. "The jury is dismissed."

As the public area erupted in loud chatter, the judges left the courtroom. Two police officers grasped Justin, one on each side, and escorted him out, and the crowd funneled through the exit door.

Soon, all was quiet, save for my own heartbeat as I stood alone in the barreau. A firm hand compressed my shoulder. Marc Noël stood next to me, his face gray and grim. "You did the right thing."

"Thank you, but I'm not so sure."

He patted me on the back. "Come to my house. We'll have a bottle of wine and talk."

"I would like that. Thank you."

That evening, Marc and I sat in the same room where Justin had claimed Joan of Arc joined us not long ago. It seemed odd that Justin's account contained this irregularity—that I was able to see Cameron, Justice, and Jean but not Joan. Perhaps if Justin had a chance to explain, he might say that Joan's visibility had faded along with her vitality, that losing her young charge to the flames of damnation had altered her essence, or maybe wearing the ring veiled her post-earthly form. Who could tell what rationalizations a tortured mind might conjure?

While Marc and I shared an excellent bottle of red wine, I showed him the French version of Justin's account and pointed out some of the important highlights. Enthralled, he asked to read it all. I let him borrow it, knowing that I had the English version for safekeeping.

We then talked about the possibility of an appeal. It seemed that Justin had resigned himself to his fate, which meant that he probably forfeited his rights. If so, he would be dead in one week.

When I returned home, I read Justin's English account again, studying each phrase, each word. Why? I did not know. Something about the story entranced me, captivated me. I couldn't get it out of my mind.

I dozed at times, awakened by nightmares of the ghosts in Justin's tale. Joan of Arc called out from the flames, begging for water. Yet, no water was given to her.

Michael, a crown of thorns on his head as he stood in a separate fire, shouted for mercy. Yet, no mercy was shown to him.

In Justin's mind, his ghosts were innocent victims of persecution. Why would he identify with them? Why would he conjure phantoms of virtue to cover his murderous actions?

Justice returned to mind, the younger one who played with Jean, then the older one who stumbled blindly through a storm-swept alley.

I turned to the page where she appeared at Francine's table and, as Justin claimed, though he did not see it, switched the wine goblets before they drank. Since she was supposedly not immaterial, she could have done so, but why? In Justin's warped mind, what was her motive? Revenge? If so, for what?

Also, Cameron Trotter said that his ward was never human. What could he have meant by that? Or, a better question, what did Justin mean? After all, this work of fiction came from his delusions. What symbol did he hope to create by pairing his father and sister in such an odd way?

In any case, there was only one rational explanation for the Justice I found in the alley—a third sibling. Of course, a second blind sister would be an incredible coincidence, but maybe she was feigning blindness or was blinded by darkness and the storm.

While searching for evidence about Justin's family, it didn't occur to me to look for a third sibling. Perhaps that was a mistake on my part, but it was too late to return to England. My only hope of finding her lay in personally searching for her in Paris.

I rose from my reading chair and put on my cloak. I had one week—six days, really—to search. Of course, I couldn't mention my new quest to anyone. Since this girl seemed to age at an impossible rate, the idea seemed like madness. Still, for the sake of my own sanity, I had to try to solve the mystery.

Thinking that this second sister might visit Justin's previous haunts, I searched the area around the Noëls' home each morning, the schoolhouse and catacombs in the afternoon, and Justin's flat in the evening before returning home for the night. Then, before going to bed, I reread every portion of the tale that included her, hoping to find a sliver of a clue as to her whereabouts.

The nights grew successively warmer, making the effort easier. The bitter wind that chased Justin into the catacombs had departed, at least for a while.

Finally, on the night before the execution, I again read the portion about Siobhan being in the cell to help Justin remember the tale. Might the second sister have visited him as well? It would do no harm to find out.

I drove my carriage toward the prison with Justin's account in my dossier case. Taking a longer-than-normal route so I could first visit my daughter's grave, I traveled through the heart of the city and passed the Palais de Justice, a court building under reconstruction at the time. A clock at the northeastern corner displayed a statue of a woman on each side, symbolizing Law, who carried a stone tablet, and Justice, who held a set of scales.

While in England, I saw a similar statue of Justice, a blindfolded woman. The Paris version had nothing covering her eyes. Since Justin mentioned scales during the trial, could it be that he had also seen both statues? If so, might they be the catalyst for his idea of two sisters named Justice?

Yet, that couldn't be true. The two girls were not merely ideas or figments of Justin's imagination. They were both quite real.

When I arrived at the jail, because of my office and rank, I was able to enter the prison at the late hour and proceed directly to Justin's cell. He lay asleep on a straw mattress next to a table and chair, the cell layout exactly as he had described in his account. A single sheet of paper lay on the table, though nothing appeared to be written on it.

I reached between two bars and picked up the page. I turned it over and found the following written in a hasty script: *Justice is coming. I will see her in the morning. All will be well.*

I set the page back in place. What did Justin mean by those words? Had the second sister visited him? Might she come to the execution site in front of the prison and proclaim his innocence? Or was this idea yet another conjured phantom? I didn't have the heart to awaken him with such bizarre questions.

My mind swirling with possibilities, I stayed all night at the guards' quarters and read the tale once more. I dozed at times and again dreamed of ghosts, murders, and blind girls. Perhaps the madness was addling my own brain.

When dawn neared, I walked out the main gate and stationed myself in front of the guillotine's platform, a full hour before the scheduled execution time. Already, a few dozen people had lined the area's perimeter, staking out territory with blankets held down by baskets of food.

They were here for entertainment, a spectacle, something gory to make them gasp. They cared nothing for justice. It was merely a concept to be applauded, a platitude to be celebrated with words alone. Deeds were another matter.

Rain began to fall in a downpour, and a new cold wind set in, sending most of the squatters scattering. Apparently their lust for bloodletting wasn't as strong as their desire to stay warm and dry. The crowd dwindled to no more than five filthy men who had probably spent the night in a nearby alley. They didn't seem to mind the elements.

As the dreaded moment neared, a carriage dropped Marc Noël off nearby. With a dossier case tucked under his arm, he walked toward me, his expression melancholy and his hair already wet.

"Why here so early, Inspector?"

"I slept at the prison, not that I got much rest."

"I couldn't sleep at all."

"Why not?"

He extended the case. "I was reading this for the fifth time."

"Captivating, isn't it?" I took the case and set it against my own.

"Very much so. Haunting, really."

"It should be. It's filled with ghosts."

Marc laughed. "As are my dreams."

I tapped on the case with a finger. "Do you believe what you read?"

"Much of it. Not the ghost parts, of course, but I was confused by Justin's claim that you saw two of the ghosts. Are those claims true?"

I nodded. "The boy he called Jean and the girl he called Justice. I cannot verify that they were ghosts."

"Of course not, but what about your rescuing Justice during the storm and then her appearing at my house?"

"Trust me. I have pondered that paradox ever since it happened. I have to believe that they were two different girls, that he had a second sister, perhaps."

Marc shook his head. "Justin never mentioned another sister."

"Then a girl who merely resembled his sister. I saw her at night during a storm. My vision was compromised."

"So you might have been mistaken."

I nodded. "I hope Justin decides to explain before he dies. He will be given the opportunity to speak some final words."

Marc looked at the ground. "I am not looking forward to it."

"Then why did you come?"

He gazed at me with teary eyes. "Justin was my friend. We were closer than brothers. I need to say good-bye."

"In all the time you knew him, did he ever show a tendency toward anger? Violence? Revenge?"

"No, Inspector. I never saw any hint of darkness in Justin. He was a source of light to me countless times."

A thump from the guillotine jerked our attention toward it. The executioner crouched next to the fallen blade, apparently examining it after a test.

My heart seemed to skip a beat. Justin would be arriving in moments. Unless the second Justice arrived, nothing could save him. Or might there be one more option?

I glanced at Marc's hand. He wore no rings. "What did you do with Joan's ring?"

"I have it in my pocket, and I intend to place it with our family's heirlooms along with the pendant. I never want anyone to know the legend about the ring's protective power, whether true or not."

"I suppose if you gave it to Justin now, the truth would be revealed."

"Perhaps so, Inspector, but friend or no friend, Justin needs to die. He poisoned my sister. Justice demands that he pay for his crime."

Moments later, two officers marched from the prison gate with Justin. His hands and feet bound, he shuffled in small steps. His shirt had been cut away at the collar to expose his neck, another sight that made my heart beat erratically.

Marc and I walked closer. The executioner stopped us with a raised hand. "You should stay behind the splatter boundary."

At the thought of flying blood, my legs trembled. Although I had seen many gruesome murder scenes after the fact, I had never witnessed a live killing.

I searched the area for anyone who resembled Justice. If she planned to come and declare Justin's innocence, that she had switched the wine goblets, she had to arrive soon. In my heart, I hoped she would, though I knew it was impossible.

While the executioner raised the blade, a guard announced the charges against Justin and asked him if he had any last words.

"I do." Justin cleared his throat. As rain drenched his body from head to toe, he looked at Marc. "I loved Francine. I didn't want her to die. I hope someday you will believe me."

Marc's lips trembled as he spoke with passion. "Rest assured that I will arrange for you to be buried next to your dear sister. I leave judgment to God and hold no hatred toward you. Depart this world in peace, my friend, knowing that I have forgiven you."

Justin's head bobbed as he wept. "Thank you."

With the officers standing guard, the executioner lowered Justin to the chopping block. Above his neck, the blade hung poised. Only the release of a rope stood between him and death.

I searched again. A young woman who looked exactly like Justice walked into view from the direction Marc had come. Hand in hand with a little ginger-haired girl and holding no cane, she seemed able to see where she was going without a problem.

As they approached the guillotine together, the rain ceased. Both wearing traveling clothes, including hats, long skirts, vests, and boots, they bore only a few splotches of wetness, as if they had been in the rain for a mere few seconds.

When they passed us, I eyed them closely. There was no doubt about Justice's identity, but who was the little girl? And would this Justice, whoever she was, be able to speak in time to stop the execution?

She and the girl halted in front of the platform, only a few steps in front of Marc and me. Justice folded her hands at her waist and waited. But for what?

I called out, "Justice, will you speak on Justin's behalf?" She ignored me and kept her vigil, though the little girl turned her head and smiled.

Marc squinted. "Justice? What are you talking about?"

I turned toward him. "Don't you see her? She's in front of us with a little girl."

"No. Just the guards and Justin."

As the executioner reached for the rope, I pointed. "The girl with dark hair. She and a little girl are standing close to the chopping block."

"You're hallucinating, Inspector. No one is there. Certainly not Justice."

"No one?" I spun toward the guards and shouted, "Stop the execution!"

The rope reeled out. The blade plunged. In a splash of blood, Justin's head dropped into the basket.

My heart seemed to stop. I felt my mouth drop open as I stared at Justice. She neither flinched nor wept. She and the girl stood quietly, as if waiting for something.

Marc grasped my shoulder. "It's over, Inspector. You should get out of those wet clothes. You might have a fever."

"I … I …" My throat caught. I couldn't speak another word.

Tears streamed down Marc's cheeks as he said with a trembling voice, "Come to my house. Dry off. We'll have dinner and some more wine. I'll tell you stories about Justin. Help me grieve for him and my sister. It's not a good time to be alone."

I finally forced a weak, "Very well. I will come soon."

While I stood in stoic silence, Marc accompanied the executioner and the guards as they carried Justin's body and the basket containing his head into the jail. The five other onlookers strolled away and blended into the dismal surroundings. Now only Justice and the girl remained.

I walked to Justice's side. "May I ask who you are?"

She turned and looked at me with bright, piercing eyes. "My name is Justice Trotter. Who are you?"

"Inspector Paul Fortier."

She blinked. "You didn't recognize me?"

"I did. I was just ..." I touched my chest. "You can see me?"

"Yes, of course. In heaven all eyes are renewed. All shadows flee. Every broken heart is mended."

"So I have heard." I lowered my head. "If only I could see for myself."

"That day will come. Constance is looking forward to your arrival."

I stared at her. "*My* Constance?"

Justice nodded. "She hopes her papa will stop worrying about her. She is happy, and sickness can never touch her again. All is well."

My throat tightened. My thoughts scrambled. Again, I couldn't speak.

She turned toward the guillotine. "I apologize, Inspector, but I must go now. Farewell."

Again hand in hand with the girl, Justice walked toward a man who stood in front of the platform. He, too, wore travel clothes—a fine suit and cloak as well as a new beret. When Justice joined him, they embraced warmly, weeping as they kissed each other's cheeks. Then the three walked toward me, the girl in the middle.

As they drew near, I eyed the man closely. He was Justin Trotter, almost unrecognizable due to the delighted smile on his face. The girl, perhaps seven years old, pulled her hair back from her shoulders, revealing an oval birthmark on her neck.

I whispered, "Francine."

Before they passed, Justin tipped his hat to me, then the trio walked away hand in hand, slowly fading to invisibility. And for the first time in months, my heart was glad.

Readers in the future, I leave it to you to divine the meaning of this trio's appearance as well as the Justice I found in the storm-afflicted alley. I have my own thoughts on both, but I think it best to keep them to myself. I prefer to leave drawing conclusions to better minds than my own.

I looked at the two dossier cases. Every word of Justin's account was true. And, as his final penned words had predicted, Justice did come. The brother and sister were together at last. As Justice said, "All is well."

I turned toward Marc's home and plodded along the wet street. These mysterious phenomena shook me to the core. If ghosts were on this earth as an opportunity for martyrs to teach their persecutors love, then why were they allowed to interact with the living? Justin had said to let the ghosts speak as a way to learn charity, but who showed him charity when he needed it most? Certainly not Paris's version of Justice, a justice that could see all too well.

I looked up at the shrouded sky. This veil prevented a view of the heavens above, a barrier to communication. Had divine messengers visited us, piercing the veil to deliver revelations? Joan of Arc had her angels. Pierre Cauchon had his demons. Michael brought a message of love. Jean countered it with suspicion and guile. And Justice opened my eyes to hope, even in the midst of my darkness.

Perhaps Justin was right. We do need to let the ghosts speak, but we must take heed. Every messenger of light is accompanied by a countering darkness.

And sometimes they walk hand in hand.

This concludes my addendum, respectfully submitted by Inspector Paul Fortier. May those who read it find enlightenment and understanding. Perhaps you will be able to perceive what the blind cannot. I fear that we in my era lack the wisdom to see beyond the veil.

Author Note

This story originated in a dream that included many of the events in the first two chapters. Most of my dreams fade by afternoon, but this one stayed with me, gnawing at my mind for more than twelve years. In a sense, the story demanded to be written.

When I finally heeded the call, the story gave birth to its own themes, which I will not identify here. I prefer that readers discover themes for themselves. Yet, I will say that my being an author likely contributed to their genesis.

This story drove me to conduct a great amount of research, including books about 18th century French history and culture, biographies about Joan of Arc and Michael Servetus, and Youtube videos of the Paris catacombs. I felt immersed in Paris to the point that I began thinking in a French accent from time to time. It was loads of fun.

As a result, I learned more than I could ever use in the story, including fascinating aspects of the martyrs' lives. Inserting these would have provided educational benefit, but it would have slowed the pace too much. My favorite resource was Mark Twain's biography of Joan of Arc, one of the best books I have ever read.

If you enjoyed this book, I hope you will provide a review, whether on a retail website like Amazon, in a blog, or in a social media post. I thank you in advance for doing so.

You can connect with me on the Internet in the following ways:

Website – www.daviscrossing.com – You can sign up for my email newsletter there.

Facebook - https://www.facebook.com/BryanDavis.Fans

Twitter - @bryandavisauth

Blog – www.theauthorschair.com

Email – author@daviscrossing.com

I look forward to hearing from you.

Made in the USA
Columbia, SC
03 February 2020

87386709R10146